"HOW DID YOU KNOW WHO I AM?" ROSE ASKED COOLLY.

Oh, she was good, Thornton thought, leaning nearer. "My bailiff gave you away, Lady Roselyn."

She put her arms against his chest and pushed, but he didn't move. "What do you mean, *your* bailiff?"

"Are you so foolish that you didn't read the contract that binds us together?" he demanded. "Everything here is mine, by your father's own command."

Horror stole across her features. "You are lying. I did not marry you!"

"Believe me, I am more and more thankful of that—but our contract is still binding. You have made sure I can never legally marry, but I am damn well entitled to the lands and moneys promised me."

Her back to the door, Roselyn stared up at Thornton. This was the man she remembered: He used his strength and size to intimidate her, just as long ago he'd driven her away with a casual, dismissive look. He was dark and foreign, and maybe even a Spanish spy.

Would he hurt her now that he didn't have to pretend anymo

Other **AVON ROMANCES**

GAYLE CALLEN

His Betrothed

AVON BOOKS
An Imprint of HarperCollinsPublishers

This is a work of fiction. Names, characters, places, and incidents are products of the author's imagination or are used fictitiously and are not to be construed as real. Any resemblance to actual events, locales, organizations, or persons, living or dead, is entirely coincidental.

AVON BOOKS
An Imprint of HarperCollins*Publishers*
10 East 53rd Street
New York, New York 10022-5299

Copyright © 2001 by Gayle Kloecker Callen
ISBN: 0-380-81377-7
www.avonromance.com

First Avon Books paperback printing: June 2001

Avon Trademark Reg. U.S. Pat. Off. and in Other Countries, Marca Registrada, Hecho en U.S.A.
HarperCollins ® is a trademark of HarperCollins Publishers Inc.

Printed in the U.S.A.

10 9 8 7 6 5 4 3 2 1

To Elisa Konieczko,
my high school "editor,"
my best friend

Prologue

London
October 1586

On the eve of her wedding, at a party to celebrate the joining of their families, Lady Roselyn Harrington laid eyes on her betrothed for the first time—and felt like tearing the flowers from her hair.

Oh, Sir Spencer Thornton was handsome enough, with his dark, foreign, brooding looks. His mother was Spanish, but he'd been born and raised an Englishman, and would someday inherit his father's title of viscount. But courtesy was beyond him.

He was nothing like Philip Grant, her father's stable groom, who accompanied her on her wild gallops through the London parks as she tried to outrace her future. Philip was blond and lighthearted, with sea blue eyes she could gladly drown in. He understood and cared for

1

her, and to be alone with him holding hands was as romantic as any poem.

Thornton had obviously been drinking before he'd arrived at the celebration, because his laughter was too free and too loud. He stood across the room with his friends, looking the very picture of the court dandy, from his silk doublet to his high neck ruff to the pearl earbob dangling from one ear. Yet where his friends wore their beards dyed in outrageous purple or orange, Thornton was clean-shaven.

He smiled broadly at every lady who passed him, be she maiden or dowager, and his teeth glimmered like moonrise in his dark face.

But he spared not a glance for his betrothed.

Smoldering with fury, she watched him and catalogued the sins he'd thus far committed during their short betrothal. He had never come to visit, never brought gifts. While every other young maiden was at least being wooed by her family's choice in husband, Thornton treated her as but a distasteful business.

Philip's gifts might be only a handful of wildflowers and the pleasure of his company, but she felt cherished by his adoration, beloved.

Thornton, on the other hand, had come early to their betrothal ceremony the previous week, and after signing the contract, had left before she'd even come downstairs. She'd caught only a glimpse of his back as he slammed the front door.

Roselyn should have expected no better, since her parents had chosen her husband because of his money. When they had taken care of the contract without her, her father had said only, "Don't worry yourself, dearest."

When she'd tried to ask about Thornton and his family, her mother had asked in a frigid voice, "Are you questioning our choice of your husband?"

Roselyn had been so offended by the whole process that she went along with them, for after all, she didn't need to read that ornate tiny script when every marriage contract was the same: the groom would be well paid to marry the bride.

But the groom could have made a small effort to *pretend* to court her, for the bride's sake!

She had heard stories of Thornton's wild revelry, his attachment to Queen Elizabeth, his Spanish ancestry—which no one ever let her forget. And to think there might soon be a war with Spain, and she would be married to the enemy! She suspected every female friend of laughing behind her back, and every gentleman friend of deserting her.

Finally, Thornton's father led him forward for the First Meeting, and her own father, the Earl of Cambridge, gripped her elbow as he escorted her to the center of the hall.

"Lady Roselyn," Viscount Thornton said, his

brown eyes filled with hope, "this is my son, Sir Spencer Thornton."

Spencer Thornton glanced at her with those hooded, dark eyes, and a tremor of something—probably shock—jolted her. Then he looked away and swallowed another mouthful of wine. He was as dark as Satan himself, and she wondered if on the morrow the church would burst into flames rather than admit him.

"Sir Spencer," said her father, "allow me to present my daughter, Lady Roselyn."

Full of affronted pride, she wasn't even going to curtsy until her father squeezed her hand in warning. With her chin high, she sank into a deep curtsy. Viscount Thornton gave her a warm smile, while his son stood stone-faced until his father elbowed him. Even then, he only nodded to her.

Roselyn's outrage flamed higher, and she felt humiliated, knowing everyone was watching.

Her betrothed and his friends left the celebration without waiting for the first dance. Alone, Roselyn watched them go from her place near the wall, her arms across her chest. How could she marry such a man? she wondered, glaring at her preening parents as they accepted the congratulations of the nobility. Thornton would probably send her off to his family seat in Cumberland, as far from London as one could get without crossing the Pict's Wall into the wilds of Scotland—just when she was finally of an age to attend the queen's court.

As the party guests began to dance, her mind returned to Philip, who just this day had sworn his undying love for her, vowing to help her escape this forced marriage. She'd told him it could never be, but as she stood alone and contemplated a loveless match, she was more unsure than ever of what she should do. He was forbidden to her by class, by betrothal, but it made their time together wildly exciting. Could she have the unthinkable—a man who loved her for herself?

On his wedding day, Spencer Thornton waited on the stairs of the church, his head pounding, his throat dry, and prayed for the nausea to subside. Sometime before dawn he'd fallen into his bed roaring drunk, but that was still not enough to make him forget the disdain in his betrothed's eyes.

He'd handled the entire affair badly.

But what choice had he? Spencer had done his best to ignore the poor girl his parents had picked for him, hoping that her family would end the courtship. But short of outright disobedience—and he loved his parents too much for that—there was nothing he'd been able to do but drown his rage in his cups.

But he did regret his treatment of her last

night. It wasn't her fault that his parents had resorted to the blackmail of needing an heir. If only they understood that he would never have the kind of marriage they had.

Through the crowds gathered to stare, Spencer saw the approach of Roselyn Harrington's gilt carriage. A tight feeling of despair clutched his chest, but he straightened grimly.

The bride was helped from the carriage, and her wedding garments glittered under the sun. Again he saw that pale face, remembered the vulnerability of freckles scattered across her nose. He found himself hoping that they wouldn't hate each other.

Roselyn took a step toward him and stopped as their gazes clashed.

Suddenly she turned and ran.

Spencer stood in stunned silence as he watched her dodge past people on the street, pull off her headdress, and throw it into the mud. Both sets of relatives moved about in pandemonium, shouting, pointing. Someone ran after her, but it wouldn't matter even if they caught her. The damage was done.

Spencer stood as if he'd been turned into a statue, unsure what he was feeling. Shouldn't it be relief, exaltation?

Everyone turned and looked at him, mouths agape, and a chill shuddered through him. He was used to creating scandal, and enjoyed making sure the nobility knew he was there.

But not this way. His gaze darted frantically from person to person, and soon they were whispering behind their hands. His own friends started to laugh, and the ensuing uproar reverberated through him.

He'd forever be a laughingstock, an object of ridicule—and it was all Roselyn Harrington's fault.

He looked at his parents, whose disappointment must be even worse than his humiliation.

"Am I too late?" said a familiar voice. "Just got into town for the wedding of the year."

Spencer glanced aside to see his brother Alex, lurching up the church steps with a giggling, dressed-up doxy on his arm.

"She left," Spencer said, wondering if his brother would take satisfaction in the rejection. "There will be no wedding."

"But I wanted to meet her," Alex said with an exaggerated sigh. He slung his free arm around his brother. "Come on, Spence, let's go. There's this tavern by the river . . ."

For the last time, Spencer looked down the street where his bride had disappeared, feeling the bitterness inside him freeze and become brittle. Then he turned and walked away.

Chapter 1

◦◦◦◦◦◦

July 1588

In the growing darkness, Spencer Thornton stood by the rail and watched the frantic sailors scrambling up the masts of the Spanish ship, loosening the ropes and sails in a desperate effort to alter their course. The English fleet still sailed behind, sending cannonballs screaming through the sky to topple masts and puncture ships.

Death had been stalking him for days now. He was so weak from lack of food that his pretense of being a seasick soldier seemed real. He couldn't allow himself the solace of sleep because one by one, other British spies were being murdered—and he might be next.

He gripped the rail and stared hard at the Isle of Wight, with its shadowed cliffs and beaches. He had made plans to jump ship there, where he now owned dower property from that ill-fated betrothal.

At least some good had come from his last London scandal.

He would have done anything to escape the notoriety of his missing bride, and the British government had presented him with a way to be needed—a way to prove himself loyal. He'd spent over a year pretending to be Spanish, gathering information on the pathetic condition of the Spanish soldiers and sailors. The armada's food and water were spoiled, and they lacked ample supplies of powder and shot. He was all but certain the Spanish couldn't invade England. All he needed to do was get his information to the queen—unless the traitor killed him first.

The ship was in an uproar: soldiers huddled in sobbing groups, while sailors crawled through the rigging. Now might be his best—and only—chance to get the proof of treachery he needed.

Spencer leaned over the side to check that the boat he'd lowered earlier was still lashed to the hull. Then he headed for the cabin of Rodney Shaw, a highly placed British spy—and the man Spencer believed was betraying his country. As he reached the door, an explosion rocked the ship and the shouting intensified.

He ducked inside the dark cabin, feeling his heart pounding against his ribs and the sweat rolling off him in the stale air. Footsteps pounded overhead; the ship shuddered with the impact of another cannonball. He frantically ran his hands over the table, through the trunks, beneath the bedclothes. He found only one sealed letter, and by the light of gunfire outside the porthole, he was able to make out the first few sentences. It was written by Shaw's Spanish superiors—just what Spencer needed.

After stuffing the letter in an oilskin pouch, he strapped it to his chest beneath his shirt and was soon back in the shadowy corridor. He had taken only one step when he felt the prick of a sword in his back.

"*Señor*?" said a voice.

Spencer held his hands out to his sides to show he was unarmed, then slowly turned around. He looked into the dark, smirking eyes of a Spanish soldier.

Spencer braced himself against the bulkhead and wiped his shaking hand across his forehead. "Forgive me, sir. I am sick, and I was trying to find my way below deck to rest."

The soldier leaned closer, keeping his sword at the ready. "My master is looking for you. And where do I find you? Right outside his door."

Unease spread through Spencer's chest. This man worked for Shaw—but did he know what Spencer had found in the cabin?

He allowed himself to be prodded on deck, where the growing darkness was lit with gunfire. He could just see the island disappearing off the port side—so much for his plans to jump ship before he was caught.

The bow was all but deserted except for the shadowy figures of two men. Spencer approached warily and received another sword prick in the back to hurry him up.

Rodney Shaw—dark-haired and still amazingly well dressed—stepped forward and smiled. "Lord Thornton, how good of you to deliver yourself into our hands," he said softly in English.

Spencer answered in Spanish. "You didn't cover your treachery well, Shaw. Did you not think we would discover your secret?"

"There is no longer a 'we,' Lord Thornton. Every other spy is dead."

Spencer kept his rage contained. "I don't understand why you would do this. Surely you knew that your loyalty would have been well rewarded by the crown."

Shaw only shrugged. "Now I can be well rewarded no matter which side wins. And imagine how grateful the queen will be when I hand her the name of the traitor—Spencer Thornton. I'll tell her what a shame it was that I had to kill him before he could kill me. And then of course, when the Spanish invade with my help, I shall be a hero to them as well."

Spencer's arms were suddenly gripped from behind. Before he could do more than briefly struggle, he felt a blow to his stomach, then to his face. Pain shot through him, and he tried to pull away. Shaw and another of his henchmen took turns pummeling him, and Spencer knew they intended to beat him to death. He deliberately sagged in their arms, and when one of the henchmen leaned over him, Spencer plucked the man's sword away and rolled to his feet.

Shaw's own sword suddenly glittered in the moonlight, and he laughed. Swaying, Spencer blinked his eyes as his vision blurred, but he fought to hold his hand steady. When their swords arced overhead and rang together, he felt the rippling shock of it clear down to his chest. He desperately fought on, wondering which blow would be his last.

His breath came in labored gasps, and sweat dripped into his eyes. When he stumbled to one side, he felt Shaw's sword pierce between his ribs. And even if he managed to defeat Shaw, the Spaniards were just waiting to take Shaw's place.

With one last blow, Spencer knocked Shaw a

step backward, then grabbed the rail and vaulted overboard. For a moment, the wind whistled past his ears. He landed in a crumpled heap in his boat, feeling a shattering pain in his leg where it slammed into the wooden seat. Somehow he managed to pull the knife from his boot and cut the ropes holding the boat against the Spanish galleon.

Dazed and nauseated with pain, he rowed out of reach of the ship's guns, watching the fleet veer away from the treachery of the island.

"I'll find you, Thornton!" echoed across the water, and a bullet whistled past his head.

Once out of range, Spencer tried to staunch the blood flow at his side using his shirt. Then he rowed northwest, to where the chalk cliffs of the island rose out of the sea to guide him through the darkness.

On dark nights, on the low cliffs overlooking the English Channel, Roselyn Grant could almost forget that the English and Spanish fleets were resting at anchor, waiting for dawn to renew their battle. The moonlight tonight wouldn't allow that, illuminating the masts rocking out on the waves. Occasionally the flash of a lantern winked at her, and she could hear a sailor's shout, sounding eerily close.

Many of the island's people had fled to the

mainland, leaving the villages half deserted.
But she had rebuilt her life here, and she would
stay until the Spanish invaded, if necessary.

She had no other place to go.

The wind off the channel was as chilly as the
rest of the cool, wet summer had been. Roselyn
tugged the kerchief closer about her shoulders
and closed her eyes, breathing deeply of the
salt air. Her usual nighttime peace eluded her.

When she opened her eyes, she stared in
shock at a small boat silhouetted in the moonlight, rocking wildly in the breakers close to the
beach. For a moment she thought they were being invaded, but the solitary boat looked empty
as it was tossed ashore and overturned.

She told herself to run away, but the impetu-
ous Roselyn of old suddenly appeared, as if the
last two years hadn't happened. She found herself descending the path to the beach, skidding
on gravel, grabbing clumps of weeds to steady
herself. Her curiosity had awakened from its
long dormancy, and could no longer be ap-
peased. After all, it might be a perfectly good
boat.

She walked unevenly down the sloping sand,
stepping over broken spars and split casks,
remnants of the sea battles. She slowed as she
reached the boat, which was resting against a
boulder, but it was empty. Then she heard a

low, ragged moan. Roselyn froze, taking a deep breath before peering cautiously around the far side of the boat.

For a moment she thought her mind was playing tricks on her, that it was only the gulls she'd disturbed. In the roar of the waves she could imagine anything.

But she heard the sound again, and this time a dark shadow moved. It was a man, sprawled facedown across the wet sand, his lower body buffeted by the surf. Roselyn cautiously crept forward as he moaned more softly, as if his strength were ebbing with the tide.

She crouched down beside the man's body, gathered her courage, and tugged on his shoulder to roll him over. His arms splayed out to his sides; his head lolled. Above a ragged beard, his face looked distorted, misshapen, and she saw the darker shadow of welling blood below his eye.

With a groan, the man shuddered, and Roselyn scrambled away from him.

"Help . . . me."

He was an Englishman, not a Spaniard. Relief flooded through her, and she sagged to her knees at his side. "I'll go for help. I promise I will not be long."

Before she could stand, he reached a trembling hand toward her. "No! Please . . ."

He gripped her fingers with a strength that surprised her. His skin was wet and frigidly cold as he seemed to will her with dark eyes to heed him. She felt caught, trapped in his gaze as the moist wind swirled around them.

Roselyn licked the salt from her lips as she released his hand. "I cannot carry you alone, sir, and I think there's blood soaking your shirt. You might be badly wounded."

"No . . . the Spanish . . . they'll be coming . . ." With a groan he rose up on one elbow. "I can . . . walk."

She knew she should go for help now, before the man injured himself even further, but he had already dragged himself up into a sitting position. Resting his chin against his chest, he took ragged, deep breaths that convulsed his entire body, as water ran in rivulets from his long dark hair.

"Sir . . ." Roselyn began doubtfully.

The sailor groaned as he rolled onto his hands and knees. She gave up trying to persuade him to be still and reached down to help him. He clutched at her shoulders and almost knocked them both to their knees in the surf, but somehow she withstood his weight. He smelled of brine and sweat and blood, and as he threw his arm across her shoulder, the cold ocean water seeped into her clothing.

When he reached his full height, she realized that even injured he could be formidable.

Together they took a few staggering steps across the sand. She could tell that something was wrong with his right leg by how little weight he put on it.

Roselyn cursed herself with every exhaled groan he blasted in her ear. He was too big for her—what was she supposed to do with him, take him all the way to the lord-lieutenant?

Though she thought every staggering step would be his last, he never faltered. During the climb up the cliff path, they had to stop several times as the sailor braced himself against the rock wall and gasped for breath.

"Let me go for help," she pleaded again.

"No." He could barely whisper, but still he clutched her skirts to keep her with him.

She wondered what kind of man he was, to force himself beyond his strength. She could see only the barest outline of his profile in the dark—a bold nose over an unkempt mustache and beard. He wasn't even using his right leg anymore, just her body as a crutch.

They reached the meadow above the cliffs, and she thought the sailor would sag to his knees in relief. Instead his entire body trembled as he held on to her, resting.

Roselyn's own legs were weak, and she felt

disoriented. She was helping a strange man through the stark, moonlit field, and she didn't know what to do next. He hung from her shoulders, head down, his bare feet buried in the high grass.

Though he was a British sailor, she did not dare bring him to her own cottage. She would take him to a shed on her father's lands, where she could tend to his wounds before going to the lord-lieutenant. Not that the militia in the nearby village of Shanklin would have much time for one stray sailor; they were busy digging trenches and scouring the island for powder and shot in case the Spanish invaded.

They half limped, half staggered through the night. Hours could have passed and Roselyn wouldn't have known. She would have been grateful to run into one of the patrols, anything to have help with the ever-increasing burden of the sailor. She was exhausted by the time she reached Wakesfield, her father's estate, where the outbuildings loomed in the distance.

" 'Tis . . . not far," she gasped.

But speech was beyond the sailor's capability as he clung to her. She could feel the bones of his hips and ribs against her, as if he hadn't eaten in a long time. By the saints, what would she do if he died?

When they reached the shed, Roselyn shouldered open the wooden door, and the sweet smell of drying grasses from the mill pond wafted out toward them.

Without a sound, the man dropped onto his knees, then face forward into the pile of grass, almost disappearing into the black shadows of the shed. She could see nothing without a lantern, so she rolled him onto his back and listened to his shallow breathing.

"I shall return in but a moment," she said slowly, hoping he understood. "I'll bring bandages and food."

Roselyn left him and ran across the grounds, past stables and barns, the orchard and the gardens. Her father's manor was dark and silent, with only the bailiff, Francis Heywood, and his family living there. The moon reflected off the panes of the windows like a single bright eye, following her.

Her parents had no idea that she'd sought refuge here. If they knew, they would banish her. She'd refused to jeopardize Francis's position by living in the manor, and instead lived in one of the cottages.

A candle glowing in the small glass window of her home welcomed her inside, where the faint smells of supper still hung in the air. She retrieved a bucket of hot water off a hook over the fire, then put linens, salves, blankets, bread, and a horn of drinking water in a sack she hung over her shoulder. Next she searched for some of Philip's garments buried at the bottom of a chest.

When she returned to the shed, she set about removing the sailor's sodden clothes. Finding an oilskin pouch strapped to his chest, she set it aside in the grass. As she tugged down his breeches she told herself that he was just another man to heal, but feeling his naked skin beneath her hands made her oddly unsettled. After a quick, wide-eyed stare, she put a towel discreetly across his hips. Then she examined the jagged gash in his side, obviously caused by a knife or sword. He groaned when she touched his right leg, and she felt a swelling at his shin—he must have broken the bone. Though his body was leanly muscled, it was obvious that food had not been in plentiful supply on board ship, for his ribs were too evident.

Roselyn cauterized the bleeding wound in his side, cleaned the rest with wine, and applied salve. Then she bandaged his ribs and made a splint for his leg. The sailor's trembling eased as she covered him with a blanket.

Before dawn, the man began to toss and groan in a fever-induced delirium. He seemed panicked, desperate, and she wondered what horrible memories plagued him. When he began to mumble, she froze in stunned surprise.

The words were not English, but Spanish.

She had grown up near seaports and knew

the language enough to recognize it, but not enough to translate.

With a chill of foreboding, she lifted the lantern and held it above him. His hair was black, unfashionably long, and she realized now that his skin was not the pale color of an Englishman. By the saints, could he be a Spaniard?

She hung the lantern back on its hook, reminding herself that he had spoken perfect English up to this point.

Yet wouldn't a Spanish spy know English? Had he arrived to ready the island for invasion?

Roselyn reined in her panicked thoughts. He had been in battle and was barely clinging to life, which was not how a spy would come ashore. He had been fleeing from the Spanish—or so he'd said. And since many Englishmen knew Spanish, she couldn't label the man an enemy with so little proof.

"What is your name?" she whispered, knowing he couldn't hear her.

For two days the sailor moved in and out of consciousness, and Roselyn began to regret that she hadn't brought him to her cottage. She was constantly running for supplies, for broth to dribble between his lips, for soap to clean his body and his matted hair and beard. She deliberately chose his most unconscious moments for such "baths," then tried to tell herself that her hands weren't shaking from performing such intimate acts on a strange man.

He occasionally mumbled unintelligible words, though once he asked a lucid question: "Do you live on my land?"

Before she could even think what to reply, he was asleep again.

But always she worried about being discovered by the Heywoods. She could never put them in the way of a possible Spanish plot. Francis had been like a father to her, his children were practically her siblings, and they had been nothing but kind in the year since she'd fled to the Isle of Wight. She couldn't involve them in this new problem she'd created for herself—not again. She could last until the sailor was well enough to turn over to the militia.

Late in the afternoon, Roselyn returned to the shed with a thin stew for the sailor's meal. She paused in the doorway, watching his face in a shaft of sunlight. The swelling from his bruises had subsided, and beneath all that long hair and beard, he seemed to be a handsome man. In his sleep, he turned his head, and his hair fell away from his brow.

She frowned, feeling a prickling sensation on the back of her neck. She walked forward as if in a dream and knelt beside the man, setting her tray on the dirt floor.

Roselyn felt a dim sense of panic reach her, grasp her, until she almost couldn't swallow. With a shaking hand, she pushed the hair off his hot forehead, as a nobleman would wear it.

Beneath the mottled purple and green bruises and the ragged beard was the face of Spencer Thornton—her betrothed.

Chapter 2

Roselyn scrambled away from Thornton, accidentally kicking over the bowl of stew. She pressed her back against the wall and stared wildly at him, waiting for him to awaken and remind her of all the sins she'd committed.

She suddenly had a vivid recollection of the eve of her wedding, remembered his face looking her over with a casual cynicism and then looking away in disinterest. Her guilt for her own part in that disaster was swallowed by a sudden flaring of outraged anger at him, at her parents, for what they'd all forced her to do. Remembering it made her stomach clench.

Just when she thought her life was proceeding at an even pace—she had a place to live, a way to earn her livelihood, and a few friends who cared about her—she had to face a ghost out of her past.

Not a ghost, she told herself, but a man who'd

wronged her—a man she, too, had wronged, she forced herself to admit.

And he was no common sailor.

Roselyn thought again of the foreign words he'd mumbled. His mother was Spanish; naturally he knew the language. Yet what was he doing with the fleet—and which fleet was he with? Did he hold alliances with Spain that she knew nothing about?

Sliding down against the wall, she buried her face in her hands and shuddered. Why was this happening to her? She had tried to escape Thornton—and ended up shackled to Philip, a man no better, who wanted her only for the same reasons Thornton did: money and power.

Just when she'd come to terms with living her life alone, Thornton reappeared. She remembered the words he'd mumbled, *Do you live on my land?* Could he have bought property near Shanklin?

That night Roselyn couldn't sleep. Questions and fears raced through her mind, but she didn't want to confront them. She rose and dressed by firelight, then went out into the night with only the moon to guide her. She wanted to walk in peace, to feel the breeze on her face, to inhale the soothing smell of flowers and the sea.

Yet when she found herself near the shed

where Thornton lay, she was not surprised. Everything she wanted to escape had to do with him. With a heavy sigh, she opened the door.

A shaft of moonlight cut across the pile of drying grass—but Thornton wasn't lying upon it. The blanket she had covered him with lay in a heap on the ground.

For a moment she remained frozen with shock, then came back to herself and quickly searched the shed. He was gone.

Had someone discovered him and taken him away? Surely Francis Heywood would have been notified, and the sound of men's voices as they trudged to the shed would have alerted her.

Could Thornton have left on his own? He was weak from his injuries, and he wouldn't be able to stand with a broken leg.

But he'd also been delirious with fever.

Roselyn searched the moonlit ground outside the shed, and found dark stains in the grass. She touched them with her fingers and felt wetness, then lifted her hand to her face and smelled fresh blood.

She straightened and looked out across the estate. For a moment she was torn with indecision; should she let him go?

But she couldn't allow him to bleed to death

in the grass, or fall off the cliff onto the rocky beach. She wouldn't be able to live with the sin of her cowardice.

So she followed the trail of crushed grass made by Thornton's body. Every moment she expected to catch sight of him, but he'd crawled farther than she would have imagined. Her nervous fears increased, and the darkness seemed to wrap around her, with the wind picking up to tug at her unbound hair. She thought she heard the sound of voices, but it faded so abruptly she knew she must be imagining it.

Where was he?

Just as she began to wonder if she'd followed the wrong trail, she saw a glimmer of something parting the grass before her. She knelt down and found Thornton, whose bare chest gleamed by moonlight between the bandages. He wore only Philip's old breeches. He lay on his side, trying to struggle up onto his knees.

Though she didn't want to touch him, she forced herself to place her hand on his arm. She felt the fire of his fever as he suddenly grasped her wrist and yanked her to the ground. She twisted onto her back, but before she could move he was upon her, his forearm against her throat. She tried to yell, but her voice came out as a muffled gasp.

Kicking her heels into the ground and thrashing, she caught his arm and managed to pull it enough to breathe. His eyes were narrowed; his teeth were bared in a grimace above her.

"Thornton!" she rasped. "I'm not your enemy!"

She rolled and tried to push him off her, and in their struggles his free hand caught her waist. He immediately went still. All she could hear was his breath rattling in his chest. Slowly, his hand skimmed up her rib cage.

"Yes, I am a woman!" she said in outrage, before his touch could become too intimate. She slid out from beneath him, and he allowed her escape, collapsing forward onto his elbows.

"Mr. Thornton," she whispered regretfully, "you must come back with me."

He got one knee beneath him and tried to crawl away from her, but ended up sinking down into the grass with a moan. He was muttering, and when she leaned closer, she realized that he was using Spanish again.

Suddenly Roselyn felt a whisper of gooseflesh rise across her arms, and she stilled. Again, she heard voices, and realized with dawning horror that there were men out on the cliffs. She collapsed onto her stomach at Thornton's side, her breath coming rapidly.

She stared at his flushed face and his fluttering eyelids as the men came closer. What were they doing out in the middle of the night?

Slowly she lifted up until she could just see over the swaying grass. A group of men hovered like dark shadows near the cliffs, moonlight glittering off them.

She realized they were wearing swords. Could it be the militia from nearby Shanklin?

Or the Spanish, ready to invade England?

Roselyn dropped down again, only to find Thornton's eyes open as he stared at her in exhausted bewilderment. What was she to do? If she crept away, they might find him and take him off her hands. He'd wake up soon and be able to explain everything. He might not even remember her.

But if those were Spaniards out there . . .

Thornton suddenly gripped her arm and pulled her closer. She smothered a gasp as she stared into his wild, dark eyes and felt the heat of him burn her. His lips moved, and she heard his hoarse mutterings—again, in Spanish.

What should she do? If the militia saw him like this, with his black hair, olive skin, and foreign words, they would surely take him for a Spaniard.

And if the soldiers were Spanish, then everyone on the island was doomed.

Roselyn had no choice but to wrap her arms about him and try to keep him quiet. The patrol was closer now, and a gruff laugh carried on the wind—and the sound of the Queen's English. She shuddered with relief as one fear faded.

"Shh," she whispered, holding Thornton's face to her neck, praying he would stop struggling. He stiffened, and she worried that his strength would yet prove too much for her.

Then with a sigh, his whole body relaxed, going heavy against her. She felt his arms tighten about her waist, and a new fear rose in her mind as he slid his knee between hers.

Everything in her wanted to rebel, to slap him and push him away. Instead she lay against him seething with anger, feeling his mouth move on her throat, then lower to her collarbone. She shivered. Every rumor she'd heard of him over the last year blazed starkly in her mind: his affairs, his mistresses, the scandals he caused wherever he went. Only wild, foolish women would fall for the seductive words of a man like him.

She bit her lip and squeezed her eyes tightly shut as his lips nibbled the high neckline of her gown. She tried to insinuate her fingers against his mouth—anything to distract him—but immediately pulled away when he tried to kiss them. Kiss her fingers, by the saints! She pressed his head even harder against her, almost wishing she could smother him into unconsciousness.

She was caught in her own scheme, for if they were found together . . .

A cold dread chilled her.

Spencer felt that he existed only in his dreams, and they were hot, feverish nightmares of battle: choking smoke, burning sails hanging from the yardarms, cannonballs screaming overhead. He felt again the slice of the sword at his side, and the pain of it awakened him.

The sun in his eyes seemed out of place, and he squinted as it lanced through his head. But he couldn't lift a hand to shield his face; he could do nothing but lie still.

There was something he had to do, some urgent mission that eluded him.

"Would you like some water?"

He tensed. It was the voice he'd been hearing in his dreams—a voice speaking English.

He opened his eyes to see a small barn with windows opened to the daylight. He turned his aching neck slowly and saw cobweb-strung beams dwindling into the darkness of the roof, then the hazy shape of a woman, silhouetted against the bright window.

She leaned over him, small, delicate, concerned, but with perhaps a touch of fear in her eyes. She wore a white apron over a country gown of black homespun. Her light brown hair was pulled back severely from her face and tucked beneath a plain white cap. She wore no face paint, no elaborate headdresses or jewelry to distract a man from the absolute perfection of her smooth skin. Her small nose held a smattering of freckles, and above it she had wintry gray eyes.

"Would you like some water?" she asked again, a soft, deeper voice than he would have imagined coming from such a delicate throat.

And then Spencer realized that his mouth was parched. In growing dismay, he wondered how her face had made him forget his discomfort. He tried to speak, but managed only a nod.

The woman put her arm beneath his head and held a drinking horn to his mouth. His cheek brushed her breast, and she smelled of wildflowers and baking bread, images that soothed him, comforted him.

Then the cool water touched his tongue and he swallowed it frantically.

"Slowly," she murmured, and he felt the vibration in her chest.

"What's . . . your name?" His voice was gravelly and hoarse.

The woman sat back on her heels and clasped her hands together in her lap. "Rose Grant," she said softly, with a refined accent that did not match her garments. "Who are you?"

For a moment he almost said the name he'd been living under for a year and a half, but re-

membered in time. "Spencer Thornton." His
real name sounded foreign, forbidden. "I owe
you my gratitude for saving my life."

Rose Grant nodded, then propped his head
against a cushion and fed him like a babe. It
had been so long since he'd had a hot stew that
he actually didn't mind.

She set the bowl aside too soon, and as he
looked at it longingly, he saw her first uneasy
smile. It softened her features into a shy prettiness.

"You can have more later," she murmured.
"First let me examine your wounds. You were
bleeding again last night after your little adventure."

"My adventure?"

"You were determined to leave." She hesitated. "Have you no memory of it?"

"None," he whispered, his eyes feeling
heavy. "What . . . did I do?"

"Crawled away. I found you near the cliffs."

"I guess I'm lucky to be alive." He finally remembered the reason he was trying to escape:
his battle with Rodney Shaw, his plunge overboard instead of death at the hands of traitors.
And Shaw's promise to find him. Spencer had
to get to London.

But when Rose pulled off the bandages
across his chest, he fought a sudden rushing
wave of pain and sank into unconsciousness.

Roselyn sat back and exhaled a trembling breath. He was once again asleep, and she didn't have to look into those dark, mysterious eyes for another moment. Her hand still rested on his chest, and though she had long since lost her pale London complexion, her skin stood out starkly against the olive hue of Thornton's.

She snatched her hand back, remembering that she had misled him about her name.

She was a coward.

But then she remembered eluding the militia, and the terror of keeping him quiet, while his hot mouth moved intimately against her skin. It had taken bravery of a sort not to turn him over to the patrol and be done with him, especially since he'd tried to choke her to death!

And it had taken all of her endurance to drag and half carry him back to the shed as the gray of dawn rose at the edge of the island like mist from the sea. He had collapsed into a deep sleep, while she had slept only fitfully on her own pallet.

Still tired, she finished changing his bandages, then leaned back against the wall and studied him. They would have been married almost two years now, if she hadn't run away.

Lady Roselyn Thornton would have been an entirely different person from Roselyn Grant.

She remembered her girlhood and cringed at her selfishness, at the impulsiveness that had made her throw away her family and her life because she thought she knew best.

Now she lived her days at peace, alone—but Thornton could ruin it all.

Whenever Francis came back from the mainland with the latest London scandals, she was always glad she hadn't married Thornton. His name was often involved—in fact, she had heard a tale recently of how he had escaped a married woman's husband by climbing over roofs. She frowned as she adjusted her patient's blanket, feeling again his thin ribs. He did not seem as if he had recently been living the wild, dissipated life in London.

But it was none of her concern. She just hoped he didn't remember her, since they'd only looked upon each other twice. Then she'd worn her finest, costliest garments woven with jewels, with a farthingale that widened her hips stylishly and a headdress that allowed her long hair to tumble free. And she'd been plumper from the easier life she used to lead.

Thornton could not possibly remember her. She would speak little, make him well, and turn him over to the militia when he was better able to defend himself against their questions. She was not made to seek out the truth about spies, or meddle in politics. She was just a village baker now, and she no longer wanted more.

*   *   *

The next time Spencer awoke, dusk was falling, drifting through the open windows like gray fog—the gray of Rose Grant's eyes.

Now where had that come from?

He saw her then, sitting beneath the window, watching him. Again she wore a black gown, but this time with a kerchief around her shoulders. Was it even the same day? He expected her to lean over him, to fuss, but she sat still, her arms about her knees, watching him in a way that startled him.

For a moment he had the strangest sensation he'd seen those piercing eyes before. But she'd been caring for him for who knew how many days, so he must already be familiar with her face.

She fed him fish soup, never once complaining about his slow pace. When he was finished, Rose stood up to light the candle in the lantern. She reached for the tray of food and turned toward the door.

"Don't go," he found himself saying gruffly. "I don't know how I got here—I don't know where I am."

Her shoulders seemed tense as she kept her back to him just a moment too long. Then she set the tray on a stool and turned to face him. She did not seem a tall woman; her shoulders were narrow, almost delicate. The lantern caught and glistened in tendrils of her hair where they escaped her cap. Her apron was cinched about her waist, making her appear fragile. How had she gotten him to this shed by herself?

"This is your fifth day on the Isle of Wight," she said. "I found you on the beach, next to a wrecked boat."

Spencer closed his eyes and remembered hard, wet sand beneath his cheek—and a woman rolling him over, her face as pale and lovely as the moon in the night sky.

"Did you see another boat?" He held his breath, knowing the importance of her answer.

"No."

He dropped his head back onto the cushion, feeling a meager amount of relief.

"You said you needed my help," she added, "that the Spanish might be coming for you."

He narrowed his eyes, and the rehearsed words suddenly came easily to him. "I was aboard the *Newcastle*, and she took a lot of shot that last day. I remember her sinking . . . but that's all."

Rose continued to study him, and for a moment having to deceive this woman left a foul taste in his mouth. But he'd been lying for so long that a lie to protect someone seemed like redemption.

"What happened on the channel?" he asked. "Is there still fighting going on?"

"The fleets sailed away the second day you were here," she said. "They fought, and we heard rumors that they would invade, but they never did."

She hesitated, watching him with eyes that almost didn't blink. "Should I send word to your captain?"

"I am useless to him now. I'll rejoin when I'm able to serve."

Did she believe him? The last was the truth, after all.

"Rose, I owe you my life. Why did you help me?"

She looked down and shrugged her shoulders. "I couldn't leave you to die."

"Others would have."

"I have seen enough death," she said, and he thought he heard a touch of fierceness in her voice.

Spencer's curiosity was roused, but why should he ask a country maid about her life? He was frustrated by his weakness when he really needed to be in London. He rubbed his shaking hands over his face and felt each bruise begin to ache.

"Rose," he said, surprised to find his voice faltering, "whose land are we on? Are there others who know I'm here?"

She repositioned the cushion under his head.

In the meager light she looked as tired as he felt. Had taking care of him cost her so much?

Roselyn sat back on her heels, praying that Thornton would fall asleep before she had to answer. He looked paler by the moment, and she lifted the blanket, but saw no fresh blood on his bandages.

"Over half the people have left the island because of the Spanish, leaving the villages strangely quiet," she said. "Besides myself, only the bailiff and his family are on this estate, but I have not told them of you."

His eyes closed, his mouth relaxed, and then he was asleep.

With a shuddering sigh, she dropped her chin to her chest. How long could she keep this up, holding off his questions, revealing as little as possible? And why didn't he want people to know about him?

She remembered the way his eyes had not quite held hers when he told her about serving on the *Newcastle*. That look had been burned into her the first time she'd met him two years ago. Her father had introduced her, and it was as if Thornton didn't *want* to see her. She'd been overcome with anger and mortification. Even though she disliked having to deal with him again, she was also curious, because she sensed there were truths he held in reserve.

She pressed her eyes closed—and saw his eyes: dark, fringed with heavy lashes, hiding his thoughts yet penetrating enough to see through to hers.

Chapter 3

Late the next afternoon, Roselyn worked in her bake house preparing supper. She felt tired and uneasy, and told herself the cause could only be Thornton.

At the sound of footsteps outside the door she gasped and whirled, holding a knife, her heart pounding.

John Heywood stopped in the doorway, his smile fading. "Roselyn?"

The knife dropped from her shaking hands and barely missed her foot. She ran her hands over her face and gave John a tremulous smile. What had she been thinking? Was she so on edge that she imagined enemies following her about the island?

"John, you startled me," she said lamely, picking up the knife. "I have felt . . . uneasy all day."

"It is understandable with a war going on so near."

41

He came toward her and she tried to relax, to remember how happy she usually was to see him. He was the eldest Heywood son, of average height and spare from hard work, and his hands could work miracles out of wood. More and more he had taken to visiting her, to dropping hints about marriage, even though he knew they could only be handfasted, not legally married in the church.

She felt comfortable with him, and she'd begun to think that that was as good as love could ever get.

But to see him now, when Thornton was so near, only made her nervous.

"We've been worried about you, Roselyn," he said, taking the knife from her hand and setting it on the table. "We've missed your morning visits."

"The bread," she said, shaking her head. "I haven't brought your order lately."

" 'Tis not the bread we miss. Mother and Charlotte have baked what we need." He smiled and leaned down to press a quick kiss to her cheek. "We've barely seen you. It's almost as if you've gone back into mourning. Twice now, Charlotte has come to practice her baking with you, but you've been gone."

Charlotte was John's fourteen-year-old sister, and her cheerful companionship had eased Roselyn's loneliness when she'd first returned to the island. What if the girl had followed her to the shed?

"You must be working too hard," John said with a smile. "I'll have to keep a closer eye on you."

She usually enjoyed their banter, but now his words made her worry. She could not risk the Heywoods finding Thornton, not if the man could be an enemy. How could she bring such danger on the family she loved?

After John left Roselyn approached the door to the shed, but she could see at once that Thornton wasn't lying where she'd left him. She felt a moment of absolute panic, wondering if he'd truly killed himself this time.

She entered the doorway and gave a sharp cry as a hand grasped her upper arm and pulled her inside. The tray bobbled in her hands as she recognized Thornton, bare-chested and imposing.

He leaned against the wall, standing on one leg and bracing himself with the palm of his hand. His whole body trembled as he looked down at her. She realized how truly tall he was, how easily he could overpower her if he chose. In the growing evening darkness, perspiration glistened on his face.

"My leg is broken, isn't it?" he whispered.

His big hand slid behind her head to tilt her

face up to him, and Roselyn caught her breath
on a gasp at the shock that went through her.

"I must leave here." His whisper was almost
a hiss. "It's been five days! I've never been so
incapacitated. I'm sorry . . . the word means—"

"I know what it means," she said coldly.

He held her still, his fingers spread across her
skull, his eyes delving into hers. "Yes . . ." he
said softly, "I can see that you do. You're not a
typical country maid."

"And six days have now passed."

"Six days? I cannot even keep track of such a
simple thing!" His mouth turned up in a grim
laugh. "I don't even know whose clothes I'm
wearing, or how I got into them."

"I helped you."

His gaze focused on her again, and she felt
herself tremble as it dipped to her mouth.

"You are quite the nursemaid," he murmured.

For a moment Roselyn could only remember
lying beneath him on the cliffs, his hand just below her breast. Suddenly she couldn't bear to
be near him, because it only made her remember that their fathers had tried to force this intimacy on them. "Please let me set the tray
down."

He released her at once, and she placed the
tray on the ground.

"You need to lie down. You're not strong enough to be about."

Again he laughed with little humor. "But you're strong, aren't you? I must have been dead weight when you . . . disrobed me."

She felt a blush steal across her features and thanked God the sun had set so Thornton couldn't see. She could barely admit to herself that she'd studied his nakedness as if she'd never seen a man before.

"If you saw everything," he continued, the quirk in his mouth dying, "was I wearing a pouch strapped to my chest?"

"No."

She didn't hesitate to withhold the truth, even though she saw the brief look of despair in his eyes. She had forgotten all about the pouch, and hoped it was still buried in the grass beneath him. She needed to examine it before she gave it back to him, to determine if he was a spy.

She put her arm around his back, and he half hopped, half dragged himself to the stool.

Thornton had already wandered away once—he had almost done so again. What if he told people she was caring for him? Her parents could discover where she was, and make her leave the only place she'd ever felt safe.

Roselyn took a deep breath. "This arrangement isn't working out."

"Arrangement?" His black eyebrows rose. "You sound as if I'm renting lodgings from you."

"I'm sorry, but it's getting too hard to keep running down here. I'm the village baker, and I have duties I can no longer neglect. You need to come home with me where I can better . . . care for you." And she could retrieve the pouch.

But she felt heat suffuse her body at the thought of having him alone in her cottage. She vividly remembered the feel of his leg between hers. What was wrong with her?

"You should eat, regain your strength a bit, and then we'll go."

"Now?"

"We cannot go during the day; someone might see you."

He questioned her no more, just looked thoughtful as he ate his meat pie. After lighting the lantern, she felt that watching him eat was suddenly too intimate, so she glanced out the window.

He took a last swallow of ale and handed her the tankard. "Are you ready, Rose? Forgive me, but I'll have to lean on you."

Now he treated her cordially, though she was but a stranger to him. When she was his betrothed, a frightened young girl, he'd been cruel. She would not forget.

"Very well, Mr. Thornton," she said, remembering not to use his title, which simple Rose Grant wouldn't know. She took his hands and placed them on her shoulders, trying not to notice the warmth of his callused palms. "Use me to stand."

With a grunt of exertion he rose up on his good leg. Wincing at the pressure on her shoulders, she slid beneath his arm.

She reached for the lantern and blew out the candle, saying, "I can't have the bailiff seeing us—unless you'd like to be taken in and nursed by his family."

"You are doing a fine job," he said—too quickly.

He obviously didn't want anyone else to know where he was.

Together they set off across the estate, guided only by the moon and Roselyn's sure knowledge of her home. In every shadow she thought she saw the villagers watching them, prepared to spread the word that she was housing a strange man. Perhaps John had been suspicious, and still lingered nearby. It was difficult to put her nervousness aside, especially when the hair on the back of her neck prickled with strange awareness. *Was* someone out there in the darkness?

A quarter hour had not passed before Thornton's breath was rasping in his chest, and his perspiration soaked her clothing. Finally she saw the faint light in the window of her cottage, and she breathed a shuddering sigh of relief. She pushed open her door and almost dragged him inside.

Awkwardly holding him while leaning over, she pulled a bench away from the table. "Sit here, Mr. Thornton. Give me a moment to prepare a pallet for you."

She brought her own goose-feather mattress from the loft and made his bed in the corner closest to the hearth. She could make herself another mattress on the morrow.

As she helped him to his feet, he staggered forward and slung both arms over her shoulders in the semblance of an intimate embrace. She felt herself blush as her face was pressed to his chest, and she had no choice but to grip his waist to keep him upright.

"Forgive me," he murmured into her hair.

She remained silent, frozen, too aware of him.

"You smell wonderful."

When she didn't answer, his chest shook in a laugh. "I'll wager I don't."

Roselyn couldn't stop the smile that fleetingly crossed her face. Why did he have to be charming, even in sickness? She hadn't suspected he had this side to him.

Together they managed to get him onto the pallet, where he collapsed back and closed his eyes as she covered him with a blanket.

"I must leave you for a few moments," she said. "I have to return for the tray and the lantern."

When she reached the shed, she began to dig in the pile of grass for his pouch. She found it quickly, then held it up in the meager light. It was still damp, and tightly tied at the neck. It took her endless minutes to loosen the leather laces.

She found herself opening the pouch slowly, not eager to know what was inside. She had nursed Thornton and held off death for him, and though she longed for him to be gone from her peaceful island, she didn't want him arrested for treason.

And yet—that would be proof that she'd made the right decision in not marrying him.

Her hand shook as she pulled out several sheets of parchment, folded and sealed with an unfamiliar wax imprint. Only hesitating for a moment, she carefully lifted the wax and spread open the letter. Her stomach sank in immediate distress.

The words were in Spanish.

Roselyn stared at the unintelligible letter and gritted her teeth; anger raged through her as quickly as gossip at court. Would an English viscount actually betray his country for the sake of his mother's people?

She told herself to remain calm, that this

could be just a letter to Thornton's mother. But would he have asked for such a simple thing the moment he had his wits about him?

She couldn't give it back to him; she'd already lied and told him she didn't have it. She couldn't give it to the militia, either. If no one understood Spanish, they could very well arrest him as a precautionary measure—or God forbid, hang him as a spy on his appearance alone.

She couldn't allow that to happen. She would have to be satisfied that he wouldn't betray his country before she allowed him to leave her home. She would watch him, even make him feel comfortable around her. And she would listen to every word he said, in hopes of piecing together the puzzle that was Spencer Thornton.

She reburied the oilskin pouch and its questionable contents beneath the cut grass.

When Roselyn returned to her cottage, she stood above Thornton and looked down on him. He was deep in an exhausted sleep, with shadows darkening his eyes.

She dreaded bathing him again. It would be better to do as much of it as she could while he was asleep.

Spreading towels about him to catch the soapy water, she began to wash him. But removing his breeches this time was more embarrassing and intimate. She knew who he was

now, what he could have been to her—husband.
He was different from Philip, darker and larger,
and part of her wanted to stare.

Instead she concentrated on removing his
splint and washing his legs, pretending she
didn't feel overly warm and flustered. It was
only as she moved up his body that she realized the effect her ministrations were having on
him. He was becoming . . . aroused.

Her face shot with heat, and she didn't know
what to do, where to turn. She wasn't through
bathing him, yet she couldn't keep looking
at . . . it. She dropped the wet cloth over his
groin, then gasped as he awakened with a start
and came up on one elbow.

"What the—" Thornton began, then gaped at
his barely concealed nudity.

"I needed to . . . bathe you," she began, faltering with an embarrassment she wasn't used
to. "I thought it would be better if you were
asleep."

He pulled a towel over his hips. "Aren't you
a little young to bathe strange men? Surely
your husband couldn't approve."

"My husband is dead. You've been wearing
his garments."

"I'm sorry for your loss," he said in a gruff
voice.

There was something absurd about a naked,
aroused man expressing his sympathies.

An awkward silence hovered between them, and she should have looked away—but couldn't. They seemed caught, their gazes bound together, their bodies too close.

Thornton finally cleared his throat, and his eyes dropped down her body before he looked away. "Let me finish this . . . bath, if you don't mind."

"You're still weak—"

"Then let me take care of . . . certain areas."

Roselyn waited outside in the darkness, her back against the cottage, hugging herself against the night wind. The stars overhead seemed distant, cold, and she had the strangest feeling of exposure. She closed her eyes and tried to pretend that she didn't feel watched.

When Thornton called for her, she stepped inside and closed the door quickly. He had a towel wrapped tightly about his hips.

After wringing out the cloth in the soapy water, she washed carefully about his bandages, holding his long arms while she soaped them. When she looked up into his face she realized with a start that he was again watching her.

He gave her a crooked grin. "I don't suppose you'll allow me to return the favor someday."

A slow heat burned her face. How dare he tease her after he had rejected her? But he didn't remember her—and she had rejected him in the end.

She managed to look coolly into his face while she worked soap into his short beard. "Shall I shave this for you?"

His smile fled, and his eyes narrowed, leaving her with a strange chill.

"Why would you ask such a thing?" he said in a low voice. "Do not most men of your acquaintance wear beards?"

She had seen him without one two years before, and merely made the error of thinking he still wore it that way. Why did he take offense?

"I did not know if you wore a beard. I was merely granting you the courtesy of asking."

She didn't break his gaze until he finally smiled and shook his head.

"Forgive me. I am not used to being so . . . coddled by a woman."

"Have you no wife, Mr. Thornton?"

"No. The uncertainty of war delayed any thought of marriage."

She longed to see some signs of guilt in his face, but he showed nothing. She placed towels about his head and proceeded to wash his hair, trying to quell her unease at this strange intimacy.

Chapter 4

Spencer told himself he should feel uneasy having Rose bathe him as if they were longtime lovers instead of strangers. But her hands rubbing his scalp were strangely soothing, washing away months of sea life.

He focused his gaze on her determined face as she finished drying his hair and began patting his arms with a towel. He guessed she'd not been married long, though there was a weariness about her that seemed to indicate she lived a hard life.

She slid the towel down his torso, and he willed his body not to react or the towel at his hips would become recognizably snug again.

"Allow me to help you dress," she said.

Her deep, mellow voice suddenly seemed . . . intimate. If this were any other time or place, he would be welcoming her help and turning it to his advantage. It had been well over a year since he'd shared any intimacy with a woman.

They compromised. She slid clean breeches onto his lower legs, then turned her back while he struggled to pull them up.

"I was wondering if you'd like me to send word to your family that you're alive," she said suddenly.

That doused his lustful thoughts.

"No. You can turn around now."

She stood uncertainly in the center of the room. "But won't your parents wonder if you're hurt?"

"My mother will only worry more if she hears of my injuries," he said softly, still studying her. And then he said something unplanned, foolish. "My father died last year."

"My condolences to you," she murmured.

Why had he felt the need to say something so personal to this woman he barely knew?

"Maybe it was for the best," Spencer said, looking up into her wide, gray eyes. "I don't want him to know—I don't want him to see—" What—his shame? The humiliation he'd soon suffer in London? "I would be a disappointment to him," he finished lamely.

"I'm sure that is not true."

He seldom allowed himself to think of all the ways he'd disappointed his parents. As a child he could do nothing to help his mother, a Spanish noblewoman. Whenever his father took him and Alex to London, his mother usually stayed home alone. He still could see their heads together as they spoke in low voices in the great hall of their Cumberland estate, the loving way they held hands, the wistfulness on her face as she kissed her family good-bye. She was not as welcome everywhere as her husband was—Spencer and his brother had paid the same price.

His father didn't see it—didn't *want* to see it. But Spencer and Alex knew what it was to walk into a room and have gazes slide away from them, to hear whispers, to know that every smile was false. He was used to feeling like a foreigner in England, ashamed of his heritage, hurt and angry when he and his brother were ignored. But it hadn't taken long for either of them to realize that people were forced to notice them if they caused a scandal.

Rose helped him finish dressing, then said a quiet good-night, and carried a candleholder as she climbed a rope ladder up into the loft. The candle threw crazy shadows across the beams and roof as she undressed. When she blew it out, he listened for her breathing, then cursed himself for a fool.

He tried to distract himself by examining her home, looking for clues to the mystery of Rose. Drying herbs and baskets hung from the beams supporting the thatched roof. Though the timber-framed cottage had only one room, it boasted a fireplace and chimney, and glass in the windows.

She seemed to live alone, but how did she support herself? The only people he'd ever met who were this generous to strangers were his parents, but they had money to support their good deeds.

Remembering his parents unfortunately made him think of his wedding day. He had warned his parents that proper young ladies would have nothing to do with him. But he hadn't been prepared for the tears in his mother's eyes, and how badly he'd felt to disappoint her once again.

With a groan, he imagined her reaction when Rodney Shaw claimed her son was a traitor. The pouch had been all that stood between him and a hanging, but it was gone now. Shaw would beat him to London and whisper whatever lies he wanted to the queen, blaming Spencer for his own crimes. Perhaps Shaw would even create convincing proof—or bring along a "witness."

He *had* to get to London. He propped himself up on his hands and swung his broken leg to the floor, but pain and weakness could not be overcome by will alone. He had barely been able to walk *with* Rose's help. He dropped back on the pallet and punched the wall.

* * *

At dawn Roselyn was in the tiny bake house behind her cottage, with eight loaves of bread in the large courtyard oven. Though she had sold most of her baked goods in Shanklin before the Spanish threat had driven away the villagers, she had steady customers at Wakesfield Manor—another reason to bless the Heywoods.

It was past time to deliver bread to the manor, as John's visit had reminded her, so she couldn't avoid them any longer. She returned to her cottage, set bread and cider beside the slumbering Thornton, picked up her baskets, and left.

The manor house, more windows than walls, glittered like a jewel amid the rolling green fields and trimmed hedges. She followed the gravel path to the rear of the manor.

When she entered the kitchen, the Heywood family had already gathered around the trestle table used by the servants. Without her parents in residence, only Francis and his family lived at the manor.

Francis's long, bushy mustache tickled when he kissed her cheek, and he took the basket of bread from her hand. His wife, Margaret, plump and white-haired as a mother should be, patted the bench beside her, and Roselyn sat down. She thought of her own mother, her hair dyed yellow, her mouth always too painted to give her children kisses.

As Margaret hugged her, Roselyn suddenly felt an overwhelming desire to tell the older woman everything, to relieve herself of this burden of Thornton. But if he was a spy, how could she put the Heywoods at risk?

So she bestowed a bright, forced smile on Charlotte, who often spent hours in the village with Roselyn helping her to sell her pastries and bread. Thomas, Charlotte's elder by a few years, also smiled back as his face turned red.

"Where is John?" Roselyn asked.

Francis and Margaret exchanged smiles, as if she had just asked when she could marry him.

"John had carpentry work in Shanklin today," Margaret said.

Roselyn concentrated on her porridge. "Tell him I said good day."

"We will!" Charlotte bubbled with so much amusement that Roselyn gave her a narrow-eyed look of warning.

The girl only grinned back, and Roselyn couldn't stop her own reluctant smile. Was her own sister like Charlotte? The girls were close in age, but Roselyn hadn't seen her sister in two years.

Francis sat down opposite her and pulled a piece of bread from the loaf. "We missed you at supper Sunday, Lady Roselyn. You should not keep to yourself so much. A year has passed now; you must go on with your life. I had thought you were doing better when I didn't see you at the graveyard Sunday afternoon."

For the first time she had missed her weekly visit. The sorrow struck her hard, and tears came to her eyes.

Charlotte touched her hand. "John wanted you to know that he put flowers on the grave for you."

Roselyn could have groaned. John even *acted* the part of her husband.

And now she was lying to them all, risking her place among them.

The Wakesfield chapel graveyard was empty when Roselyn arrived, and she wound her way through the well-worn paths between the head-stones. At her husband's grave, there was only a simple stone, carved with his name—and their baby's.

She dropped to her knees and put her palm on the grass and earth that covered their bod-ies. Of Philip, she thought little—he had made her miserable in repayment for her parents dis-owning her.

But Mary, their daughter, had been only two months old when the plague took her, too. Though Roselyn had protested, the Heywoods had buried father and daughter together, as if Philip had ever held the baby while he was alive.

She laid the wildflowers she'd brought across the grave, beside the dying flowers John had left. The misery she had suffered as Philip's wife had been worth the joy of carrying her daughter inside her body and in her arms, though it had been for only months instead of a lifetime. She realized that her grief was no longer so overwhelming, but had become a part of her.

If she had married Spencer Thornton, she'd never have known the warmth and peace of holding Mary. A rational part of her knew that she would have had other children—but in her heart, another child couldn't replace Mary.

Spencer had never lain abed for so many days. His frustration and weakness infuriated him—and sent him one step closer to despair. He knew he could not leave within the next week, but surely a fortnight would be enough time . . .

Then he looked down at his broken leg, which flared to painful life along with his ribs even when he sneezed. How could he mount a horse? How would he defend himself?

The door opened and he tensed. Though it was only Rose, carrying an empty basket, he would be dead if Shaw had come for him.

She seemed almost . . . relieved.

"Did you think I would flee?" he asked.

"I had hoped you would not be so foolish again." She leaned over him to check the splint on his leg.

He inhaled the natural perfume that was all hers. When she raised his shirt to look at his bandages, he imagined pulling the plain cap from her head and watching her hair fall down around them. He must be bored, to find a country girl so fascinating, but there was something about her honesty, her serenity, that intrigued him.

She rubbed salve into his wound, her touch firm but gentle. He found even the chapped skin of her hands fascinating.

After Rose finished bandaging his chest she pulled his shirt down again, and he suddenly noticed that she had a lush, full mouth.

Disgusted with himself, Spencer concentrated on sliding the knife she'd used beneath the pallet as she stood up.

"Rose," he said, propping himself up on his elbow. "I am going to walk today."

"But your leg—"

"I won't put weight on it—but neither will I regain my strength just lying here."

Roselyn was fighting a losing battle with herself. How was she to discover the truth and be free of her past?

His dark eyes hid secrets behind their friendliness. She found herself strangely fascinated by the differences between him and other men. Even when she played her role of healer, she saw not his wounds but his body, so large and different from Philip's.

Her palms were suddenly damp, and she had a hard time meeting his gaze.

Thornton tried to lift himself onto his good leg, but even across the room she could see his arms tremble. Roselyn found herself at his side, putting her arms beneath his shoulders, bracing herself against his weight. He finally rose up on one leg—and would have gone down again if she had not slid beneath his arm and held him steady.

She absorbed the lean, muscular length of him along her entire body. His hip pressed against hers, and she could feel the faintest touch of his breath against her cheek. She couldn't look at him, knowing she must be blushing. Why did her body betray her like this, when all she wanted to do was remember how cruelly he'd once treated her?

Thornton was tall and imposing in her tiny cottage, but even more intimidating was the penetrating way he studied her. She couldn't look away as his gaze roamed her face, alighting on her mouth for just a moment too long.

She was trapped by his awareness of her as a woman. Why had he never bothered to treat her this way when they'd been betrothed?

Those long-ago memories stiffened her resolve and she coolly asked, "Shall we begin?"

Together they managed something more than a hop, but not quite a stagger. When they reached the end of her one-room cottage, they turned and started back toward the pallet. She knew he must be in pain, but he never showed it.

"I'd like to go outside," he said.

"I'm not sure that's wise." She thought of John appearing in her bake house, of Charlotte's habit of stopping by.

But when she tried to steer him away from the door, he wouldn't be moved. His strength only reminded her of how quickly he could turn against her if he knew her identity.

"Allow me to sit in the sun for just a little while," he said, reaching for the door latch.

For a man who wanted to stay hidden, he was proving stubborn in his recklessness. Roselyn had no choice but to give in, knowing that only kindness would win the revelation of his secrets. "Then we must walk as quickly as possible to the courtyard behind the cottage. It looks out over empty cottages, and you won't be seen."

Their journey seemed to last forever, and she had to constantly resist the urge to look over her shoulder. When they reached the courtyard, she helped Thornton to a bench near a tree heavy with green apples. He sat down with a sigh and stretched his leg before him.

"I'll be weeding the garden," she said. "Call if you need me."

"Rose?"

She looked back, and in the sunlight he seemed a reminder of the night, dark, full of shadows and shades of truth. He leaned back on the bench, and in his relaxed pose was power restrained. She felt something strange uncurl into life deep in her belly. She didn't understand what she was feeling; she only knew she wished she could run to safety, to the time before he'd come.

He cocked his head as he studied her in return. "I don't think you ever told me the name of this estate."

She wanted to lie and live with the consequences later. But she couldn't keep secret the name of a place like this, so well known on the island.

"Wakesfield Manor," she said, lifting her chin.

His eyes narrowed, and as he opened his mouth to speak, she braced herself.

She suddenly heard a voice shouting greetings from the front of the cottage, and felt the shock clear to her fingernails—it was Francis Heywood.

Chapter 5

Spencer watched Rose Grant lose all the color in her face at the man's shout.

What was going on? One moment he was relaxed, imagining the peace of being married to a woman like her—pretty, capable, easily satisfied. In the space of a heartbeat, his suspicions of Rose flared back to life. Why hadn't Spencer brought the knife with him, even if it was only an eating knife?

"You must hide!" she said, her voice higher than normal.

"Where shall I go? Who is this man?"

"I—oh, just wait here," she said, both hands raised as if by sheer will alone she could keep him where he didn't want to be. "He mustn't see you!"

He watched her unlatch the gate and flee the courtyard as if hell itself had opened up to summon her.

Before he could even try to stand, he heard their voices and froze.

"Francis," Rose said, her tone bright and forced, "it is a fine day today. What can I help you with?"

"I wanted you to know that John and Thomas will be coming tomorrow to begin harvesting your fields, Lady Roselyn."

Whatever else the man said was lost in the red haze of a long-buried rage that rose to engulf Spencer's mind.

Lady Roselyn Harrington?

Lady Roselyn Harrington and Rose Grant were the same woman.

How could he have been so stupid not to see it? She had been hesitant, distant, almost afraid of him. He'd put it down to a reaction to his Spanish looks.

Instead, she'd been playing him for a fool. She had known his identity from the beginning, and she'd never said a word. What was her game? He had thought for the first time that he'd met a woman of compassion, when all along she'd had her own selfish reasons for helping him.

Maybe it was guilt for what she'd done to him, Spencer thought, wishing he could pace his frustration away. More than likely she'd enjoyed humiliating him further and was just waiting for the right moment to laugh in his face.

After all, she'd done that to him before, when every friend he'd had was there to watch her turn him into a laughingstock.

He had thought service to his country would help him and the rest of London society forget, but even that was denied him. By now the queen must think that Spencer was a traitor.

And he had just been imagining marriage to a woman like Rose. If she knew, she'd laugh in triumph.

There was no "Rose," the feminine, sweet woman. There was only Roselyn, the lying bitch who'd succeeded in humiliating him a second time—the last time.

As Roselyn emerged alone from the side of the cottage, Spencer was unprepared for the shock of hatred that surged through him. It was as if all the anger and uncertainty and fear of the last few months suddenly had a focus.

Now that he knew her identity, he could see why he hadn't recognized her. She was thinner than he remembered; she wore no face paint or jewel-studded garments, no corsets or farthingales—and her hair was always hidden.

She looked almost fragile, vulnerable in her widow's black, but it was all an illusion, and he'd fallen for it. Had her lover died, or had he just deserted her when he'd found out what a fickle woman she really was?

She opened the gate and walked slowly toward him. "You don't have to go inside. He's gone now."

It was a struggle not to snarl his anger at her. "Who was that?" he asked, surprised at how normal his voice sounded.

"Francis Heywood."

"The bailiff of Wakesfield Manor."

"Yes," she answered uncertainly.

Spencer could tell that she wondered how he knew that. He continued to stare at her until she finally walked down a row of the kitchen garden and knelt in the dirt, to weed.

He should confront her now, but as he watched her on her hands and knees, it gave him a dark feeling of satisfaction. Was this her punishment, a lifetime of the meanest labor? Or was she biding her time, waiting for her father to rescue her?

He watched her for at least an hour as she toiled in the hot sun, her black gown clinging to her back. He thought he should feel victorious, but as she put aside the vegetables she meant to use for his meal, he suddenly wanted it all over with.

He rose up, bracing his hand against the apple tree, angered anew by how weak and trembling even his good leg was. "I'd like to go back inside," he said, unable to use the name she'd called herself.

Roselyn sat back on her heels, wiping the perspiration from her forehead with her sleeve. "I have one last row—"

"I need to go in now," he interrupted, watching as she flinched and her expression grew uncertain. If she had been born a boy, her acting could put her on the London stage.

She walked toward him, carrying the basket of vegetables. It sickened him that he would have to depend on her.

Spencer lifted his arm, and she stepped against his body. He wanted to feel revulsion, but instead, as she reached around his back, he felt the pressure of her breast against his ribs, smelled again the natural perfume of her garden and her kitchen.

The walk from the courtyard around the cottage seemed long as he looked down at her bent head and thought of all the things he wanted to say. He was angry at her, and angry at his body for reacting to her as a woman.

Hastily she opened the door, guided him inside, then shut it. When she turned toward him, Spencer used his body to push her back against the door. The basket of vegetables tumbled from her arm and spilled across the floor. She looked up at him with wide gray eyes as he braced his hands on either side of her and used all the menace his height allowed him.

"Mr. Thornton, what—"

"Be quiet, Lady Roselyn," he said, his voice a soft, rumbling growl.

Terror widened her eyes, then she wiped all expression away.

"How did you know?" she asked in a cool voice.

Oh, she was good, he thought, leaning nearer. She shrank back against the door almost imperceptibly—but he saw.

"My bailiff gave you away, Lady Roselyn."

She put her hands against his chest and pushed, but he didn't move. "What do you mean, *your* bailiff? And move away from me. Now!"

"All in good time, Lady Roselyn. Have you been sleeping in my manor home? Is this cottage just to make me feel sorry for you?"

"You mean my parents' home. I live in this cottage. Surely you remember they wouldn't want me at Wakesfield—or anywhere near them."

"Are you so foolish that you did not read the contract that binds us together?" he demanded. When would she tremble and cry and beg for his understanding?

"I broke our betrothal; nothing binds us now."

"You don't sound certain, my lady—and with good reason. Everything here is mine, by your father's own command."

This time she didn't try to hide the flash of horror that stole across her features. "You are lying. I did not marry you, so you are not entitled to a dowry."

"Believe me, I am more and more thankful that you didn't marry me. But our contract is binding. You have made sure I can never legally marry—but I am damn well entitled by law to the lands and moneys promised me."

She took in a harsh breath, and Spencer thought tears would be next. But she was so calm it was unnatural.

Roselyn vowed she would not scream, she would not give Spencer Thornton the satisfaction of knowing that once again he had hurt her. Her father would never give away her childhood home, her only sanctuary. His words could not be true.

But her parents hadn't let her read the marriage contract.

With her back against the door, she stared up at Thornton. This was the man she remembered. He used his strength and size to intimidate her, just as long ago he'd driven her away with a casual, dismissive look. He was dark and foreign, and maybe even a Spanish spy.

Would he try to hurt her now that he didn't have to pretend anymore?

"Is that why you came to Wight?" she demanded, pushing again on his chest, feeling muscle as solid as any wall. "Do you want to disrupt my life with your lies just for revenge?"

" 'Tis not a lie—this is my estate now."

"You made it clear you didn't want to marry me. I did both of us a favor by running away, so I owe you nothing, and certainly not my home."

"A favor?" he said, giving a harsh laugh. "I knew my duty; I would have married you."

"I didn't want to be your duty! I knew nothing about you—I most certainly didn't love you."

"You are naive if you think love has anything to do with marriage. It was about our families taking what they could from each other, merging into a strength no one but the queen could touch. But your stupidity cost your father the dowry he'd promised for you. 'Tis mine now, and I'm here to take it. If you don't believe me, go ask your father."

"I don't speak to my father after the way he treated me," Roselyn answered, ducking beneath his arm to escape the prison he'd created for her.

"Don't you have that in reverse?" Spencer said as he awkwardly turned around and rested his back against the door. He gave her a cold smile that made her want to shudder. "*He* won't speak to *you*. He disowned you, didn't he?"

The pain she'd caused herself and her family was too private to show anyone, especially this man. She clenched her jaw and spoke through gritted teeth. "You obviously know this already. Does it make you feel like a man to taunt me with it?"

He took a deep breath and didn't answer immediately. She saw that the strain of standing was beginning to affect him, but she'd rather let him fall than offer him help now.

"I am not taunting you," he said stiffly. "I am only trying to make you understand that you are an intruder on my land."

"I refuse to believe you. And even if it were true, would you be so cruel as to make a widow leave her home?"

"Widow?" he said with a sneer. "You are not a widow. Your lover may have died, but that still only makes you his whore."

Roselyn's hard-fought calm vanished beneath an onslaught of wild, pent-up rage. She slapped him hard, using the weight of her body behind her arm. She heard his head hit the wooden door, watched with dawning uncertainty as he fell—luckily onto his own pallet.

She almost ran to help him—until his cruel words reverberated through her brain, closing up her throat with tears she refused to shed. He could help himself.

Thornton rolled onto his back and lifted himself up on his elbows. His cheek had darkened from the imprint of her hand. "Striking me won't change the truth. You made sure I can never legally wed another, that I can never give my family an heir. I will at least take all the property owed me."

She didn't answer, just clenched her fists to keep from hitting him again.

"I'll wager your father doesn't even know you're here. Is the bailiff in on your deception?"

"The Heywoods are good people—they run this estate better than anyone else my father could hire."

"So they house you, and you bake their bread. Do they enjoy watching you serve them?"

He might as well have struck her, and she gasped. "They are my only family—if you dare to make trouble for them, you'll answer to me."

They stared at each other, both breathing heavily, the air between them thick with anger and mistrust. Roselyn finally turned away. Sobs pressed against her ribs, tears stung behind her eyelids, but she would not let Thornton know how terrified she was.

Why hadn't she just left him on the beach, like any sensible woman?

She knelt down and began to pick up the scattered vegetables with hands that shook. She felt his mocking gaze on her, but she refused to look at him. She didn't know what to do, had no one to turn to. Now that he knew who she was, there was nothing to stop him from hurting her, especially if he was a Spanish spy.

But what if he was only an angry, rejected bridegroom? Regardless of the cruel things he'd said, she had humiliated him before all of London society, which seemed to matter to him.

But that didn't give him the right to force her to leave her family home. She would *not* believe that her father would part with Wakesfield, where she'd spent so much of her childhood.

Roselyn didn't look at Thornton as she hung another cauldron of water over the fire. She kept her back to him as she chopped vegetables and checked on the salted mutton she'd left soaking in a bowl. With each repetitive stroke of her knife, she became even more numb to the despair she thought she'd long ago buried—

Until she turned around and saw him watching her with black, fathomless eyes. A knowing smirk turned up the corners of his mouth. She froze, barely keeping herself from flinging the vegetables at him.

But it would only make more work for her.

She put the vegetables and mutton and seasonings in the cauldron, and tossed the bowl back on the table. Without looking at him, she calmly opened the door and went outside, where she took one step, then another, and another, until she started to run, as if she could outrun the coming darkness.

Roselyn didn't stop until she fell to her knees in the tall grass overlooking the ocean, and finally let the sobs escape her aching chest.

Chapter 6

The uncertainty and anger poured out of Roselyn in bitter tears.

Was she always going to live in fear, with never a place to call home? She couldn't believe the gall of Spencer Thornton to threaten to send her away from Wakesfield.

How could she go back to her cottage, with him there, ready to reproach her for his humiliation, when he should be bearing much of the blame?

When her tears finally ended she felt drained. She would not allow him to destroy her life, not when he and his family had already tried once. And to think she had recently thought him capable of charm! He had a lot to answer for—especially his part in this war with Spain—and she would not rest until she knew the truth.

She suddenly realized it was not yet full dark, that anyone could have found her sob-

bing. Her face and hands—even her gown—
were stained with dirt, and she needed to
cleanse away her sorrows the only way she
knew how.

It was but a short walk down the cliff path to
the beach, and beneath the waning moon, Roselyn walked into the waves and submerged herself. She rose to the surface with a gasp,
shaking the cap and pins from her hair until it
fell long and tangled down her back. The chill
salt water soaked through her garments, numb-
ing her emotions until she felt only tired, no
longer full of despair. For a moment, she again
experienced the odd sensation of being
watched, just like the night she'd brought
Thornton to her cottage. But she heard nothing
but the crash of the waves, saw nothing but the
muted shadows thrown by the moon.

She had handled so much in her life—she
would be able to deal with Thornton.

Spencer lay back on the pallet, smelling the
stew that bubbled above the fire, wondering
what he was supposed to do next.

He held his anger restrained, simmering just
beneath the surface. The prospect of *at least* two
more weeks with Roselyn Harrington seemed
intolerable.

In his mind flashed images of the humiliation
he'd had to bear: standing on the church stairs,

watching his bride flee from him. The looks of shock on his family's faces, the laughter in his friends' eyes.

He had done his best to have the courtship called off honorably by being the scoundrel that he was. But Roselyn had gone too far and committed an offense no one—least of all he— would forget.

With a growl of anger, Spencer slid the knife from its hiding place and pulled the mattress back a couple inches from the wall. With quick, angry strokes he slashed seven small marks in the wooden floor, one for each day he'd been trapped in this cursed cottage on this cursed is- land. Fourteen more days and he would leave, he promised himself, as he slid the knife back into its hiding place.

Inside the cottage it had grown darker, with only the dying fire for light. Soon he heard foot- steps outside and he tensed. The door opened and Roselyn strode in, closing it behind her.

She was a mess—water streamed from her body and puddled on the wooden floor. Her long brown hair looked black with water, and it clung to her back and breasts. If possible, she looked even more slender and fragile, but she held her back straight and her chin lifted, as if she defied him to speak.

Spencer refused to ask her what had hap- pened; she'd probably fallen into a creek somewhere. Clenching his jaw, he watched her bend to stir the stew, then climb the rope stairs to the loft, dripping water as she went.

Sometime later she descended the ladder, wearing black as usual, her wet hair bound tightly to her head. She looked composed, if pale, as she removed the kettle of stew from the fire and placed it on the cupboard. He almost expected her to tell him to help himself, but she poured two helpings into wooden bowls and brought him one.

She stood above him, silent, while bitterness overwhelmed him. He couldn't understand why she felt put upon, when she was the one who had refused to marry, who had refused to accept someone of his heritage.

"Would you rather starve yourself," she said, "than eat the food made by my hands?"

"There is little likelihood of that," he said, propping himself into a sitting position. "I'll need whatever strength I can get to foil your little schemes."

"I have no schemes." Her gray eyes were deceptively calm. "You are the one threatening me."

"I make only promises, not threats."

She ignored his outstretched hand, setting the bowl on the floor so hard that some of the stew spilled over. They ate their meal in strained silence.

When Spencer finished eating, he lay back on his pallet. Roselyn came to stand above him again, and though he glared at her, she didn't go away.

"I have to change your bandages," she said, without a hint of any emotion in her low voice.

"Are you sure you're not going to salt my wounds?" he asked sarcastically.

"When I realized who you were, I could have put you back on the beach where I found you."

She knelt down, placing a basket of medicines and bandages beside him. Spencer scowled, suddenly not even wanting the touch of her against his skin. She reached for his shirt, and he gripped her small hands to hold them still.

"So you didn't know who I was on the beach?"

She didn't try to free herself, as if he wasn't worth the effort.

"I thought you were a wounded sailor, that it was my duty to help you. I even help wounded animals, you know, though they might bite me."

He rolled his eyes. "So you would have left me there, had you known my identity."

She didn't say yea or nay, but he could imagine, couldn't he?

"How long did it take you to recognize me?"

She looked down at where he held her, and

he noticed the strength and sturdiness of the hands that had taken care of him. He let her go, and she quickly sat back on her heels.

"When the swelling in your face went down several days later, I recognized you."

"Then why did you keep me here?"

She seemed taken aback by his question. "I already told you that I didn't think you deserved to die for your fickleness."

"*My* fickleness?" he began, then shook his head. "No, I'll leave that nonsense for another time. You could easily have called the authorities to take me away. Why didn't you?"

Her tone stiff, she said, "The people of Shanklin would shun me if they found out I was housing a man."

"I don't believe you," he said flatly. "You cared little what people thought of you two years ago."

"Believe what you wish. Now may I finish this chore so that I may sleep? I have to bake in the morning."

"For my estate again?"

"For the bailiff and his family on my parents' estate."

She put her hands on his shirt, and suddenly her ministrations seemed too intimate.

"You are naive, Roselyn, or you do not understand the way the world of the nobility works."

"I understand well enough how little a woman matters to men," she said, with only a hint of bitterness.

She unwrapped the bandages from his chest. Though the tugging was painful, Spencer didn't complain. He searched her face for a clue to her real feelings.

"Like you, I had no say in the marriage," he said.

"You made that perfectly clear the eve of the wedding."

He watched her fingers rub a smelly salve into his skin. He remembered little of that night. He'd been drinking with his friends beforehand, and he hadn't stopped drinking at the party. Since he barely remembered meeting her, what could he have said or done wrong?

As Roselyn leaned over him, he smelled the brine of sea water. "Did you go swimming in your clothes?"

"I'd rather smell of salt than your odor."

"Then I guess 'tis time for another bath. The last one showed you what you missed by not wedding me."

"I only discovered how *little* I missed."

She coolly stood up and turned away, leaving him speechless. He was used to women giggling at his outrageous talk, not shooting it back at him.

Clenching his jaw, he watched her climb up

into the loft. Only a few moments later she came back down, carrying clothing over her arm. Without looking at him, she went outside and closed the door behind her.

Roselyn marched around the cottage to the bake house, where she'd earlier put water on to boil. Seething over Thornton's rude comments, she added hot and cold water to the half barrel she used to bathe in during the summer. Thornton's presence wasn't enough to stop her; the salt was itching her skin and scalp too badly.

From a crate, she stepped down into the barrel and submerged herself, knees close to her chest, sighing with pleasure. It didn't last long. Though the stars above usually made her think peaceful thoughts, tonight they only reminded her of the glitter of Thornton's dark eyes. She even felt ill at ease being alone outside, somehow.

Roselyn scrubbed herself hard, seething with anger. How dare he make rude comments about the wedding night they'd never had?

And why had his words made her remember his naked body beneath her hands as she'd washed him? What was wrong with her, that she could think of him as a man, when he'd behaved like a monster, calling her a whore just because she'd followed love?

When she was finished bathing, she donned her smock and dressing gown in the dark bake house. After walking to the cottage door, she took a deep breath to fortify herself, then stepped inside.

She had hoped Thornton would be asleep, but in the low light of the dying fire, she could see him propped against his cushion, watching her. Since it was a warm summer evening, he'd removed his shirt, and his white bandages glowed against his dark skin.

Ignoring him, Roselyn laid more wood on the fire and headed for her loft.

"I heard a lot of splashing outside," he said.

She froze halfway up the ladder, suddenly remembering the window overlooking the bake house.

"Don't worry yourself; I didn't look. I wasn't even tempted."

She climbed up into the loft, ignoring the tightness in her chest.

Roselyn made sure she kept herself occupied all morning, disregarding the cold silence between her and Thornton. For dinner she left the plate of ham, bread, and fresh-picked peaches beside him, while she ate her own meal at a wooden table in the courtyard.

She was staring out across the fields, brooding, when she saw two figures walking toward her in the distance.

She had forgotten all about John and Thomas

Heywood coming to harvest her fields. Dismay bowed her shoulders as she remembered that she usually provided their supper. How would she keep them out of the cottage?

She put on a fixed smile as the two of them reached the low rock wall surrounding her courtyard, but when she went over to greet them her smile became as genuine as theirs. They were such good men—good to her and to their family. They would never dream of treating a woman the way Thornton had treated her.

Thomas, only eighteen, blushed and nodded his head to her, while his brother John gave her a good-natured grin. He opened the gate and came toward her, and she let him kiss her cheek. For a moment she remembered Thornton's heated black eyes raking her body, then she was ashamed of thinking of any man but John.

He smiled. "Good afternoon, Roselyn. It is a good day for the harvest."

She could only agree as the two men took her by the arms and led her out into the fields.

As the afternoon hours passed and Roselyn did not return, Spencer lay flat on his back and battled frustration. He had practiced walking— hopping—for as long as he could, and he was drenched with sweat. He should be thinking about strategies to hurry his recovery, and what he would say to the queen when he arrived in London.

But he couldn't stop thinking of Roselyn, a woman who swam in the ocean when she was troubled. Two years before, he had known nothing about her, and even now she was an enigma—but she had saved his life.

He hadn't helped matters between them by wounding her with sharp words.

He tensed when he heard voices outside. Was she angry enough to turn him over to the authorities? She was already suspicious of his presence on Wight.

Slowly he sat up, cursing his weakness as he got up on one knee. Roselyn had earlier opened the glass in the window, and Spencer leaned out just enough to see the distant fields and the orchard.

Two young men scythed in the wheat fields, and Roselyn followed behind them, gathering the stalks of grain. Across the rolling fields her laugh carried: deep, throaty, painfully intimate to hear. Something uncertain tightened inside him in reaction. He didn't think of her as a happy person, but stoic. Maybe that was only with him, though.

Was even a menial life better than marriage to him?

The two men must be the Heywood brothers,

part of this paragon of family perfection she so defended and adored.

He watched uneasily as the men lowered their scythes when Roselyn came up to talk to them. She waved as she left them, and they continued to watch her as she walked away. Were these the next lovers she was trying to en-snare?

By the time she entered the cottage, Spencer was sitting on the pallet with his back against the wall and his legs stretched out before him.

She didn't even glance his way as she pinned an apron to her dress and began to prepare supper. The silence stretched out, taut, until he couldn't contain himself.

"Who are those men?" he asked in a bored voice.

Though she didn't stop what she was doing, she said, "John and Thomas Heywood."

"They help harvest your crops, and in return you give them . . . what?"

Roselyn set her wooden spoon down hard, and Spencer told himself it made him feel better to provoke some kind of reaction from her.

"What are you implying?" she demanded. "They are good men, raised as closely with me as my own brother."

"But they're not your brothers, especially the older one. Surely it is getting too difficult to live alone. A woman like you needs a man—any man."

Keeping her head lowered, she put the last meat pie on a tray, then lifted her face to look at him. It was devoid of all emotion; even her eyes were ice gray, hiding her thoughts.

"But there you're wrong," she said softly. "If I needed just *any* man, I could have had you, and the luxury that went with our respective titles. I can see now that I made the best decision."

Carrying the tray, she swept past him, leaving Spencer close to gaping. He was used to having the last word, making outrageous statements sure to immortalize him in everyone's memory.

But this foolish girl implied that poverty and disreputability were preferable to him.

And hadn't that been exactly what he feared, when he tried to convince his parents that he didn't need to marry?

Two years before, he'd consoled himself with the notion that Roselyn was young and stupid and headstrong when she'd convinced herself she was in love with a stable groom.

But it had been *him* she'd fled, his heritage, his position just on the edge of society. It only confirmed Spencer's thoughts—so why did this tight ball of a lifetime of misery still linger in his chest?

Chapter 7

Roselyn strode to her bake house, carrying her tray of meat pies, trying to wipe Spencer Thornton and his cruel words from her mind—but it was no use.

How had he dared to imply that she needed a man to take care of her? She had spent the last two years learning to rely on herself, not her family's riches. She'd gone through abuse and heartache and despair, and she would not turn back into the girl she used to be.

She would not allow Thornton to make her forget that considering John Heywood's suit was actually a courageous decision on her part. She was willing to try to love again, even if it meant a safe sort of love—the only kind that seemed real anymore.

After she put the meat pies in to bake, she arranged the courtyard for a simple supper. Off to the side of the cottage, a small window was open. She hoped Thornton would hear the entire conversation, so he would know she didn't need a man with a title and wealth. She could be content with good friends—and a man who cared about her. Life needed no more than that.

Except the courage to unmask a spy, and in her anger, she was forgetting her purpose with Thornton. Was he deliberately trying to distract her?

As dusk was falling, the Heywood brothers returned from the fields, stopping at her well to wash away the dirt. Roselyn studied John as he wiped down his face and neck. She thought she should feel something more for him than affection, but then, she hadn't had much practice being a wife after Philip had so coldly rebuffed her. She should be moved by John—but in her mind flashed the memory of Thornton naked beneath her hands, his large body at her mercy.

The sun had long since set when Roselyn said good-night to the two brothers, cleaned her supper dishes, and went into the cottage. She brought the last meat pie to warm by the fire for Thornton.

As usual he was sitting on his pallet in the shadows as she came in. She tried not to look at him, but she sensed his tension, his anger, and she wondered how she had ever thought him easygoing.

Kneeling before the fire, she said, "Your supper will be ready in a moment."

He didn't answer.

As she lit candles around the room and cleaned away her supper preparations, she couldn't help wondering how he felt lying motionless all day. Did he dream of Spain or England?

When the meat pie had heated through, she started to bring it to him, but he said, "No," quite forcefully. She watched him brace himself and rise onto his good leg. He didn't ask for her help, nor would she have readily offered it. As he hopped toward the table on one bare foot, he used the stone chimney to brace himself, then a cupboard, and lastly the table. She pulled out a bench for him and he sat.

Even dressed in Philip's old garments, Thornton looked every inch the nobleman holding court. His bruises were gone, showing the classic strength of his face and his proud, strong nose. His beard and hair needed trimming, but other than that he looked aloof, above his meager surroundings.

Roselyn was once again thankful she had not married him.

When Thornton finished eating, he stood up again, and this time swayed. She took a step forward without thinking, then stopped. He

caught hold of the table and slowly straightened.

"I have to regain my strength and learn to
walk again," he said, eyeing her. "If you want
me gone, you'll help me."

"I was helping you without your threats. I'm
not about to stop now—especially with the
added temptation of your imminent departure."

He gave a cold laugh. "Then come here."

She approached him slowly, uncertain why
she hesitated. Their gazes remained locked together, even when she was forced to arch her
neck to see his face. He seemed surprisingly intent, distracted from his anger.

Sliding her arm so intimately about him was
dangerous to herself and everything she believed in. His rib cage was broad and strong,
and already he seemed healthier. The muscle at
his waist made her feel strange and fluttery and
uneasy.

His arm came about her shoulders until she
was pressed to the warm length of him. She
looked away, breathless and uncertain.

And so they started to walk, back and forth
across the room until even Roselyn grew tired.

"Since we both want me gone as soon as possible," Thornton finally said in a tight voice,
"how should I get off this cursed island?"

"You can take a ferry at Cowes, on the north

side of the island," she answered, trying to sound calm instead of burdened by his weight. "Take the one to Southampton, where the road to London is better. There's a decent inn right by the dock, should you need to eat or rest."

"Trying to make my leave-taking as enticing as possible?"

Not bothering to answer, she bit her lip and struggled to hold up his weight. Showing weakness would only please him.

But he wouldn't stop walking until he staggered and almost sent her tumbling to the floor with him.

She helped him down to the pallet, put her hands on her hips, and studied him. "You need to wash now."

Slowly he opened his eyes. "Enjoyed my bath, did you?"

"Enjoyed—!" She clamped her mouth shut and whirled away from him. From the kettle over the fire, she poured hot water into a basin, tossed towels and clean garments onto his pallet, blew out the candles, and climbed up to her bed.

In the darkness she lay awake, listening to the splash of water.

After Roselyn had left for her morning chores, Spencer came up on his elbow and stared at the closed door. He wondered how many times a day, as she milked cows or baked bread, did she wish she had not left him at the church on their wedding day? Did she long for servants to attend her, or would she have been content had her stable groom lived? He thought of the two of them alone together in this room, and his gut churned with nausea. Was he even lying on the pallet they had shared?

He couldn't remain on his back for another moment. He angrily slashed another mark in the floor for the ninth day—only twelve left—got unsteadily to his feet, and, clutching the furniture, hopped across the room. He repeated the process until he tripped over Roselyn's chair before the fire, and on his way to the floor hit his forehead on the stone chimney—another new bruise, he thought in anger and disgust.

Of course Roselyn arrived at just that moment, so she could see him on his hands and knees, his aching head dropped between his shoulders. Clenching his jaw, he looked up at her.

She had come to a stop just inside the door, carrying her basket full of round loaves. She said nothing at first, her face so proper and prim she probably *bored* her family into abandoning her.

"What are you looking at?" he demanded in

a low voice. "If I do not work on my strength, we'll never be rid of one another."

"If you insist on forcing yourself into things you're not ready for, you'll reinjure yourself. *Then* we'll never be rid of one another."

She set her basket on the table as Spencer failed to raise himself up onto one foot, while the room swam about him and his head throbbed. He felt frustrated, despairing, raging with anger at the things he couldn't control, at the way his life might soon end.

The last thing he needed was Roselyn Harrington taking hold of his arm as if he were an infirm old man. He tried to shake her off and couldn't even manage that.

"Release me," he said, his voice a low growl.

"You need help, even though I don't want to give it."

She dropped to her knees and when he tried to push her away, she toppled over onto her back. She didn't even look rattled to be lying there, and he despised her serenity.

"Are you used to lying on your back?" he said, the angry words tumbling unbidden from his mouth.

He wanted her to fight, to scream, to hit him, but instead she raised up on her elbows, her eyes glittering and her lush mouth mutinous, kissable.

Kissable?

Leaning over her body, he braced himself with one hand. He didn't know why he felt this need to wound her. "While we're on the subject of your back, tell me about your stable groom. I never did hear his name."

Her chest rose and fell at a quick pace as she glared at him. "Philip Grant," she said between her teeth.

"How long ago did he die?" Spencer watched her eyes narrow. He had a sudden memory of her hair long and wet, reaching to her hips.

"I owe you no answers."

"You owe me much more than that."

"So it's back to our betrothal again, this contract you say you never wanted. If you are convinced you're owed this land, why don't you just go up to the manor for Margaret Heywood's care? She helped me when I nursed—"

Roselyn knew she should not even mention the Heywoods to him, let alone Philip, but the threat of his body above her made her nervous. Thornton had trapped her in her cottage, trapped her in lies, just as he now trapped her with his body. He was large and strong, and every day he seemed more powerful to her.

But at the mention of Wakesfield and the Heywoods, he narrowed his eyes at her, then looked away—almost guiltily.

"Why do you hesitate?"

When his eyes returned to her face, she felt the fire of his regard. "I do not need to force strangers to care for me—*you* owe me."

Her heart pounded within her ribs so loudly he must certainly hear it, as her every inhalation pressed her breasts to his chest. She was flustered, unable to stop the awareness of him as a man.

"But never forget," he continued, leaning even lower until their breaths mingled, "that this estate is mine, that all this is mine." His gaze swept down to her breasts as if he owned her, too.

"What are you implying?" she demanded as a curious, excited tension shivered through her stomach. When his gaze settled on her mouth, she couldn't help licking her lips as if they were suddenly parched. Pressed so close to him, she felt his muscles tense, could see the smoldering heat of his coal black eyes, and suddenly she knew she needed to distract them both from these mad thoughts.

"Thornton, I don't understand you. You claim indignation, abandonment, yet even the night before our wedding, you wouldn't make an effort to speak to me."

That certainly distracted him, and he straightened away from her, letting Roselyn come up on her knees.

The sunlight streamed in the open window,

almost blinding her, but Thornton sat behind it, in the shadows of the cottage, dark, remote. He could have hurt her as she lay beneath him on the floor, but never once did she think he would use violence. Was she being foolish?

He finally met her gaze. "I handled our betrothal the way I thought best," he said in a bitter voice.

But you hurt me, she wanted to cry. How could he do that to a young girl who would have accepted any kindness, when she had known so little?

"Well, your handling of our betrothal made sure you had no bride," she said, "so I guess you succeeded."

"You had your lover all ready, did you not? And I can only imagine what lure you used."

She took an angry breath to reply, but he continued before she could.

"But none of it worked as you planned. So Grant had to be nursed before he died, did he? You bargained for a malleable husband and wealth, not this life," he said, glancing around her cottage with obvious sarcasm. "Were all your choices still worth *this*? How will you feel when I go to court to break this betrothal by naming you an adulterer?"

"An adulterer! I was married."

"And we know how legal that was. This might be our only chance to be free of one another. Don't think I won't do it out of some misguided notion of pity."

Roselyn stood up, her fists clenched at her sides. "I am sick of your snide comments and your threats. I have saved your life, and instead of gratitude, I get bitter sarcasm. When are you going to let go of the past? Don't you think I have paid enough for what I did to you? My family has cast me out; I work for every morsel I put in my mouth. I am done paying, Thornton. Go ahead and slur my name at court if that makes you feel better. It can't be any worse than what I've already gone through."

Without offering to help him up, she left a loaf of bread and piece of cheese wrapped in cloth on the table, poured him a mug of cider, then left to make her delivery to Wakesfield Manor. She muttered angrily to herself as she marched down the sunlit path, knowing that constant argument was not the way to discover the truth of his loyalties.

Roselyn knew that she eventually had to go back to the cottage. Daylight was almost gone, yet still she worked in her bake house by candlelight, preparing the pies ordered by the village tavern.

She couldn't forget how Thornton had looked at her bosom, as if she should freely give herself to him to repay her debt. She should be disgusted, revolted—but instead she remembered the glimmer of hurt in his eyes.

Suddenly, she heard a noise behind her, and before she could even turn around, a filthy hand covered her mouth.

Chapter 8

Roselyn's gasp was smothered as she was pulled against a short, wiry body. She struggled, trying to elbow her assailant, but the man cruelly pinched her breast and she froze.

She was alone in the coming night, and Thornton would not be able to help her against whatever this man intended to do. She blinked back hot tears and tried to think how to escape, but her terrified thoughts were spinning out of control. For days she'd foolishly ignored her suspicions about being watched. Never had Wakesfield been unsafe—until the war, until the battle had been within sight, until Thornton had washed up on the beach.

As if echoing her thoughts, the man spoke against her ear in heavily accented English. "I have been watching you, *señorita*. I saw the wounded man you keep hidden. Who is he? Where did he come from?"

She made a muffled sound against his hand,

and almost retched at the bitter taste of his skin.

"I will let you speak, but if you call out, it will not go well for you."

His hand moved away from her face and settled threateningly on her breast, which still hurt. Roselyn took a deep lungful of air and tried to still her trembling. For one wild, cowardly moment she wanted to tell the Spaniard to take Thornton away, to end her troubles for good.

"Please," she said, surprising herself with how calm her voice sounded, "I don't know what you mean. He is my husband, William. He was injured during the harvest."

The Spaniard pinched her other breast so hard that she cried out. From behind her, he reached to slap her face.

"*Señorita*, do not think me a fool. That man is no Englishman."

"Please, just go! I will tell no one that you were here."

But her desperation was only answered with his laugh. "Then let us talk to him together."

The Spaniard dragged her outside and through the courtyard. She suddenly kicked backward between the Spaniard's feet, then flung herself sideways as he tripped and fell. With a low growl he reached for her skirt, but she rolled to her feet and began to run, leading him away from the manor and toward the beach. She had no idea what to do, where to go, but she had to protect the Heywoods.

With the moon only a sliver in the sky, she had an advantage. She dodged through the orchard, raced between the barns, but always she could hear him panting behind her. Wild panic filled her throat, making her breath come in wheezing gasps. She'd made a horrible mistake—she couldn't outrun him, and he might kill her out of anger now.

Just as the ground sloped down toward the low cliffs above the ocean, the Spaniard grabbed her from behind. Roselyn fell, slamming her head against a rock, and her world tilted as they rolled in a wild heap. When they came to a stop he was straddling her, his hands at her throat. She struggled for air as spots of light danced before her eyes. His face was frightening in the dark—black hair, black ragged beard, wild eyes.

"I could kill you now, *señorita*," he said, gasping. "But I think not. He wouldn't like that, eh? Every man needs his *puta*."

Suddenly she could breathe again, although his hands still threatened her. He pulled the cap off her head and ripped the pins from her hair. Each scrape across her scalp made her want to scream.

"You're a pretty little *puta*. Perhaps he will share you, since I have been long at sea."

He put his mouth on hers and held her down until Roselyn was reduced to whimpering and gagging at the foul taste and smell of him. His beard rubbed raw patches against her cheek and chin.

With a dramatic sigh, he climbed off her and pulled her up to her feet. "Our pleasure must wait, *señorita*—but not for long."

Taking her by the arm, he began to drag her back through the dark, deserted estate. Her head ached, and she veered between wishing someone would rescue her and praying no one else would get hurt.

Just before they reached the cottage, the Spaniard caught her hair in his fist and yanked her head back, covering her mouth with his hand.

"Say nothing or you die!" he hissed into her face.

He slammed open the cottage door and dragged Roselyn inside. She heard a low grunt behind her, and suddenly she was yanked sideways toward the pallet. She whirled around and saw Thornton behind the Spaniard, his arm around the man's neck. Thornton's face was hard and cold and frightening.

Then she saw the knife in the Spaniard's hand.

Before she could even cry a warning, she was flung across the room, and heard Thornton curse. He fell back against the wall, blood streaming from his arm. The Spaniard crouched, waving his knife before Thornton, laughing as he glanced back at Roselyn, then shouting something in Spanish.

Her mind raced with useless ideas; there was little she could do against an armed man. And the way Thornton was bleeding, his strength wouldn't last much longer.

Just as the Spaniard started to speak, Thornton launched himself forward, catching the man's arm to hold the knife wide. They toppled over, and the Spaniard gave a hoarse cry as his head struck the hearth. Though the Spaniard went limp, Thornton quickly pinned his arms wide, and Roselyn scrambled for the knife.

She shook horribly but forced herself to remain near, waiting to hand the knife to Thornton. He pressed his hand to the man's chest for a moment. Then, using the chimney, he pulled himself to his feet.

Trembling from exertion and fear, Spencer stumbled back in pain and bumped into Roselyn. Without thinking, he caught her hard against him in a tight embrace. Her arms clasped his waist; her face pressed against his chest. All he could hear was his own gasping breath, the crackle of logs on the fire—and Roselyn's sobs.

"Roselyn?" he said softly, close to her ear.

"Did he hurt you? Is there another man still out there?"

She shook her head emphatically but didn't lift her face. Her sobs quieted, yet still her shoulders trembled, and she clutched him even harder.

"I have rope," she said. "We should tie him up—"

"That won't be necessary. I felt no heartbeat. He's dead."

Spencer was stunned that his first thought had been outrage at the assault on Roselyn. As she shuddered, he was aware of how she felt in his arms, so small and slight, suddenly so vulnerable.

He didn't understand his own reaction to her.

"Roselyn, tell me what happened. What did he do to you?"

She wiped her tears with her palms, then lifted her face to his. Her stormy eyes were uncertain and fearful.

Just the sight of him seemed to change something inside her—the naked emotion on her face was wiped away as if it had never existed. She pulled back, leaving him to rest a hand against the chimney.

For a moment, he almost resisted letting go of her.

"He slapped me, but I'll be fine," she said,

with only a little hitch in her voice as she
looked down at the Spaniard's body. "And he
was alone. But what will we do with—with—"

"First calm yourself and tell me what happened."

"No, no, not with . . . *him* here."

Spencer looked down at the Spaniard, one of
Rodney Shaw's henchman. Could Shaw have
discovered he had taken the pouch?

But it was at the bottom of the channel,
where it could not exonerate him.

"Do you know him?" Roselyn asked in a soft
voice.

He lifted his head to find her watching him,
and he realized she was suspicious. What had
the Spaniard said to her?

"I've never seen him before," he said, the lie
coming easily.

She nodded and caught her lip between her
teeth as she looked down at the dead man.
"What shall we do with him?"

"If I had two good legs, I'd heave him into
the ocean where he came from."

"But you don't. I can't . . . can't . . ." She
started shivering and her face looked bleak.

Again, Spencer felt a strong need to hold her.
Why the hell would he want to protect her, after all she'd done?

But she'd been threatened and injured be-

cause of him. He couldn't tell her the truth, and
now he couldn't do much about the dead man
in her home.

Roselyn clasped her hands together and
stared at the body with a helplessness that
made Spencer uneasy.

"We cannot bury him," he said. "I'd be useless with a shovel, and you can't do it alone."

"I'm strong," she insisted.

He almost smiled at her stubbornness. "It
would take all night, and someone would be
bound to notice a fresh grave. No, I think the
ocean would be best. Do you have a horse?"

She shook her head but looked at him with
the first spark of hope in her eyes. "Wakesfield
does. The stables are behind the manor. In the
middle of the night I could bring a horse here."

"Excellent idea. We can last until then." And
now he knew there were horses nearby to use
when he escaped.

Her faltering gaze dropped to the body. "Can
we take him . . . outside?"

"I don't think we could drag him far. I'd
rather save my strength to get him on the horse.
Let's go out to the courtyard instead. I'm starv-
ing."

It was the wrong thing to say—her wide eyes
fastened on his face in shock.

He sighed. "After you've been in a few battles, Roselyn, you start to realize what's impor-

tant. This man is dead. He tried to hurt you, but he didn't succeed. There is no point in worrying about what can't be changed."

She gave a slight nod. "I'll gather bandages for your arm."

He glanced down at the wound he'd forgotten, then back up to Roselyn, who watched him with a wariness she didn't bother to hide. He noticed a rash of red marks across her chin and cheeks. He knew it was caused by a man's stubble—he'd done such a thing himself, many a time. But he'd been carried away by passion, not brutality.

Spencer rubbed his thumb across the raw skin on her chin, and she stared at him almost wildly.

"Did he kiss you?" he demanded. "What else did he do?"

"It's not a kiss when a man forces his mouth on mine," she said softly.

"He did nothing else?"

Lowering her eyes, she shook her head. She crossed her arms almost protectively across her chest, and he thought perhaps more than her lips had been touched.

"He . . . he called me your '*puta*.' What does that mean?"

He opened his mouth, but no words emerged.

" 'Tis the same as whore, isn't it?"

"Roselyn—"

"You called me that, too." Her voice held no emotion, but her face was as white as bleached bones scattered on the beach. "He said the two of you would—share me."

Nausea twisted his gut. "I shouldn't have called you that. I was angry."

"He was angry, too."

He flinched as if she'd struck him, just by the comparison. "I *am* sorry."

She pulled away. "But that doesn't make it right, does it?"

Spencer refused to apologize for anything else, if that's what she wanted. After fetching the bandages and helping him put on one of Grant's wooden-soled boots, Roselyn guided him outside. In the dark courtyard she cleaned and bandaged his forearm, and then they ate a silent meal of cold chicken.

Alone with his thoughts, he didn't know whether to be relieved or frustrated. Though the pouch was gone, Shaw didn't know that. One of his men was now dead. Would he send another man looking for the Spaniard and him?

Chapter 9

Battered and bruised, Roselyn ached with exhaustion, but she couldn't rest until the body was removed from her cottage. It would be hours before she could risk going for a horse.

Thornton sat silently across from her, his food long gone. Was he thankful to have escaped death, or had he killed the Spaniard only to protect himself from exposure?

When he'd washed up on the beach, Thornton had been worried that someone would follow him. She had no proof that this assailant was doing anything else, and she would drive herself mad with endless speculation. But would another Spaniard follow when this one didn't return?

Thornton's voice startled her. "Now will you tell me what happened?"

She shrugged. "He came upon me in the bake house and wanted to know who you were, said that he'd been watching us. He said you are no Englishman."

Thornton's only response to that was a gleam of a smile in the darkness. "I've heard that on more than one occasion, although often the word 'proper' preceded 'Englishman.' "

She didn't smile. "When I wouldn't bring him to the cottage, he grew angry." She was glad it was too dark for Thornton to see her protectively cover her bruised chest with her arms. "I escaped and ran from him, trying to lead him away from the estate. He caught me and fell on top of me and—" She broke off, wiping her mouth and shuddering.

Thornton didn't speak, but his tension was clear.

A sudden memory was sharp in her mind, and she spoke slowly. "When he was . . . insulting me, he said he'd been long at sea."

"Which is only natural if he came from the armada," Thornton said. "I was worried that one of the Spanish ships had seen me survive and sent someone to follow me."

"But why would they? How could one lone Englishman matter to them?"

He disappointed her by not even hesitating. "Perhaps they thought I carried information to be used against them. Did anything else happen before you arrived at the cottage?"

She shook her head, then propped her chin in her hand.

"You're certain he mentioned no one else who'd come with him?"

She nodded.

Thornton studied her closely. "You seem exhausted," he said in a grudging voice. "You've done well today. Lay your head down, and I will awaken you when the time is right."

She didn't even bother to protest as she put her head in her arms and fell asleep.

When Roselyn was shaken awake by Thornton, she came up with a gasp, having had vivid dreams of the Spaniard's leering face.

The peculiar stillness of deep night enfolded her, though off to the east she could hear the faintest crash of waves on the shore.

She stared at the pale outline of Thornton and realized she had not asked him the question that most concerned her. "What did he say?"

"The Spaniard?"

"Just before he died, he spoke to you in Spanish. What did he say?"

"Just that he was going to kill me."

His voice was deliberate and too controlled. She didn't believe him, and her doubts threatened to overwhelm her.

"I'll go for the horse," she said, pushing herself off the bench.

He looked up at her. "Know that I would do this for you if I could. Be careful."

She stared into his dark, solemn face, wishing she could read his expression as she said softly, "I'll be back soon."

Once she had reached the stables, Roselyn selected the gentlest mare she could find. Angel had been hers as a child, and would obey her without shying away.

For just a moment she put her arms around the horse's neck, letting memories of long ago comfort her. Francis had taught her to ride on Angel. She'd spent hours every day exploring the island on horseback, making endless plans for her life.

She never rode Angel anymore for fear of painful memories, just as she never visited any other room at Wakesfield but the kitchens. She was no longer the favored child, only a tenant.

She saddled Angel and led her away from the stables. When she reached the cottage Thornton was waiting for her in the doorway, silhouetted by the firelight. The Spaniard lay behind him.

She gazed down at the body for a moment, caught again in the terror of what had happened. Thornton's voice distracted her.

"Why aren't you riding the horse?" he asked.

She glanced up to find him watching her speculatively, as if he knew her every thought and was amused.

"Because she's not mine," she said firmly. "Let us finish this, please."

Roselyn steeled herself against the horror of dragging a dead man. While Thornton pulled awkwardly on one arm, she tugged on the other, feeling that at any moment the Spaniard would awaken and grab her.

Standing on one leg, Thornton lifted the body and boosted it behind the saddle, over Angel's haunches while she braced him for balance. When it was done, he sagged against the horse's flank, then roused himself enough to tie the body behind the saddle.

"She's a calm horse," he said afterward, stroking the animal. "What's her name?"

"Angel."

She heard his soft chuckle in the darkness. "This angel will be leading a Spaniard to the gates of hell."

His penchant for inappropriate humor was infuriating and improper, and she told him so.

"Lady Roselyn, your lack of humor is much of your problem."

"How would you know, Lord Thornton? You never bothered to find out."

He was silent, then said coldly, "Let's go."

"First you must return to the cottage," she said, attempting to slide beneath his arm.

He held her away. "I'm going, too."

"You most certainly are not. That is the last thing I need, to be seen riding so . . . intimately with a man."

"But riding intimately with a corpse is acceptable?"

She shuddered. "You're right; I'll walk."

"Don't be a fool; that would take most of the night. And you aren't going alone. What if a ship is at anchor out there, waiting? Then you'd need my help."

She hadn't considered that there might be a Spanish ship hidden nearby.

He grasped the pommel, then pulled himself high enough to get his left foot near the stirrup, but it kept bouncing out of his reach.

"Will you help me?" he demanded, his voice strained.

Shaking her head, Roselyn guided his foot into the stirrup, and he swung up into the saddle. By the light spilling out of the cottage, she saw him grimace in pain.

"This is not a good idea," she said. "You might aggravate your injuries."

"I'm not letting you clean up a mess that's my fault. Go close the cottage door."

So he thought he was heroic, helping the poor maiden in distress?

She pulled the cottage door closed. "There isn't room for me—I'll walk."

"Put your foot in the stirrup and give me your hand."

"No."

"Give me your hand," he repeated firmly.

"The poor horse will—"

"Roselyn!"

He reached for her, and with a sigh she clasped his hand and put her foot in the stirrup. She didn't realize until she was straddling the saddle that he meant her to sit before him. She was pinned between the pommel and his body, and she watched in growing worry as he placed his arms around her to reach for the reins.

"I can guide the horse," she said swiftly.

He didn't answer.

"You can't even use your right foot." She was mortified to hear her voice rising.

"I'll make do."

His voice rumbled with amusement, and to her surprise she could feel it against her back. She had been resting against him, and she straightened so fast he chuckled.

Thornton guided the mare away from the cottage.

"You're heading for the village, not the shore. You were barely conscious the last time you came this way."

"Very well," he said, allowing her to take the reins.

That ended up making matters worse—he rested his hands on her waist. She could feel the heat of him through her clothes.

"Please let go of me."

He spoke softly into her ear. "I'm feeling dizzy. You wouldn't want me to fall."

She hated his sarcasm, his superiority, especially the way he enjoyed tormenting her. It only made her more aware that he was not a gentleman. She had to distract herself—and him.

"Earlier you said this soldier would be going to hell, but perhaps he was just doing his duty. Surely you have followed orders as well."

If she hoped for any truths from him, she was disappointed.

"There is no excuse for abusing a woman. That is proof of what kind of villain he is."

Didn't he realize that although he had never physically harmed her, he had abused her just the same during their betrothal? Didn't he know that his treatment of her now was in many ways worse?

As they neared the cliffs, they could hear the pounding of surf on the rocky shoreline below them. Though Roselyn was keeping her back straight, she still felt Thornton's thighs pressed to the length of hers. His hands tensed at her waist and she knew it must look as if they were riding over the edge, but even in the darkness Angel knew her way. As they began the descent to the beach, she heard Thornton release his breath.

There was almost no moon this night, and the water seemed an endless black.

"Do you see a ship?" she whispered, looking over her shoulder at him.

He shook his head, but he still looked intent, worried.

"Do you think the Spaniard arrived the same night you did?"

"Probably, and it took him this long to find me. Perhaps he has a boat hidden on the shoreline nearby, or he was going to steal one. I think we're safe for the moment."

Nothing seemed real to Roselyn, as they rode into the dark water until the waves soaked their legs. She clutched the pommel as Thornton untied the Spaniard's body and pushed it off the horse. She flinched at the splash, and didn't protest when he took the reins and guided Angel back onto the beach.

"Someone will find the body in the morning," she said, shivering.

"Perhaps not. The tide could drag him farther out. But if he is found, well, he was just another casualty of the war."

Angel herself guided them back up the cliff,

and when Thornton would have headed for the cottage, Roselyn stopped him.

"Wait." She took the reins back, and turned Angel toward the channel. They looked out over the dark water, and she couldn't help but remember the night she'd found him, when the moon had been full, and enemy ships threatened the island.

She took a deep breath. "Do you remember anything more about how you arrived here?"

She was so close to him she could feel the slight stiffening of his muscles.

"Only what I've told you."

"It must bother you to have a piece of your memory missing. How long were you with the fleet?"

"Almost three months." The tension in his voice grew. "What is the point of these questions?"

"I'm curious. This island is not so remote as you imagine; Francis goes to the mainland often and brings back stories he hears in the taverns. It might surprise you to know that your . . . exploits are talked of even there."

"My exploits?"

He sounded suitably bewildered; she was impressed.

"The only reason I asked how long you'd

been with the fleet, is because Francis heard talk of you that sounded quite recent."

Thornton said nothing.

"Perhaps Francis heard incorrectly," she continued.

"That could be," he said mildly. "I've had so many exploits that stories of them could easily take a while to spread."

"Why do you feel the need to behave in such a way?" she asked, trying to mask her disappointment that she couldn't trap him.

She thought he would laugh and make light of his behavior. Instead his hands tightened where they rested on her waist.

"How else will society forget how you humiliated me?" he said coldly.

She gritted her teeth together. "You're claiming that your actions are my fault?"

"Who else?"

"You didn't want to marry me, either!"

"Perhaps not, but after the contract was signed, I was committed."

"Thornton, your scandalous behavior proves to one and all that I was justified in not marrying you—and it began long before you met me."

He leaned against her, suddenly reminding her that she was alone with him on a deserted cliff in the darkness.

And no one knew where she was.

"Rationalize your own behavior all you'd like, Lady Roselyn, but we both know who was doing his family duty, and who was selfishly destroying lives."

She elbowed him in the stomach, and with a grunt he straightened. "I haven't harmed my family," she said, "and though it has taken me time, I've found my own peace. Can you say the same for yourself?"

She tapped her heels into Angel's sides, and let the horse's hooves drown out anything else he might want to say. At the cottage he dismounted without a word, and she continued on to the Wakesfield stables, walking the last few hundred yards.

After unsaddling Angel, she rubbed the horse down, then spent a moment petting her, not knowing when she'd get the chance again. After a last look around to make sure everything was as she found it, she left the stables for home.

Francis Heywood arose before dawn, certain he'd heard someone near the stables. After he dressed, he crept outside in time to see Lady Roselyn returning Angel. Instead of confronting her, he hesitated. She never rode the horse, no matter how far her business took her.

So why had she borrowed Angel in the middle of the night? Why had she been acting so distant? Whatever secrets she was keeping, he wanted only to help her. But how could he help if she wouldn't confide in him?

Chapter 10

❦

Spencer awoke at dawn, having slept poorly. He couldn't stop thinking of the rumors Roselyn had hinted at. He'd been gone from England well over a year, and his brother was supposed to be taking care of everything.

What was being said about him in London, and how could he pry for more information without sounding suspicious?

He heard the wood creak above as she dressed, and he cut another mark in the floor. Eleven days left.

She descended the ladder, giving a start as she looked at him. "You're not usually awake," she murmured, turning away.

"I couldn't sleep well."

She hesitated, glancing toward the door he'd barricaded with the cupboard. "Neither could I."

He waited to be overwhelmed by his usual anger toward her, but couldn't summon it as easily. She brought him bread and cider before he could come to the table, and he pushed himself to a sitting position.

She straightened, and in the firelight he saw a shadow on her neck that disturbed him. "Come here," he said, frowning.

She seemed too tired to protest as she knelt down. "Is something wrong with the food?"

He ignored her words, reaching out to lift her chin, making himself ignore the softness of her skin. She inhaled swiftly, but didn't pull away. Spencer saw faint bruises around her throat, the kind that could come only from a man's hands.

"The Spaniard tried to strangle you," he said, as a wave of frustrated rage swept through him.

She tried to pull away but he grasped her arm and held her near. He brushed the back of his finger against a bruise and she flinched, the pulse beating at the hollow of her throat. Her skin was translucent, delicate.

"Are you going to finish the deed for him?" she asked.

"Of course not!" He let her go, not quite certain *what* he'd meant to do.

She stood up and he took a quick gulp of cider, unable to meet her eyes. For a moment he'd felt fiercely protective, outraged that someone had dared to touch . . . whom? His nurse? His betrothed? What was Roselyn to him now, that he should feel such emotion?

He didn't like it, but seeing the wounds she'd suffered because of him made things . . . different.

"Roselyn."

She looked over her shoulder at him.

"I need to walk again today."

She raised an eyebrow and waited. Why didn't she just nod her head in agreement?

He let out his breath in a sigh. "Would you help me, please?"

She leaned back against the cupboard and folded her arms over her chest. "I could return from my chores in an hour or so and work with you, and then perhaps later in the afternoon again."

"Thank you," he said, studying her until she turned away. "And Roselyn, if you must go outside, be very careful."

He saw her stiffen, saw the shudder she couldn't hide. "Do you think another Spaniard could be out there somewhere?"

"I doubt it. If he had a partner, they would have come together to overwhelm us."

"I won't go farther than the bake house," she murmured, sitting down at the table to break her fast.

After milking the goats, Roselyn was kneading dough in the bake house, wondering if she would ever get over the feeling of being watched. Just when she was starting to relax, instead of looking over her shoulder constantly, she heard footsteps in the courtyard.

Her heart suddenly pounding, she picked up a knife and whirled toward the door.

Francis Heywood stood in the doorway, gazing at her in concern. "Lady Roselyn? Is something amiss?"

She set the knife down quickly, hoping he didn't see her trembling. "No, Francis, you merely startled me."

He took a step toward her. "I have done that before, and you've never felt a need to defend yourself, my dear."

She gave him a weak grin. "The battle in the channel must have upset me more than I thought."

He set his hand on hers, his eyes full of concern. "Is that all that's bothering you, my lady? You have not seemed yourself, and John agrees with me."

For an insane moment, she wanted to fall into his arms and tell him about Thornton, and spying, and the Spaniard. She was tired of feeling alone and wondering if she was making the right decisions.

But just the memory of the dead Spaniard was enough to keep Roselyn quiet. Francis would insist she come to the house; he would turn Thornton over to the garrison. Since it was frightening to contemplate bringing such danger to the Heywoods, she would have to continue doing this alone.

She smiled and squeezed his hand. "I'm having a hard time realizing that Mary and Philip have been dead a whole year already. I still can't believe I forgot to visit their grave."

Francis looked almost disappointed, as if he expected her to say something else. "I was worried you felt this way, my lady. It is only natural for you to go on with your life."

"I know. Sit with me awhile and keep me company. I've missed talking to you."

The sun had already risen before Roselyn returned to the cottage, with flour covering her apron and a smudge of it across her cheek. She stood above Spencer as he sat at the table, and he was amazed that he felt an urge to chuckle. He would *not* be swayed by her. She took his elbow to help him up, then pulled his arm across her shoulders. She felt small and fragile, and it made him imagine that Spaniard straddling her, his hands about her neck.

She should still be frightened from her trauma of the previous night, but she seemed no longer affected, and he couldn't help being impressed by her fortitude.

Outside, she helped him walk from the courtyard to the bake house and back. He noticed that she constantly watched the surrounding estate. Was she worried about another Spaniard—or the Heywoods?

Since he didn't feel as weak as before, he said, "Let's walk to the orchard."

She stiffened.

"I honestly don't believe there are any more Spaniards lurking in the trees. And this boot of Grant's is almost comfortable. Do you not want me to get well quickly?"

He knew that would work. And he was so desperate to regain his strength that he would gladly risk discovery. With a long-suffering sigh, she opened the gate and led him from the courtyard.

He hadn't imagined the distance as great as it really was. Soon he was perspiring, and his good leg felt afire. When they reached the orchard, he gratefully leaned against an apple tree.

"Why don't we rest awhile?" she said.

We? Spencer told himself he should feel affronted; instead he sank down to the ground, keeping his broken leg carefully out before him. Roselyn walked a little away from him and stood looking out over the estate.

In the distance, he could see Wakesfield Manor. She had grown up there, yet claimed she would never live there again.

He wondered about the woman behind the reserved face, who defied her parents for the love of a man beneath her, who could be content living alone, doing menial work. She stood alone now, the wind catching her black gown, teasing strands of her light brown hair loose.

He tried to put himself in her place—hell, two years ago he *was* in her place, told by his parents whom to marry. He wanted to hate her, but he couldn't—nor did he forgive her, either.

Roselyn told herself that she should not have brought Thornton to the orchard, especially not with Francis dropping by so unexpectedly.

But last night had changed things between them, and she no longer knew what to expect, or how to treat him. For the last few days he'd spoken to her with bitter, angry words, but now his voice sounded grudging, reluctant. Did he feel guilty for the Spaniard's attack? What was she to make of that except that he was guilty of treason?

She looked over her shoulder and found him staring at the manor, a pensive look on his face. Why was it so difficult to admit to herself that he could be a spy? So he had expressed sympathy for the bruises she'd suffered; it could merely be the result of a guilty conscience.

He'd even apologized for that harsh word he'd called her.

Yet he'd been almost defensive when she'd told him of the rumors about him. He was such a puzzle to her!

Thornton glanced at her and their eyes met. She wanted to look away, but she lifted her chin and refused to give ground.

He nodded toward the manor. "You grew up there?"

After a moment's hesitation, she nodded. "When we weren't in London, we were usually here."

"Does it not bother you to live in a cottage, forever staring at a manor you claim you'll never live in again?"

For once, he seemed sincere instead of sarcastic. Where could these questions be leading?

"No, I was grateful for a place to live. I've only been back a year."

"A year?" he said with a frown. "Has it not been almost two years since"—he broke off, and this time his smile had the faintest tinge of mockery—"since you decided not to marry me?"

Her brows rose in surprise at the tactful way he spoke. "We lived in London at first."

"But I was there—I never saw you."

Roselyn hadn't thought he would be capable of such naiveté. "You wouldn't have, unless you frequented Southwark."

Thornton leaned his head back against the tree and studied her with narrowed eyes.

She went to stand above him. "Do you think I'm ashamed? When I make decisions I live by them, no matter the consequences."

"Are you implying I didn't?"

She sighed. "I was implying nothing, merely answering your questions. Philip was a baker before he worked for my father, and he went back to that trade."

"And he taught you?"

"I worked alongside him, yes. Our home was also our store." She could still remember how cold their front parlor was in the winter, with the shutters opened onto the street so customers could peruse their baked goods.

"Then why return here? Surely there were more customers in London."

"We came here to escape the Black Death, but it was too late."

His eyes widened before resuming their shuttered, suspicious look. "Your stable groom died of the plague?"

She nodded, noticing that he did not call Philip her husband. But she couldn't bring herself to argue about it.

"And you . . . ?" he continued.

"Though I nursed him, I did not become sick." She still thanked God each night for not letting her spread death to the rest of the islanders. She would never have forgiven herself if even one other person besides her husband and child had died.

He studied her for an uncomfortable moment before he looked back toward Wakesfield Manor. "Have you tried to see your parents since his death?"

"No, they made their feelings clear."

Spencer was rather shocked that she had made no effort to mend the rift. "But it might change things."

Roselyn seemed genuinely puzzled. "Why should it? My parents are not people who forgive, let alone forget, nor do I wish to return to their treatment of me. Though this last year has been difficult, in many ways I am more content."

"You can't be serious," he said, studying this serenity she wore like a garment.

"You are a man, free to do as you please. For the first time, I, too, can shape my own destiny."

"Few people can do as they please. Like anyone, I have obligations—and my family is one of them."

"Mine no longer are," she said softly.

"Yet this is your destiny? Up before dawn to bake for strangers, harvesting your own food, exhausted and spent each night?"

"Do not mock my life!" she said, leaning over him.

"But I'm not—"

"I know the contentment of providing for myself. Can you say the same?"

Using the tree for support, Spencer struggled up onto his good leg. Her usual serenity was replaced by unexpected fire in her wild gray eyes.

"I do what's necessary," he said slowly. "I can be proud of that."

"Not from the things I've heard and seen."

"You don't know everything, Lady Roselyn. And if you believe rumors, then you are too naive."

"So you're denying these stories?"

"I have heard nothing to deny."

Though there were enough true stories about him to make a virgin quake in fear. Roselyn wasn't a virgin—and he found himself wanting to shock her out of this prim, sanctimonious frame of mind.

"Go ahead," he continued, smiling. "I want to hear one of these rumors."

"This is hardly a rumor, not when all the court knows what you did six months ago."

Spencer felt an inkling of disquiet. Six months ago he'd been in Spain, spying for the queen, but no one knew it.

"How can you stand here and pretend you do not remember such a scandal?" she said, throwing up her hands and stalking away from him.

What had his brother done?

"Lady Roselyn, I pretend nothing. There are just so many . . . rumors to choose from."

She looked disgusted with him, and suddenly he noticed the blush stealing up her neck and reddening her pale skin. She was *embarrassed*—he could hardly allow her to back down now.

"Go ahead, Lady Roselyn."

"Stop calling me that," she said crossly.

"I cannot show you the respect of your rank?"

"Not when you don't mean it—and I do not go by my title anymore."

"But I heard my bailiff call you that."

"Let us go back now," she said sternly, marching up to slide her shoulders beneath his arm.

Spencer didn't quite know what came over him: he caught her against his side and held her still, until she looked up at him with wide, astonished eyes. He should avoid the subject of these recent London scandals, but he wanted to see how shocked she would be to repeat them.

"The rumors?" he prompted. Standing so close to her, he suddenly realized he could see the faint shadow of the valley between her breasts.

Color blazed across her face again, and she stared straight ahead, not up at him. "What were you thinking of to send such a statue to Her Majesty?"

That distracted him from his earthy, dangerous perusal of her. What statue? What had his brother done in Spencer's name?

His mind worked frantically. "How can one enjoy life without causing an occasional shock at court?"

"But a statue of yourself?" she said, clearly aghast, as her wide gray eyes lifted to his.

He allowed himself a smile, while inside he was laughing. *Oh, Alex,* he thought with grudging respect. "Well, the queen always said I had a fetching profile."

She made a strangled, choking sound. "Thornton, how many innocent young girls do you think this statue corrupted with your *naked* profile?"

Chapter 11

◦⟨◦⟩◦

Naked? Spencer barely held back a choked laugh, yet he didn't release Roselyn. He held her body firmly against his.

"And the wings!" she continued, rolling her eyes. "Even the queen cannot find your behavior angelic."

He tried to picture the incredible sight of Queen Elizabeth holding a naked statue of an angel that resembled him. Roselyn didn't know her very well if she thought the old girl would be offended. More than likely, the statue held a place of honor at court that day.

But *he* felt embarrassed. Alex had always been willing to go one step farther than Spencer in whatever mischief they created.

He imagined Roselyn's reaction if she'd actually seen the statue; he would have taken dark pleasure in her prim outrage.

"Are you shocked?" he asked in a low, rumbling voice.

The light played across her face between the shadow of the leaves. Again he found his gaze straying to her breasts, small but so perfectly formed. For a moment he wondered what she would do if he caressed them—as was his right.

She took a deep breath, and her eyes narrowed as she studied him. "Nothing you do shocks me."

"No?"

The nerve of her, to challenge him so! They stood side by side, pressed together from thigh to hip to shoulder. He could tell he unsettled her, by the way she moistened her lips and refused to break away from his gaze. How much further could he affect her—even to the point of desire? He looked into the depths of her eyes and thought he could use this attraction simmering between them, tease her until she found out what she had missed, arouse her until she could think of nothing but him—and then reject her, as she had done to him.

He pretended to stumble forward, and she turned to brace him, obviously without thinking. Their bodies met in a frontal assault, her breasts pressing low against his chest. His hands naturally dropped to her waist, and through her thin gown he could feel the delicate bones of her hips, which flared out with feminine appeal. Whatever else she was, Roselyn Harrington felt like a woman.

Spencer thought for certain she would step away, but she lingered, seeming flustered and unprepared. Her hands came to rest against his chest, and he imagined them sliding up behind his neck, pulling his head down for a kiss—

They both broke away at the same moment.

"We should be returning," she said in that prim, controlled voice of hers.

"Of course." He was stunned by the flash of desire he'd been unable to control, when it was she who was supposed to be overcome. What business had his body to react to a woman who'd betrayed him? And how could he be thinking of sex, when what awaited him in London might be the end of his freedom—perhaps his life?

He let anger sweep away his feelings of helplessness and bitterness. *He* would control their encounters; *he* would make her squirm with frustration.

Reluctantly linked together, they walked slowly back to the cottage, his prison.

During the afternoon a light rain swept the island, but that didn't stop Roselyn and the Heywood brothers from harvesting her grain. She walked the fields behind them, gathering the wheat in bundles, but her mind was on the morning she'd spent with Thornton.

Why couldn't she just ignore his assault on

her senses? She knew he did it deliberately, that he took pleasure in provoking her. Touching her was surely only another means to some revenge.

If only she didn't fall for it so easily. It was as if when she was near him, he cast a witch's spell over her; her common sense fled. When she looked into his dark, exotic eyes, she thought of shadows, and the illicit things one hid in them to do. The calm life she worked so hard for fell away beneath an itch that seemed to burn inside her.

She hadn't been able to keep her silly gaze off his mouth. It was far too expressive for a man, whether twisted in mockery or grinning in gloating delight.

She raised her face up to the clouds, and let the misty rain cool her heated skin. Next she'd be forgiving him for every crime and falling at his feet, she thought in disgust.

"Roselyn?"

She heard voices call her name, and she realized how far away her thoughts had been. John and Thomas were some distance ahead of her, and both had turned to look at her with exasperation.

Throughout the day it continued to rain, and Roselyn grew more and more uneasy about where she would feed the Heywood brothers.

Just when she was wondering how she could get herself invited to Wakesfield for the evening, the sun came out. She left the Heywoods to go prepare supper, knowing it would only take a little convincing to make them eat outside.

She hurried inside the cottage, and when she didn't see Thornton right away, she felt a moment of panic.

Then she saw him standing against the far wall. His dark looks and beard blended into the shadows, and she couldn't help thinking of the night ahead. He said nothing, just stared at her, and she wondered if he, too, was remembering how it felt to touch each other, chest to chest, so close that nothing else in the world had existed but the orchard, their bower.

Forcing such thoughts from her mind, Roselyn clenched her tired fingers together.

"You're wet," he murmured.

The exhaustion in his voice drew her out of her spell. She came toward him and realized that he was perspiring heavily, shaking as he leaned against the wall.

"What have you been doing?" she asked, reaching out to steady his arm.

"A lot of hopping."

Thornton's grin made her insides twist with a pleasurable sensation she'd never felt before. She wanted to step closer and explore it further—and she wanted to run as far away as she could.

She clamped down on her strange feelings and gave him a cool stare. "You will not get well if you overexert yourself."

His chest rose and fell as he took quick breaths. "So you've said. But if I spend another day on my back, I'll go mad."

Roselyn glanced down at his broken leg. "I have seen such injuries before. It will be many weeks before you can walk."

His grin faded. "No, it won't."

"Are you accusing me of lying?"

With a sigh, Thornton rubbed his face with both hands. "Let's not start this, Roselyn; I'm too tired."

"Let me get you back to your pallet. I have to make supper."

"For the boys again?" he asked sardonically.

He slung his arm a little too forcefully over her shoulders.

"They are hardly boys," she said between her teeth.

She helped him across the room and would have eased him down onto his pallet, but he didn't let go of her.

"You're damp," he murmured, his voice—his mouth—too close to her ear.

"You said that already." Good Lord, her voice

shook, just as her hands would shake if she
didn't keep them clasped together. The heat of
his body scorched her.

She knew she should shove him away, but
she had promised herself that she would discover his secrets, understand his loyalties.
Making him angry wouldn't accomplish that,
so she stood still, biting her lip, telling herself
that she only allowed this contact between
them for her country's sake.

There was a silent moment of hesitation that
seemed to stretch on forever. She could feel her
wet skirts brush her legs, as if her skin was suddenly too sensitive. The weight of him against
her body was almost pleasurable.

Why did she feel like this? She knew too well
how uncomfortable her husband's weight had
been, how he'd often taken her to bed even
when she was sick. Men thought only of themselves and their pleasure, and wives could only
submit. Philip had never shown her kindness
after she'd been disowned by her parents,
never even kissed her. Was that why she was
fascinated with Thornton's mouth?

With a shudder of self-disgust, she stepped
away from him, and he lowered himself to sit
on the pallet.

Spencer watched Roselyn busy herself with
the supper preparations. Not since he was a
boy trying to sneak sweets had he spent so

much time watching someone cook. She didn't act as if it were a chore she was forced to do. She did it like she did everything else, with a calm serenity that annoyed him.

Naturally she could be serene, he thought bitterly. She didn't have an executioner waiting for her arrival. For too many hours each day, he contemplated the bleak future that awaited him, what his Spanish heritage had brought him to—no wonder he was so easily distracted by Roselyn.

Well, he'd done as much as he could today to fluster her, and he thought it was working. He took great pleasure in upsetting this balance she'd found for herself. He only touched her because he wanted her to know how it felt to be rejected in the end; he ignored the darker, disturbing thoughts in the back of his mind.

Later that evening, he hopped over to the back window and sat on the floor, listening to the small party she made for the Heywood brothers in the courtyard. Though she laughed freely at their jokes, he began to realize that she still held part of herself in reserve, that it wasn't just him she was reticent with.

As Roselyn cleaned up the supper plates, Thornton moved about the room, hopping from window to window, peering out the shutters. He even repeatedly practiced using his arms to push himself off the floor until his face shone with perspiration. She wished he would sit still, or sleep as he used to.

Finally he stood looking out over the court-yard for a long enough time that she began to relax.

"Where do you bathe?" he asked suddenly. "In the bake house?"

Her fingers froze as she set a plate in the cup-board. In her old life she would have never discussed such an intimate subject with a man.

"I bathe in a half barrel," she said, keeping her back to him, waiting for his laughter.

"Really?" He sounded only intrigued.

"In the summer I leave it outside, where draining it is easier. In the winter I keep it in the bake house."

She briskly finished putting away the dishes, intending to next mend clothing for the village brewer, who'd just had her fourth child. If she ignored Thornton long enough, maybe he wouldn't say—

"I'd like a bath."

She closed her eyes and tried not to groan. "I'll get you hot water and towels, then go up to the loft to give you privacy." This was their usual routine—surely he didn't need it changed now.

"No, I'll take one outside. Can you help me remove the splint?"

"You won't be able to move well in the barrel—I barely fit."

"Ah well," he said with a grin and a shrug, "you'll just have to scrub my back, won't you?"

She forced herself not to glare at him, remembering that she had to be nice, to get him to relax and tell her his secrets.

But she knew he wouldn't fit in that barrel, and she had no intention of helping him.

As Roselyn knelt at his feet to untie the splint, she felt a slow anger begin to build inside her. When she arose, she saw the faintest smirk on Thornton's face as he pulled the shirt over his head. Her gaze swept over his chest. He looked healthier already, the bones of his ribs no longer prominent; dark hair was scattered across his chest and narrowed in a line down his stomach.

"May I have a towel?" he asked.

She hated the amusement in his voice, hated the fact that she had to accept it. She found him linens and soft soap, then helped him to the courtyard. The lantern she carried glimmered in the darkness, guiding their way. She set it on the half wall near the bake house, while he hopped to the barrel and looked in.

"I guess you weren't exaggerating about the tight fit," he said dryly.

She gave him a smug glance, but found herself distracted by the candlelight flickering across his face and bare chest.

"There's water boiling in the bake house. I'll add it to the rainwater in the barrel."

Thornton continued to frown. Did he think such a simple tub was beneath him? Surely things had not been so easy aboard ship—she well remembered how he had smelled before she bathed him.

When the barrel was little more than half full, he took the buckets from her hand. "Enough!" he said sharply. "You have worked hard enough today."

She covered her shock with disdain. "Surely if we had married, I would have served you like this. Isn't that what you demand of a woman?"

"I can think of other ways you would have served me," he said in a low voice.

Without breaking her gaze, he began to unlace his breeches.

Chapter 12

Roselyn was torn about her role in this farce—should she play the shy maiden and turn away, or boldly watch Thornton disrobe as if she were a wife in truth? It wasn't as if she hadn't seen him naked before.

But this was different—he was no longer unconscious, or even badly wounded. He knew what he was about as he began to remove his garments, pausing to look up at her, his mouth quirked in half a grin as if to say, *Well?*

"You forget," she said, "I have been a wife."

His smile died, and she knew with sickening certainty that angering him would not help her cause.

"And Grant did not require you at his bath?" he asked.

"He did not need such help—he was not a child." She could have also added that Philip wouldn't bathe more than a few times each season.

She held her breath, waiting for Thornton to erupt because she'd implied that he was a child.

Instead, he grinned. "The man didn't know what he was missing."

She was thankful for the dark, so he couldn't see her blush.

"But you are right," he continued. "You're not my wife, and 'tis unfair of me to shock you. Help me into the barrel, and then I'll remove the breeches."

"No," she said firmly. "I only allowed this to go on so long because I thought you would surely realize how impossible a bath is."

"Lady Roselyn—"

"I will not help you in this foolishness which, should you hurt yourself, would set back your recovery by days."

By candlelight she could see the anger and indecision in his eyes. "Very well," he said abruptly. "I shall wash outside tonight, where I can thoroughly soak myself. But don't go running off."

"And why not?" she asked unsteadily, trying to chase away the image of Thornton naked in the yard, with streams of water running down his body. "Surely you want privacy."

"What if I fall? I don't want to have to yell when I need you—we mustn't awaken the *Heywoods*."

She glanced longingly at the dark cottage, knowing that he was right.

Softly he said, "You forgot to set the soap within reach."

Gritting her teeth, Roselyn strode back to the half wall where she'd left the supplies. Keeping her gaze on the ground, she set the linens and dish of soap on the crate beside the barrel. Her hands shook just knowing that he was nearly naked, that he stood so tall and confident, affecting her in ways she didn't want to contemplate.

She returned to sit on a bench in the courtyard, beneath a black sky freckled with stars. The air was warm, though a breeze ruffled her skirts.

She glanced once at Thornton, then gave a little gasp as his flung his breeches onto the stone wall, which thankfully hid him from the waist down.

"I hope you don't mind," he called, and she could hear the smile in his voice. "After all, you tell me you've seen all this before."

She silently refused to give him the satisfaction of looking away. The lantern didn't illuminate him well, and he was only a glimmer of moving shadows as he washed himself. Very faintly, she heard him humming a tune she recognized.

With a start, she realized she didn't want to

believe the worst of him—for all his arrogance, he didn't seem like a traitor.

Yet he would be no good to the Spanish if he weren't convincing as an Englishman.

Covering her face with her hands, she tried to remain calm, something she'd perfected before his arrival. Now it was a struggle not to react to his words, to the growing temptation of his body.

"Roselyn?"

His whisper made her stomach clench. "Yes?"

"Can you wash my back?"

He quickly added, "I know I made a joke about it before, but honestly, I can't reach it well."

Spencer's skin itched from the soap, and suds trailed down his neck from his hair, but he felt almost truly clean for the first time in months.

"Put on a towel," she said in a low, tight voice.

He chuckled as he imagined the scowl she wore, but did as she asked.

He watched her appear out of the dark courtyard and into the lantern light, and was struck again by the simple prettiness he had never noticed in London. She still looked at the ground, but he thought she was not as unaffected as she appeared.

Turning his back to her, he braced himself against the barrel, then winced when she set to work scrubbing his back as if he were a dirty wooden floor.

"Roselyn, you're going to knock me over."

She eased up on him, but soon he began to think he preferred her strength. Now it was too easy to feel the cloth touch every part of his back, to imagine there was nothing between his skin and hers. The towel at his waist would be rising if he didn't concentrate on something else.

He looked over his shoulder into her frowning face. "I don't suppose you'd want to rinse me?"

Her eyes widened and lifted to his. Just for a moment she looked impossibly young and innocent, and he had to remind himself that she was otherwise.

"There is the bucket," she said briskly, pointing to the ground, "and there is still fresh water in the barrel. Help yourself."

She kept her back turned while he filled the bucket and thought of ways to make her look at him again, to remind her of what she'd given up. The first bucket of water was still hot enough to make him shudder, and the second sluiced the last of the suds from his body. He pushed the hair out of his eyes and turned to

face Roselyn, who held out a towel, in command of every situation.

He reached for the towel, then deliberately
lost his balance. With only the slightest squeak
of surprise, she rewarded him by throwing her
arms about his waist.

She made it so damn easy.

She was a small thing, he thought as he
looked down at the top of her head, but she fit
very comfortably in his arms, and she had
strength enough to bear his weight. That put
his mind in a decidedly different direction, one
he was not comfortable with.

"Can I let go now?" she asked, her voice muffled against his chest.

A shudder moved through him at the touch
of her lips on his bare skin. This little play he'd
staged was rapidly falling apart.

Spencer leaned close enough to smell the
clean scent of her hair. How often did she bathe
out here at night, naked under the stars?

"Don't step away," he murmured, "I fear the
sagging towel will drop to my feet."

She gasped and pressed even closer to him as
he fought a groan. Soon she'd know that she'd
affected him, and he didn't want to give her
that kind of power.

She leaned to the side and surprised him by
blowing frantically.

"What are you—" He started to chuckle when he finally understood. "Are you trying to blow the candle out? I thought nudity didn't bother you, that you'd been—" He was about to say "married" but the word wouldn't leave his mouth.

She gripped his arms, and he knew she was frozen, uncertain what to do next. He felt the smallest warmth move deep within his chest.

"Roselyn?" he whispered.

She looked up at him, and he could see the lantern reflected in her eyes. His arms were around her shoulders, and his hands itched to trace her back lower and feel the swell of her backside.

She looked at his mouth, and his body was no longer his to control. As his erection strained between their hips, she gave another gasp.

"I suggest," he said dryly, "that you close your eyes while I conquer this towel."

Her eyes snapped shut so quickly that he chuckled again. As he grasped the sagging towel, he wondered why she so amused him, why he enjoyed upsetting this little world she'd created for herself.

Spencer turned away and pulled the towel tight, his humor fleeing. Was it because his own world might be gone, that he'd be returning to imprisonment—and maybe death—if Shaw convinced the queen he was a traitor?

Behind him, he could hear Roselyn letting the water out of the barrel.

"Are you ready to go back inside?"

He looked over his shoulder into her shadowed face. He couldn't see her well, but knew the calm, collected Roselyn had once again returned. She had enough mastery over her expressions to make a good spy.

He allowed her to slide beneath his arm. "I'm sorry to get you wet."

"You weren't sorry moments ago."

"No, I wasn't."

She helped him into the cottage, then brought him clean breeches, looking at him with a speculation he found the slightest bit unnerving.

"Why did you do that?" she asked.

"Wash?" he answered, smiling.

She wasn't distracted. "Why did you touch me? We both know how you feel—how I feel. What purpose does it serve to annoy me?"

Spencer rested back against the door for balance and considered her. "You didn't seem annoyed."

"I don't like to be trifled with—to be teased," she said in a stern voice. "Is this a game of revenge to you?"

"No." He said the lie easily. "Roselyn, you don't know me well, so don't pretend you understand the motives for everything I do."

"But I know things *about* you," she said.

Keeping the tension from his face took all the deception he'd learned to master.

A cool gleam lingered in her eyes. "You enjoy scandal and the attention it brings you."

He let out his breath, feeling suddenly weak and tired as his tension drained away. "So what if I do?"

"I played a part in your scandals once, and I won't do it again. My life is devoid of scandal, and I intend to keep it that way."

"You 'played a part'?" he echoed, surprised at how close to the surface his anger was. "You *caused* the biggest scandal of my life, and I have yet to live down the humiliation. You don't think your life is still full of scandal? If your parents knew what you've been doing—"

"Are you threatening to tell them?" she asked coldly, stepping toward him.

"No, I only seek to show you that you're deceiving yourself; you like scandal every bit as much as I do."

She drew herself up. "Obviously you know nothing about me. Good night."

She climbed up her ladder, leaving him to dress alone.

The next morning when Roselyn left the bake house, she gave a little start as she saw Charlotte standing in the courtyard, grinning at her.

"Good day, Roselyn!" the girl called. "I tried

the cottage first, but no one answered. I should have known you'd be here."

Roselyn gave her a weak smile, leaning her hand against the apple tree to steady herself. "Have you come for a baking lesson today?"

Charlotte nodded. "Mama agreed I could finish my other duties later. But first I have a question." She glanced at the half wall. "Whose are those?"

Nervousness shot up Roselyn's spine as she realized she'd left Thornton's breeches outside all night. How stupid could she be?

She forced a smile. "Those are Philip's."

Charlotte looked uncomfortable. "Forgive me for intruding on your grief, but why do you have them out now? It has been a year."

As Roselyn frantically searched for a good excuse, she slowly folded the breeches, then put her arm around the girl. "Charlotte, you mustn't worry for me; I promise that I'm not dwelling on my grief. I was searching through a chest of my own garments and found these at the bottom. After I pulled them out, I—I accidentally spilled something on them, so I had to wash them."

Charlotte's smile was full of sympathy and trust, making Roselyn's guilt all the harder to bear.

"Just let me know when you're ready to part with his garments," the girl said. "I know the church would appreciate them, and Mama and I would help you carry them."

Roselyn leaned over to kiss her forehead. "You're too dear to me. Thank you. Now, come inside the bake house and we'll try a new recipe."

After Charlotte had gone, Roselyn found Thornton dressed in a clean shirt and breeches, sitting at the table. An empty bowl of porridge sat before him, and he leaned back on the bench, looking at her as if he'd been waiting. She suddenly remembered being pressed to his damp body, feeling his aroused manhood against her stomach. She didn't understand why such a thing had happened between them, and she could hardly ask him. Even now a flush of heat worked its way up her face, and she told herself it was embarrassment.

"Was that Charlotte Heywood?" he asked.

She nodded. "Thank you for not making a sound. She came for a baking lesson."

"The breeches—"

She raised a hand. "Do not say it. I was foolish to leave them out there."

"I was only going to apologize for the same offense. You have been good enough to clothe me—the least I can do is keep track of the garments."

She couldn't look at him anymore. Feeling a

jitter of nerves, she stacked the dirty wooden bowls from the table.

"Roselyn?"

She almost dropped everything. What was wrong with her? "Yes?"

"I'd like to go for another walk today."

She wanted to close her eyes and groan. "You exerted yourself enough yesterday."

"No," Thornton said, sitting forward and resting his arms on the table. "If I'm ever to be well, I need to bolster my strength. By God's blood, Roselyn, I could hardly wash myself!"

She felt her lips twitch and she lowered her head.

"You're smiling!" he exclaimed. "Don't try to deny it."

"I am trying not to grimace with impatience. Truly, I have much work to do."

"Are your Heywood brothers coming back?"

"They're not mine," she said crossly. "They're finished here, since my fields are small and quickly harvested."

"So where are they now?"

She wondered at such speculation, and wished she didn't have to worry about his every motive. "Probably in the estate fields. There aren't enough men on the island for a proper harvest, so they're working dawn to dusk. That probably helped in keeping your presence here a secret."

"Ah, so you enjoy being alone with me."

"You do yourself too much credit," she scoffed, carrying the bowls to the cupboard. "They've been working too hard to visit much, is all."

"So the brothers visit you often."

"No, just—" She caught herself before mentioning John. "Let us be about this walk quickly, for I have to go into Shanklin later today."

Thornton pushed himself up on one foot. "I'm ready."

"Must we go outside? Surely—"

"Open the door, Roselyn," he said sternly, but she thought she saw a wicked gleam in his eye.

When they stepped outside, the sun was so bright that he shaded his eyes with his hand. "Never again will I allow myself to spend this much time indoors."

He'd given her the perfect opening. "From what I've heard, you *like* the indoors."

"What does *that* mean?" he demanded.

She didn't look at him, knowing she'd see only his dark frown. "I told myself we would not argue today. Just ignore what I said."

He gave a little grunt, but said nothing else. That was fine with Roselyn; she didn't want her curiosity to win out over her good sense.

This time she led him away from Wakesfield,

south through the rolling meadows. In the distance were the high downs at the southern end of the island, covered in purple heather. Soon grasses swished about their lower legs, mixed with yellow vetches and thyme, forcing them to slow their pace.

Roselyn could usually tell when Thornton was tiring by his increasing grip on her shoulders. But not yet this day. Blue butterflies danced on the wind around them, and he watched it all with a small smile. Did he appreciate the beauty of Wight as much as she did— or was his the smile of ownership?

She was so busy trying to study his face that she didn't watch the ground before her. Her foot caught in a hole, sending her down onto her backside. She tried to let go of Thornton— but he crashed down on top of her.

Chapter 13

The impact of Thornton's body should have crushed Roselyn, but the grass and moss beneath her were like the softest mattress, cushioning her body—and his. She didn't feel pain, only the width of his chest pressed to hers, his thigh nestled between her thighs.

She felt like a silly fool as her breathing quickened. Surely her heart only raced because she'd been startled. Not because he smelled different from her—masculine, even with traces of her soap mingled in.

She didn't know what to do with her hands, which rested on his back. They practically shared a lovers' embrace, and when she tried to move, she felt the strangest sensation low in her belly and between her thighs, where he rested.

The sudden flexing of his arms and back made her feel as if she embraced a wild animal who struggled to be free. She lifted her hands from him, but he only propped himself up on his elbows and stared down at her.

Her hands fluttered like restless birds until they came to rest against his sides. She had touched more than this in caring for him, but it was no longer the same.

Thornton stared down at her with dark eyes full of secrets she couldn't guess. His black hair hung toward her, and she wondered how it would feel brushing against her face. Again she felt that strange heat move languidly inside her.

His gaze delved into her eyes and held her trapped, expectant with wondering. She took her first shallow breath when his eyes began a search of her face that felt as if he touched her. When his gaze lingered on her lips, a little gasp escaped her.

The high grasses made her feel as if she reclined in the most intimate, private place, where no one could see what she did.

But *she* would know.

Roselyn dropped her hands into the grass. "Thornton—"

"Spencer," he interrupted.

As his low voice rumbled against her stomach and up through her chest, a little shudder swept through her.

His Christian name held the same intimacies for her that his body did; it wasn't right.

"Thornton," she repeated.

A smile tugged at one corner of his mouth, and he leaned his weight on one elbow, freeing his hand. Her eyes widened, her mouth went dry as she held her breath, waiting for whatever he would do.

The back of his fingers slid gently down her cheek, and she felt the prick of tears in her eyes.

"What—what are you doing?" she whispered, and her voice sounded as light as the clouds in the sky.

"Hush, Rose," he murmured as his breath touched her face, "be still."

She was caught in the spell of a gentleness she'd never known. She hadn't imagined a man's skin could feel so soft as he traced her cheek again, then around her chin. His touch brought her to life like a blossom spreading open with the sunrise. Her chest tightened painfully to feel so much, to take chances she swore she'd never take again.

She looked at his mouth then. She wondered what it would be like to be kissed by a man—something she'd longed for as a silly, headstrong girl, and as a sober, married woman.

But she'd never known. It had been Philip's punishment to deny her the most basic affection between husband and wife.

Were Thornton's lips as soft as hers? Would his mouth be as tender as his fingers—or hard and dangerous? Just the thought of it sent another uncontrollable shiver racing down to her toes.

But he didn't kiss her, though his fingers stroked her throat so slowly she wanted to scream with the unbearable tension. They lingered in the hollow between her collarbone, then dipped just beneath the neckline of her gown. Once again, she felt the hard ridge of his erection.

Roselyn swallowed a gasp, and her scattered mind finally directed her speech. "You must do this often—I mean this must seem so familiar to you."

He'd been contemplating her garments—or so she told herself—but now he looked up into her face.

"What?"

"From the rumors that spread from London—"

"London?"

His puzzled frown at least let her know that he'd been as distracted as she was.

"Was there somewhere else you did the majority of your carousing?"

His eyes narrowed. "My carousing?" He suddenly lifted himself off her and rolled onto his back.

She told herself to be thankful that she had escaped from some dark knowledge about herself that didn't bear contemplation. Yet lying in the prickly grass, looking up at the wide sky, she felt vulnerable and unprotected without his body above her.

"I know how you love a good scandal," she said, thankful that her voice grew stronger.

She glanced at Thornton. His mouth was a hard slash through his short beard, and his eyes were narrowed.

"I'm good at scandal," he said softly. "So why don't you tell me the one you've been dying to share all day?"

"I just . . . heard things."

"From Heywood."

"Yes."

With a "hmph," he closed his eyes. "I'm waiting."

Roselyn felt ridiculous lying out in the open at his side but she was glad of this chance to understand the man she almost married. "This scandal took place at one of the parties you attended, but I guess you must have begun it long before."

He gave an exaggerated sigh. "Scandal and riddles?"

"How can you not remember? There was fighting and screams, and then they—they pulled at each other's hair!"

"Who?" he asked, lifting his head to look at her.

She sat up and leaned back on one arm to better see his face. "Your mistresses, of course."

"My mistresses?"

"All three of them had been invited to the party—did you know that would happen?"

"Naturally not," he said, without even a good pause that she could read something into. "I tried to keep the silly chits away from each other, but they so enjoy my company."

Thornton gave her the perfect rakish grin.

She was partly amused, partly horrified. Why would one man need so many women?

"What did everyone do when the one woman pulled off the other's wig?"

He only laughed and shook his head. "I don't tell tales, as you seem fond of doing."

He sat up so quickly, his shoulder brushed her chin. "Be a dear and help me up."

A dear? What was she, his grandmother? No, she was his nursemaid, the betrothed he hadn't bothered to woo—not when he had so many other women fighting over him.

As she stood up, a feeling of shame and embarrassment swept over her. But lives were at stake here, not her silly pride. She wasn't any closer to discovering whether he was a Spanish spy or not.

Spencer took Roselyn's hands in his own, and as he rose, tried not to pull too hard. When he stood upright, he rested his hand on her shoulder for balance, and even the touch of her collarbone sent his blood thundering through his body. Never had he thought he would be affected by her, not after what she'd done two years before. *She* was supposed to be aroused, and he was supposed to remain distant. He told himself that this . . . awareness between them must bother her more than it did him, but maybe that wasn't true. Maybe once again, he was the foolish one.

But he'd wanted to kiss her, God help him. It was getting to the point where he couldn't keep his gaze off her mouth, so full and perfect for kisses. Did she know how tempting she was? She certainly couldn't have missed how tempted *he* was.

And what would a kiss hurt? He would be gone soon—just ten more days—and she would hardly be damaged by it.

They started walking slowly back the way they'd come, his arm around her shoulders. He was forgetting what it was like to walk alone.

He tried to think of nothing but the vivid sky, where gulls wheeled about. He could hear the crash of ocean waves, and even catch sight of that endless blue expanse when they crested a small hill.

But the ocean reminded him of his mission, and his mission reminded him of his brother—and this latest scandal Roselyn mentioned.

What the hell was going on in London?

Far in the distance, a shout broke through his reverie, and his head came up in a sudden sharp awareness. He felt a tremor shake Roselyn, and he wondered for a moment if another Spaniard had been sent for him.

But it was only a young woman, running toward them across the meadow, waving. He allowed himself to relax slightly, but noticed that Roselyn didn't.

" 'Tis Charlotte," she hissed, even while she put on a false smile and waved back.

She glanced up at him, and her eyes were narrowed and thoughtful, making him uneasy with suspicion.

"Do you want to reveal yourself yet?" she asked.

Spencer felt confused and trapped as the girl drew ever nearer, wearing a large welcoming smile. If it became known he was at Wakesfield, Shaw and his men might find him before he could tell the queen his side of the story.

He felt a chill at the thought of luring even more of his enemies to Wight, where Roselyn—and the Heywoods, of course—would be in the way of danger.

But he had to play this carefully, so as to make her no more suspicious than she already was—luckily she'd seemed downright reluctant to reveal his presence to anyone. "You make the choice. You have hidden me for almost a fortnight now."

"At your request."

"Yes, but you don't seem to want my presence known, either."

Before Roselyn could answer, the girl was within yards of them. He saw a country miss on the brink of womanhood, wearing an innocent, happy smile.

"Roselyn!" she called, but her curious gaze lingered on him.

He could tell by Roselyn's reddened cheeks how embarrassed she was to be caught with him, held so intimately against his body. He let himself enjoy the moment—her annoyance, the chance that he could be discovered, even though it could be dangerous for him.

"Hello, Charlotte," Roselyn said, with warmth in her voice.

He thought for certain there would be an awkward moment as the two women decided what to say to each other. But the girl looked at him and grinned.

"Hello," she said. "I've never seen you before."

He found himself smiling.

Roselyn quickly said, "This is Mr. Sanderson, a soldier with the garrison in Shanklin. Mr. Sanderson, this is Mistress Charlotte Heywood, daughter of the Wakesfield bailiff."

"Mr. Sanderson" gave a bow. "Good day, Mistress Charlotte."

"Good day, sir," she answered, looking down at the splint that bound his lower right leg. "I do hope your wound is not paining you greatly."

"It is healing, thank you, due to the considerable help of Mistress Roselyn." Let Roselyn make of that what she would, he thought, looking down at her with a polite smile tinged with intimacy.

Roselyn quickly said, "I have not done much, merely walked with Mr. Sanderson when I am able to."

He could see Charlotte's high spirits dim as she considered the two of them. Of course, she was John Heywood's sister, and would naturally want her brother to have Roselyn's attention.

"I enjoyed our baking lesson this morning," Roselyn offered. "Did your mother like the pie?"

Charlotte's voice was subdued. "Yes, but she thought that I shouldn't have bothered you, that you might be too busy with the harvest."

"It's over now, so perhaps I can come up to Wakesfield. I've missed working with both of you."

"I don't mind coming to see you at the cottage," Charlotte said, with more determination in her voice.

"Of course," Roselyn murmured.

Charlotte glanced at Spencer with a bold challenge he found amusing. "Well, I must be off on an errand for my mother. Good day, Roselyn—Mr. Sanderson."

She walked away from them toward the village with a determined stride. Roselyn said nothing as she watched Charlotte go.

"Why did you decide to lie about my identity?" Spencer finally asked.

She began to walk him back toward Wakesfield. "I couldn't stop myself from thinking of that Spaniard, and wondering what would happen if more were sent after you. I must do all I can to protect Charlotte and her family."

He sensed she was withholding more, but could hardly confront her about it—not without revealing the things she needed protection from. "And how did you come up with a lie quite so quickly?"

"I've had that story prepared for a long time."

"It will be easy enough for her to discover the truth," he said.

"I know that. The sad thing is, I'm counting on her trust in me."

"Then why didn't you discourage the baking lessons? Surely that will only increase the risk of her seeing me again."

"I know, but she looked so . . . disappointed."

He knew it wasn't the baking lessons Roselyn was talking about.

She sighed. "And now I have to dread what she'll tell her father."

That evening after supper, Spencer stood at the window and looked out across the estate. It was getting easier to stand on one leg, and his returning strength should have cheered him.

But he was so bored and restless that he'd even begun paging through the Bible. He was tempted to ask Roselyn to find him something else to read, but he could hardly have her stealing books from Wakesfield. Yet he was getting desperate to stop his morbid thoughts.

He watched her leave the barn and walk toward the cottage as the setting sun cast the island in a hazy glow. She walked with proud grace, like a woman who actively used her body and didn't just sleep between parties like the idle women at court. He thought back to this afternoon, when she'd lain beneath him. She could have probably pushed him off, or at least struggled.

But she hadn't. She'd only come up with another scandal, as if she had known just how to upset him.

Spencer rested his chin on his folded hands and stared at her with narrowed eyes. He suddenly noticed that she carried a stick.

He turned as she entered the cottage, and raised an eyebrow. "Are you going to beat me for my impertinence?"

Roselyn held out the stick. "It's time you had a cane."

He stared at her, uncertain whether to feel chagrined that he hadn't thought of it first, or amused that she no longer wanted to touch him. He grasped the stick.

"Will this help your soldier story?" He gave her a slow smile, and though she had an uncommon mastery of her emotions, she blushed.

"If I give you a knife," she said, turning away to light candles against the gloom, "could you carve it to the correct height?"

When she mentioned a knife, he looked down to keep a straight face. "I may not be able to do as much as your Heywood brothers can, but as a boy, I was always whittling." He stood up and held the stick out before him, judging the proper height for a cane.

"What did you mean about the Heywoods?" she asked with obvious curiosity.

Why had he said such a foolish thing? "Oh, just that they're so competent at their *farm* skills." He drawled the words as if it were all so beneath him.

But she didn't look angry or offended, merely thoughtful.

When Roselyn awoke before dawn, she knew immediately that something was wrong. The cottage had a peculiar stillness that unnerved her. Perhaps she was just being foolish—it had been almost a fortnight since Thornton had barged into her life, and she was growing accustomed to the sounds of a man breathing and moving about in his sleep.

Even last night, long after she'd gone to bed, she'd listened to him working on his cane.

But this morning she heard nothing, and tension fluttered through her stomach. Wearing just the smock she slept in, she scrambled on her knees to the edge of the loft and looked down.

Thornton's pallet was empty.

Chapter 14

He couldn't have left the island, Roselyn told herself as she dressed; not when he couldn't mount a horse alone or defend himself on a dangerous journey.

She descended the ladder and walked quickly out the door. Would he go to Wakesfield Manor, now that Charlotte had met him? He'd originally wanted no one to know where he was, but he'd allowed her to choose whether to tell the truth to Charlotte.

Roselyn was so confused that she didn't know what to believe anymore.

But Wakesfield didn't seem like the right destination, so she swiftly headed through the meadows toward the ocean. The sun was just beginning to peer over the horizon, and by the time she neared the cliff, her face was bathed in warmth from running.

She finally saw Thornton, silhouetted against the dawn sky, the sun streaming brightly around him. Roselyn took a deep breath. She wasn't certain why she felt relieved—or why she'd worried at all. Surely it was just fear for his safety.

She suddenly remembered that when he had mentioned the Heywoods last evening, something had not sounded right. He'd tried to cover it up, but she had not been fooled. For a moment she thought he'd felt inadequate, but she'd put such a ridiculous idea from her mind. With his arrogance, he would hardly feel inadequate about anything.

She calmed her breathing as she came up behind him.

"Did you think I'd gone for good?" he asked without turning around.

Startled, she came to a halt at his side. He looked down at her, and when his eyes widened and a slow smile lit his face, she knew immediately how she must look to him—flustered, unkempt, with her hair down as if she couldn't take the time to dress properly in her haste to find him.

And it was all true.

She caught her lower lip between her teeth, and turned to look out over the ocean. It was low tide, and gulls swooped and darted amid the wet rocks at the base of the cliff, looking for food.

"No, I didn't think you'd gone," she said, "I

just thought it might be too soon for you to walk very far with the cane. What if you fell and hurt yourself, and I had to *drag* you back to the cottage alone?"

By the saints, she was babbling like an idiot. Her dreams last night had been full of his face above hers, his mouth so near, his thigh between hers—it was a wonder she could even look at him.

Yet Thornton drew her eyes until she could no longer resist. He was gazing out over the ocean, his face bathed in warm sunlight, his expression pensive.

"Is something wrong?" she asked.

He shrugged. "I was just remembering. It wasn't too long ago that there were ships as far as one could see."

Roselyn felt a little crackle of excitement at the perfect opening he'd given her. "Do you think the Spanish have tried to invade England by now? I heard that below London, they'd felt the need to stretch chains across the Thames to keep ships out."

He shook his head. "No, that kind of news travels quickly. Your reliable Francis Heywood would have heard by now. I'm sure the Spanish are limping toward their own ports. From the few days my ship trailed their fleet, I could tell they didn't approach this invasion very intelligently."

The tone of his voice when he talked about the enemy was particularly mocking. "But your mother is Spanish," she said.

The smile he gave her was not pleasant, but he remained silent.

"Does it . . . bother you?"

"What? To have Spanish blood which everyone hates?"

She was surprised at his open bitterness. Wouldn't a Spanish spy pretend to be happy as an Englishman? "Surely that is only due to the war," she said.

"There was no war during my childhood, but it seemed the same to me."

"Did people treat you so differently?"

"Always. Didn't you?"

She wanted to defend herself, to say that his mother's nationality had nothing to do with his poor behavior as a groom. But their betrothal was not what she wanted to explore right now.

"Did you ever see my mother before the eve of our wedding?" he asked coldly.

"I cannot say I did, but then again, I didn't see you, either."

"It was understood from my earliest memory that my mother was not welcome where my father and brother and I were."

"Oh no, surely you were just a sensitive child—"

"You think I am sensitive?" he said with angry disbelief.

"Well—"

"My mother came to England when Philip of Spain married Queen Mary. For a few years, my mother was a part of the court. Sometimes I think her life would have been much better had she just stayed in Spain."

"She wouldn't have met your father."

"No." His voice became low, tired. "And she wouldn't have been alone, either, whenever my father and Alex and I had to leave the estate."

Roselyn didn't know what to say. She had never thought that his childhood might be painful. She had only seen him as a scandalous nobleman who lived for pleasure and danger, little caring how it affected anyone else.

Yet wouldn't such bitterness be cause for a man to turn against the country that had so shunned him?

"I'm going back," Thornton said shortly, and turned away from her.

For a few moments, she watched him walk awkwardly with the cane. He maneuvered so slowly she knew he could not think to leave Wight yet. Deep inside she relaxed, telling herself she had more time to try to understand him.

She caught up and walked beside him. "I have to go to church today," she said.

He didn't respond.

"I didn't go last week—"

"Because of me."

"Yes. The Heywoods wouldn't understand another excuse. And they would like me to attend supper at Wakesfield tonight."

"Do they always tell you what to do?"

"Of course not," she said, linking her hands behind her back. "It is simply that I always attend services with them, and I always have a Sunday meal with them. I would ask you to attend, but you would have to create a whole life for 'Mr. Sanderson,' and soon enough, they would know you don't live in the garrison. I just can't risk them getting involved in this—this—"

"Scandal?" he asked wryly.

She stiffened.

"Do not worry. I don't wish to make our situation any more complicated than it already is. And as for church, I seldom go."

Roselyn hesitated, then couldn't resist asking, "Are you Catholic?"

He looked down at her, and though his smile had returned, it was wary. "Why? Think you to curry favor by revealing all my secrets?"

She blushed. "Of course not. But your mother is from Spain. Surely it must be difficult to be caught between two religions."

Spencer didn't choose to answer immediately, watching instead where he placed the cane. He was tired from not sleeping well, and the exertion of regaining his strength. He'd spent almost two years choosing each word carefully, constantly on his guard to keep himself alive. His exhaustion was so deep, he couldn't even trust himself on the subject of religion.

But he glanced down again at Roselyn. Her hair was wild and windblown this morn, and he knew she had come out of worry for him—either worry he'd escape, or worry he'd hurt himself. Suddenly her questions did not seem such an intrusion.

"My mother is Catholic," he admitted slowly. "I was raised with the religion in secret. My father loved her so dearly that he could not deny her this. But in my adulthood, would my mother consider me a Catholic? Most likely not."

He watched a brief, wistful look cross her features. "Your mother sounds like a woman I would like to meet."

"Why?"

"From what you've said, she seems to have such integrity, such bravery. She didn't care what it cost her, as long as she had her family to love."

Spencer looked toward Wakesfield in the distance. "I'm not sure if that was more foolish than brave. Surely your mother was much more practical than mine."

"Practical? Is that what one would wish for in a mother? My mother's motivations are greed and ambition, and if you consider those 'practical,' then that word suits her."

"Surely she and your father thought of your welfare when they negotiated with my family."

Her eyes seemed a vast gray emptiness, forlorn with long-accepted knowledge. "No, that wasn't a concern. Obedience was all that mattered, and I . . . didn't obey."

He remembered his own parents' reaction to his many scandals. They hadn't needed to become angry; their sad disappointment was worse than any lashing. He would probably have to commit murder before his mother would disown him.

"Someone's watching us," Roselyn suddenly said in a low voice.

Spencer's first reaction was an instinctive need to hide. Had Shaw sent another henchman? He calmed his racing heart and looked out across the meadow. Far in the distance, he saw someone herding a flock of sheep. He murmured, "Do you know this person?"

" 'Tis Abigail with her family's sheep."

Roselyn surprised him by waving at the girl, who cheerfully waved back.

"Is she coming our way?" he asked.

"No, she's heading for the village." Roselyn looked up at him. "I had to wave, or she'd know something was wrong."

"Of course. But you seem worried."

"She'll wonder who in the village is using a cane."

"Ah," he said, nodding. "You think she might talk to someone—maybe even Charlotte—and then tell everyone in the village I'm something I'm not."

She shrugged, and a moment later murmured, "I never wear my hair like this. What must she think?"

He considered Roselyn thoughtfully. The wind swept her wild hair off her face, and it fluttered about her shoulders. The severity of her normal expression was somehow softened, but a bleak sadness shadowed her eyes. Once he would not have cared; now he had to force himself to think of something else.

Why had he revealed so much of his childhood to her? He'd never before been tempted to tell a woman of his past. But there was something about her patience and calm nature that made her easy to confide in.

He wondered what she must think of him. She surely must be congratulating herself on escaping their marriage.

* * *

When Roselyn came back from services, Thornton seemed to retreat inside himself. He wasn't rude, nor did he talk much. He just walked about the cottage, getting in her way, obsessive about using his cane. She sat before the hearth and tried to concentrate on reading her Bible, but he kept knocking into her chair.

Though she felt like challenging his behavior, she had a vivid memory of the gentle way he'd touched her, of the heat and intensity of his eyes. She felt confused and overly warm and suddenly frightened. She had succeeded in burying the last of her volatile emotions when she'd buried her baby and husband—but now the wild, irresponsible Roselyn seemed to be rising up, taking over, and that frightened her more than the closeness of any man.

But she couldn't bury her awareness of Thornton, of his large body moving back and forth across the room. She didn't know what she wanted more—the truth of his loyalties, or for him just to leave her alone. Unbidden, she remembered how his eyes had gazed upon the wildness of her hair that morning. The thought of endless silent evenings by herself was no longer comforting.

Supper with the Heywoods was just what Roselyn needed to lift her spirits and make her forget Thornton and all the problems he'd

caused. She loved feeling part of such a boisterous, happy family. She helped Charlotte and
her mother with the last-minute food preparations, then sat between the women as if they
were her sister and mother. When it seemed ap-
parent that Charlotte wasn't going to bring up
the subject of Mr. Sanderson, Roselyn allowed
herself to relax completely.

Yet as the evening went on, more and more
she could actually feel John watching her.
Surely it was just her imagination—having
Thornton in her home had made her too aware
of a man's eyes.

When Thornton watched her, she felt distracted, too aware of him as a man.

But John's gaze was different. She felt nervous, exposed, wondering if he knew the secrets she now guarded. When he offered to
walk her home she tried to refuse, but Francis
insisted, and even he watched her with a
thoughtful frown.

There was no moon in the dark sky as John
walked at her side carrying a lantern. The wind
whistled forlornly through the orchard, and she
pulled her kerchief tighter about her shoulders.
She told herself she was ridiculous to feel so
uneasy.

After several quiet minutes, he cleared his
throat. "My father was talking to Abigail after
services."

Roselyn's stomach knotted with dread. "What did she have to say?"

"She said she saw you walking with a man she didn't recognize, a man with a cane." John hesitated, and in the meager light, he looked apologetic. "Charlotte said that she even met him. Normally there aren't many strangers on the island, but this is a time of war. Please don't blame me for being concerned—you live alone."

She smiled at him, thankful she had spent some of her sleepless hours concocting a story to explain Thornton. "Thank you for your concern, John, but really, you mustn't worry. He is just a soldier from the garrison in Shanklin. I've seen him by the cliffs before. We sometimes happen to walk in the same direction, and occasionally talk. He's a very polite man." She forced herself not to hold her breath.

John seemed relieved. "I'm glad. But you can understand why I—why *we* worry about you."

As they approached her cottage, Roselyn's nerves stretched taut. She could only see the barest glow of the fire through the windows, but not the shadow of a man moving about.

"Thank you for walking me home," she said, turning to face John.

"Might I come in to talk with you for a while?" he asked, and his gaze on hers was warm.

Before Thornton had come, she had often

wondered what she would do when her time of mourning was over, when John pushed his interest in her past friendship. Now she felt unprepared, too flustered knowing that Thornton was but mere feet away, possibly even listening.

She couldn't even think about marriage. Being once again under a man's control seemed dangerous.

"I'm sorry, John, but 'tis late, and I'm tired." She smiled up at him tentatively, then felt her smile fade as he took her hand in both of his.

"Then I'll visit another time, when we have the evening to talk."

Her breath caught as he leaned down and kissed the back of her hand. Wide-eyed, she watched him straighten and grin.

"Go on in, Roselyn. I'll stay until you're safe."

She nodded and fumbled behind her for the latch, unable to take her eyes off him. When the door swung open, she entered and closed it without looking at him again.

In the warm darkness she leaned her forehead against the wooden door and closed her eyes. She had known of John's interest in her, of course, but it was still a surprise to find him beginning a sort of courtship.

John's presence was soothing and pleasant. He didn't make her heart feel as if it would explode from her chest; he didn't make her thoughts lose focus. If there was anyone from whom she could protect her feelings, who wouldn't endanger her with another wild passion, it would be John.

Thornton's sarcastic voice dissolved her thoughts. "Out for a pleasant walk with your latest conquest?"

Chapter 15

Roselyn stiffened at the sound of Thornton's voice, yet the thought of verbally dueling with him challenged her. She turned around and found him sitting in her chair before the fire, watching her with a dark, knowing look.

What was wrong with her that even arguing with him made her feel more alive than she'd ever felt? It frightened her to feel like this—she wanted to be numb again, to be calm, but Thornton was always waiting to outwit her.

"John is not my latest conquest," she said, walking slowly until she stood before him, and he was forced to look up at her. "Francis insisted he walk me home."

"Did Francis insist the boy invite himself inside?"

"What is wrong with you?" she demanded, tilting her head as she studied him. "Am I not even allowed friends?"

He met her gaze boldly. "Your flirting with that carpenter risks my safety."

"I am not flirting with him—and how are you at risk? To reveal your presence would bring only *me* public scorn. After all, you claim this estate is yours."

What secrets could she lull from him? Anticipation made her shiver with excitement.

Thornton rose to his feet and leaned on his cane. "Don't play the fool with me. We already had one Spanish visitor; we don't need more."

"Fine," Roselyn said, stepping even nearer to stare up into his face. "Then do not question how I live my life."

She could tell he wanted to speak—would she finally know the truth? She sensed an undercurrent of anger moving through him, and it couldn't be because of their betrothal. He had already vowed to have her declared an adulterer to break the contract between them.

With mounting astonishment, she realized that she was *trying* to provoke him.

She was suddenly frightened of herself, of the wild Roselyn waiting deep inside her. She had worked too hard on her restraint to allow it all to be destroyed because of Spencer Thornton.

Breathing deeply, she took a step back. "How does the wound in your ribs feel?" she asked, to distract them both. "I noticed that you've stopped wearing the bandages."

" 'Tis fine," he said shortly, leaning both hands on the cane.

Even injured, he so dominated her small cottage that it sent a flutter of nervous excitement through her.

"Have you been watching for signs of infection?"

"I told you I feel fine."

Not breaking their shared gaze, she said, "Lift your shirt and allow me to look."

His mouth twisted into a smile within his beard. "Didn't quite get all you wanted with the carpenter?"

"What?" she asked, feeling confused and suddenly naive.

He stared at her for another moment, then looked away. "Never mind. Here, see for yourself."

Lifting up his shirt, Spencer watched the concentration that turned Roselyn's wide-eyed look into a frown. Briskly she took his shoulders and turned him toward the fire, and he found himself holding his breath. Of course he was only concerned about whether he was healing well.

Then her cool hands touched his ribs, and the shock astonished him, sending an unwelcome flare of heat to his groin. When had she gained such power over him? Wasn't it she who was supposed to be distracted by *his* presence? His mind was filled with her touch, her scent; he remembered her long wild hair that morning on the cliff, as the ocean breeze had played with it.

As she lowered his shirt, her palm brushed against his nipple. He could barely disguise the shudder that made him want to take her into his arms and teach her what touching a man could do.

She claimed herself a widow—wouldn't she already know how to tease him? Yet when she looked up at him, her eyes held an innocence that seemed too real. He wanted to hold her face between his hands and make her confess all her secrets, so that the puzzles surrounding her no longer drew him.

Only nine days left—and strangely it didn't seem enough.

When she moved away from him to clear his supper dishes from the table, Spencer leaned back against the door and let a smile play on his mouth as he boldly studied her. Her nervousness obviously grew with each clatter of the dishes, each distracted glance over her shoulder at him.

"Roselyn."

She caught a bowl before it crashed to the wooden floor.

He grinned. "Am I healing to your satisfaction?"

She nodded.

"Are you certain? Perhaps you should examine me again."

"What is the purpose of such teasing?" she demanded, turned to face him. Red stained her cheeks but she met his gaze coolly.

"Purpose?" he echoed, smiling as he limped forward. "Perhaps it merely gives me something to do. You keep yourself busy every moment of daylight, while I can only walk—and talk."

She tilted her head to look up at him as he stopped before her. He had to admire the fact that she didn't retreat.

"You do enough talking, that is true," she said dryly. "But I don't appreciate being used as a distraction."

He pitched his voice lower. "But you *are* distracting, even in those widow's garments. Surely you have worn them long enough."

Her face paled into an icy stillness. "My grief is not your concern, and I will not discuss it with you."

For a moment he stared into her eyes, glimpsing the heartache before she shuttered her emotions away from him. He thought of what she'd borne in the last year with such obvious courage.

It made him uneasy.

Roselyn climbed up to her loft as quickly as

she could, and lay wide awake on her pallet. He'd said she was "distracting."

She covered her ears with both hands and squeezed her eyes shut, but she could still hear Thornton moving about below. What could he be doing?

Reluctantly she lowered her hands and listened, finding herself barely breathing. It sounded like he was hopping about again, since the pounding of the wooden floor seemed to shake clear up to her loft. When she heard an occasional grunt of exertion, her curiosity became an itch beneath her skin.

Cautiously, she left the pallet and crept on her belly to the edge of the loft. She peered over only as much as she needed to, and saw that Thornton had blown the candle out. The room was dark with shadows, lit only by flickering firelight.

Then she saw him, and the breath seemed trapped in her lungs. He'd removed his shirt, and stood with the knee of his broken leg propped on a bench, holding his cane up like a sword. He wove and ducked and thrust, as if fighting an imaginary opponent. She could see the strain of his muscles, the perspiration on his back, and she felt as if the fire from the hearth had risen to engulf her. Occasionally he hopped away from the bench, and the vibration that moved through the loft made her feel dizzy and strange.

When he finally stopped training and began to wash himself from a basin of water, she told herself to go back to bed.

Yet she remained trapped at the edge of the loft, her wide eyes watching as he scrubbed his face and chest.

He grew unnaturally still, and his head lifted until he met her eyes. She wanted to retreat, but his gaze held hers, burning with a dark fierceness that enthralled her. An answering heat burst to life in her veins.

Without breaking their gaze, he slowly continued to wash himself, moistening the dark hair on his chest, leaving soap trails that dripped down his well-muscled arms.

The heat inside her grew overpowering, then spread down between her thighs, until she felt restless, yearning, close to forgetting everything she'd worked so hard to become.

His mesmerizing eyes were alive with awareness of what he did to her—and *that* finally brought her to her senses. Without a word, she backed away and lay down on her pallet. For a few moments longer he washed, and then there was only silence—except for the rapid beating of her heart.

*　*　*

For two days an uneasy truce lay between them, but there was still an unnamable tension that seemed to be slowly enveloping her. Roselyn had no way to fight it, no way to stop this awareness of Spencer Thornton as a man, rather than as a monster from her past.

Whenever they were together she felt his gaze like an intimate touch, and shivers spread out across her skin. His deep voice could make her jump and clatter dishes together as she cursed her clumsiness. When he smiled, she remembered his mouth so close to hers, his body touching every part of her as they lay in the grass. His gentleness had surprised her, and she would never forget his touch.

He could be so charming, so amusing, that sometimes she almost wanted to laugh aloud, something she couldn't remember doing since her daughter had died.

But she had every reason to be wary and distant—she could not forget the Spanish letter hidden in her shed, the possibility that he was a traitor to England.

He was dangerous to her in so many ways.

The day was hot and sultry, and a steady rain fell throughout the afternoon. Everything seemed wet, and her black gown clung to her uncomfortably. The laundry she'd done before the storm hung limply over the chairs and tables, refusing to dry.

Her nerves were frayed at being confined all day with Thornton, and he made it even worse by removing his shirt. His skin glistened with perspiration and renewed good health. When he wasn't exercising with his cane, he lounged before the bare hearth, watching her with hooded eyes.

Just as dusk settled over the island and she felt tense enough to scream, he stood up and limped to the window to look out over the estate. Her relief at being free of his gaze was fleeting.

He glanced over his shoulder at her. "You have company," he said, his mouth curling up in one corner with sarcasm. "That boy is persistent."

She groaned. "John?"

He leaned back against the wall, arms folded across his chest. She thought he would be amused, but she sensed something darker inside him.

"So you have other suitors?" he asked in a low voice.

"He is not my suitor. And don't let him see you!"

"That might be difficult."

Roselyn sighed. "We can't sit in the courtyard, because of the rain. You're going to have to hide."

"Hide? Where? There's only one room in here—and don't tell me to squeeze into a cupboard."

"The loft," she said, her spirits lifting with relief. "If you're quiet, he shall never know you're here."

"Send him away," Thornton said, with all the stubbornness of a child.

"I can't—that would only make him suspicious. He's been a good friend."

Though he rolled his eyes and sighed noisily, he glanced at the rope ladder.

"I still can't use my right leg; it will be difficult to climb."

"Just try—and hurry!"

Roselyn scurried about the cottage, catching up wet laundry, putting away the double settings of tankards and plates from supper. But when she glanced over to check Thornton's progress, she stopped as she watched his powerful arms pull his weight up each step of the ladder to the top.

The knock at the door came too quickly; she could still hear Thornton's slow steps across the wooden loft.

"How the hell do you fit up here?" he hissed.

"Just lie down!"

There was a crack of something hitting the wooden beams, and a muffled oath. The following silence seemed loud but for the muted sound of the rain falling.

John knocked again, and she heard him call her name.

"I'm coming!" She smoothed out her dress, wishing she didn't feel so hot and uncomfortable.

But deep inside her glowed the thrill of doing something so unexpected and dangerous.

She opened the door to find John standing beneath the edge of the thatched roof, his cloak soaked, his brown hair dripping as it curled beneath his chin.

"Oh John, do come in out of the rain," she said, stepping back so that he could move past her. "Whyever are you out in such weather?"

"I thought you might be lonely, trapped here all day."

She motioned to her only chair before the fire, then pulled up a bench for herself. She gripped her fingers together tightly in her lap. "You know I enjoy my solitude, John. The weather doesn't bother me."

He gave her a crooked, sweet smile. "Then you are a better person than I. I spend so much of my time in my woodshop that I'll use any excuse to escape outdoors."

"Ah, then I shouldn't feel guilty for imposing

on you to harvest my grain." She smiled, but she couldn't help wondering what Thornton was thinking.

"Never feel guilty. I appreciate any chance to spend time with you."

A blush stole across her face, though she willed it to stop. "I seem to remember a time when you preferred that I play with Charlotte."

"That was when we were children. Since you've come back—"

He broke off, suddenly seeming embarrassed. But why should he be? She and John had always had this comfortable closeness. She had even begun to accept the possibility that she might wed him one day, that this easy familiarity would be the best marriage for her. She would know what to expect, and he would never hurt her.

She felt no wild emotion when John looked at her, only friendship and respect—and she needed those to survive.

He smiled. "Since you've come back, I feel . . ."

He hesitated, and Roselyn held her breath.

". . . differently. I grew up thinking I would live elsewhere, that I would explore England and maybe even travel over the seas. But I could be content here if—"

He broke off again, and she wanted to groan

in exasperation. What had he been about to say? His gaze caught on Thornton's pallet, and her stomach seemed to plummet to her toes.

"Roselyn, you don't normally sleep down here, do you?" he asked in a puzzled voice.

For a moment her mind became an absolute blank. What could she say—that she'd been caring for a man who was possibly an enemy?

"No, I usually prefer the loft," she said, her voice almost trembling with relief as an idea surfaced, "but last night it was too hot up there beneath the roof."

"You would be much more comfortable up at the manor."

"John, please—"

"Mother keeps your room ready, in case you change your mind."

"Please tell her to use it for guests, because I will never stay there again." Her voice sounded sharp, and she forced a smile. "I won't endanger your family by claiming a place at Wakesfield that I no longer deserve."

"Roselyn—"

"And how is your mother? I haven't seen her since Sunday."

She forced him to answer mundane questions about his family, hoping he would leave. Usually she looked forward to his visits, but today all she could do was imagine that every creak of wood was Thornton announcing his presence.

"John, it's growing late," she finally said. "Would you like a lantern to light your way home?"

He rose with obvious reluctance. "No, I know the estate too well. Don't you remember the night walks Charlotte used to insist upon?"

Roselyn stood up, the pleasant memory soothing her nerves. "You're being too kind— forgetting my part in her schemes. You're such a good brother to Charlotte."

He took a step closer and she felt a momentary panic.

"I don't wish to be a brother to you," he murmured.

His gaze dropped to her mouth. When Thornton looked at her like that, she felt the wild Roselyn struggling to break free. With John, there was no sense of imminent discovery, of restlessness born of need.

He put his hands on her arms and drew her nearer. She felt like an observer, urging herself to experience her first kiss.

At the last moment, she turned her head aside and offered her cheek. His lips were soft, but there was none of the magic she experienced when Thornton merely brushed her skin with his fingers.

"Good night," she murmured, her thoughts confused. Didn't she want the safety of John's name, of such a calm, unthreatening life?

He walked to the door, giving her a regretful smile over his shoulder. "I'll return again," he promised, then closed the door behind him.

Roselyn sagged against the trestle table, then crossed to the window, looking through the murky glass at his retreating back. She put her hot face in her hands.

"He's gone," she finally called.

She could hear Thornton's sigh. "You'd better come up."

She glanced up sharply. "Why?"

"I believe I'm stuck."

Chapter 16

Spencer didn't feel a single twinge of guilt for lying—he wasn't quite sure what he felt, after listening to that country boy court Roselyn.

He tried to tell himself it was better this way. He'd return to the treachery of London in just six days and have the betrothal contract broken; then he and Roselyn would both be free of each other.

The thought of calling her an adulterer before the entire court made his stomach sour in a way he hadn't felt before. But that's what she was—why did he let her innocence and serenity make him reluctant to hurt her? It was the only way.

The other part of him felt anger churning inside his gut that she would play kissing games when her own betrothed could overhear.

Roselyn's head appeared in the loft, followed by her trim shoulders and well-formed breasts, encased in that awful widow's black. When she finally stood above him, she gave him a suspicious look.

"You do not look 'stuck.' "

A flash of some emotion—he told himself it was anger—surged through him, and he hooked his foot around her ankle. With a gasp, she tottered, and he caught her arm and pulled her on top of him. They sank down into the prickly straw pallet, and he realized she'd given him the comfortable one stuffed with goose feathers.

Her squirming hips rubbed his as she tried to pull away.

"Spencer!" she gasped.

Even her breath across his ear and cheek made him think lustful thoughts—and he'd never heard his Christian name on her lips. When she pushed against his chest and rose up above him, he turned her onto her back, her head pillowed in his arm, his leg thrown across hers to keep her still.

In the murky darkness, she blinked at him in astonishment, her incredibly full lips parted, her breath coming fast.

"Don't!" she cried.

"Why not? Touching my own betrothed is as far from being scandalous as I've ever gotten."

"But why are you doing this?" she asked in a whisper that reminded him of how intimate and alone they were.

"Has he ever kissed you?"

If possible, her eyes widened even more. "Of course he's kissed me."

With each breath, her breasts brushed his arm.

"I don't mean a brotherly kiss on the cheek." He leaned closer and nuzzled her cheek, smelling the sweet scent of her skin, feeling it arouse him more than any fine perfume.

She was trembling now. "His kisses aren't brotherly."

"But they're never on a more intimate place than the side of your face. So you admit he's never truly kissed you?"

Roselyn felt surrounded by Spencer: his half-naked body pressed down the length of her, his hard arm beneath her neck. Their legs were caught together, and when she tried to move, it only made them more intimately entwined.

Deep in her heart, she knew this was what she'd been longing for, this closeness to him. His gentle touch, his humor, were things she'd never had with Philip. They drew her far more than fine promises and misleading words.

But how to admit to him that even after marriage, she had never been kissed?

Spencer loomed above her, mysterious and dark as the shadows. She wanted to touch him, to feel his strong face between her hands, to run her fingers across that broad, sheltering chest.

She wouldn't touch him—but she didn't stop his hand from cupping her cheek. His thumb brushed the corner of her mouth and she shuddered.

He leaned over her and pressed his mouth gently to hers. She'd never thought her lips could be so sensitive, as she experienced the pleasure of light, butterfly kisses. The wonder of it was almost painful. She closed her eyes and let the sensation shiver through her. Slowly, he applied more pressure, angling his head. Was she doing this right? Could he tell that she was innocent of such a normal part of marriage?

The first touch of his tongue made her gasp and open her eyes. He lifted his head the slightest bit, grinning teasingly down at her.

"You didn't like that?"

Roselyn didn't know what to say, or even what to think. Her mind was a jumble of conflicting thoughts, of panic and desire, but the one that chorused most strongly was, *Don't stop!*

He pressed a kiss to her forehead, to her cheek, then hovered just above her lips. "Touch me, Rose," he whispered, his breath fairy-light on her skin.

She didn't stop to think, just placed her hand on his bare arm and let herself feel the warm, smooth hardness of him. Yet his mouth remained just above hers until she yearned for his lips with an ache that centered with shocking warmth between her thighs.

Her gaze clung to his face, as she ran her hand across his shoulder and up to the back of his head. He was breathing just as hard as she was, but still he didn't kiss her. She knew what he wanted, and she gave in, pulling him down to her.

His shining grin faded as he tilted his head and covered her mouth with his. His tongue slid urgently between her lips, and a hot and sinful feeling shook her as she willingly opened her mouth. The feel of him stroking inside her made her quiver even more as she clung to him. His thigh slid between hers, and she wished there were no garments between them.

He moved on top of her, freeing both of her hands to touch him as she wished. She slid her palms up his back, felt the damp heat of him, and as his kiss deepened again, she stroked his tongue with her own.

A groan rumbled through him, and he clasped her face between his hands, kissing her deeper, harder than she could have imagined. Did he feel the same way, full of wildness and daring and desire?

She had never felt like this in her life, and she reveled in it, touching him freely, moving restlessly to be ever closer to something new, something wonderful, just out of reach.

His mouth followed an invisible path across her jaw and down her neck, and she tilted her head back to give him the access he wanted. His hands slid down her ribs, his thumbs brushing the sides of her breasts, before he filled his palms with them. The pleasure that suffused her was overwhelming. Her nipples were hard and aching, and she knew that soon she'd be lost in these new sensations, letting him do anything he wanted.

Hadn't the first touch of Philip's hand on her bare skin made her quiver with excitement? But on their wedding night he'd been drinking, and *his* needs were all that mattered—all that ever mattered.

She stiffened beneath Spencer, and he raised his head to look at her with a frown.

Were his needs all Spencer considered, too? How could she so easily forget the child who'd suffered and died because of her flaws, this wildness that made her forget herself?

"We must stop," she said hoarsely, dislodging his hands and covering her chest. "This isn't what either of us wants."

"You don't know what I want," he said in a low voice.

He tried to kiss her again, but she turned her head away.

"Then tell me," she whispered. She wanted the truth, all of it, but his silence was as eloquent as the thrust of a knife.

He rolled off her.

Roselyn stood up, straightening her clothing with shaking hands, trying not to feel empty and alone without Spencer holding her. She turned to start down the ladder, but couldn't resist looking at him.

He was propped on one elbow, his hair in disarray, his mouth wet. My God, had she done that?

His eyes glittered at her in the darkness. "Is John Heywood the next boy you'll replace me with? Does he know you're already betrothed?"

"John knows everything about me," she said wearily, "which is more than you can say."

She went down the rope ladder quickly, her chest tight with tears she refused to shed. She gathered linens and a change of clothing and went out into the night to bathe.

Spencer listened to the door slam and knew just where she was going. He rolled off the pallet onto his stomach—which was an uncomfortable position since his arousing encounter with Roselyn—and inched backward until his legs hung over the edge of the loft. The rope ladder was tricky, and he almost slipped and broke his fool neck, but soon he was safely on the floor. He blew out the candles, hopped to the window overlooking the courtyard, and slowly opened it.

Roselyn had already finished filling the barrel by lantern light. The rain clouds had finally blown away, and under the starry, moonless night she took down her hair. Each pin she dropped onto the wall nailed home how this desire for her had sneaked up on him. When the dark mass of her hair unrolled past her shoulders, his skin twitched as if she'd touched him. She had glorious, womanly hair, hair that was made to curtain him as she rode his body through desperate pleasure.

Then she began to remove her garments.

Spencer knew this was only further torture, but he couldn't stop himself from watching. He'd touched parts of her through her clothing, and now his eyes wanted to devour her as well.

Her black gown fell to the ground, leaving her smock to glow under the stars. His eyes were drawn to the pale skin of her shoulders. She unlaced the smock and allowed it to sag to her waist, revealing breasts as perfect as pearls adorning the night sky.

He stopped breathing as the smock joined the gown in the grass. Though Roselyn was delicately small, the curve of her hips was lush and full and made to comfort a man. When she stood on the crate and lifted one leg to step into the barrel, he groaned and turned away, sliding down the wall to sit on the floor.

The sound of splashing water did nothing to cool his ardor.

By the time she returned to the cottage he was lying on his pallet, facing the wall, trying to keep from panting like the lustful beast he was. Six days seemed too far away—and much too quick.

Spencer opened his eyes in the morning, and was glad that the day already seemed cooler. He lay still for a moment, staring up at the loft, wondering what had awakened him besides frustrated desire.

Suddenly Roselyn appeared at the edge of the loft, neatly dressed for the day in her usual black.

He quickly closed his eyes, then peered up between his lashes. She had turned her back and begun her descent. Beneath her skirts he could see her stockinged calves, and the faintest blush of bare thighs before she reached the floor.

And he was as aroused as if she still lay beneath him. In his mind, he saw her naked, wet, her arms lifted to him.

By God, why did he allow her to affect him like this? His plan to arouse and reject her was turning back onto him.

He lifted up on one elbow to watch her, but except for a raised eyebrow, she ignored him, appearing as calm and serene as if they'd never shared passionate kisses.

Damn, but she was frustrating.

After she'd left the cottage, Spencer slashed another mark in the floor—day sixteen of his sojourn on the Isle of Wight. There were only five days left until his self-imposed departure. Five days and he hadn't been able to practice riding a horse or even wielding a dagger. Roselyn occupied far too many of his thoughts.

He broke his fast with hard black bread and hard cheese. Last night, she had said that John knew everything about her. Were there other secrets in her past, things she kept hidden from him?

He took up his cane and went outside, only to find himself limping toward the bake house. He could hear her singing softly to herself, as if nothing he did could ever bother her. He leaned in the frame of the open doorway and watched her knead dough at a stone table, a floury apron pinned to her dress.

He knew the moment she was aware of his presence, and felt satisfied as she stiffened and turned to face him. By the blush in her cheeks, he didn't think it was annoyance she was experiencing, either.

Because she was a woman of obvious passion, he couldn't help wondering what kind of man her groom was; why she'd deserted her betrothed for him, beyond the obvious reason of Spencer's treatment of her. For a woman who considered herself widowed, she seemed to have the innocence of a newly bloomed flower.

Roselyn turned back to her worktable. "Did you need more to eat?"

"No." He continued to study her until the silence between them stretched taut. "Do you miss him much?" he finally asked.

"John?"

"No, the stable groom. What was his name again?"

Her hands stilled as she softly said, "Philip Grant." She gave him a steely glance over her shoulder. "My husband."

It was a direct challenge, one he didn't wish to take up at the moment. "But do you miss him?"

"The state of my widowhood is no business of yours."

"You didn't answer the question."

"Of course I miss him," she grudgingly said, turning away.

But he thought he heard the slightest hesitation in her voice, and for some strange reason, it pleased him. "I only asked because I wondered if our kiss bothered you."

"It was more than a mere kiss," she said with sarcasm, glancing at him.

"Very well, our mutual fondling."

"Mutual—"

Roselyn turned away again, and he couldn't tell if she was withholding a smile.

She slowly began to knead the bread. "I guess those intimacies do not matter to one such as yourself."

"Such as myself?" he repeated, limping over to sit on a stool near her.

"You have surely exchanged much more than 'mutual fondling' with your mistresses."

"Ah yes, all fifteen of them."

"Fifteen—" She whirled to face him, scattering flour in her wake.

He grinned. "At the same time." It was getting far too easy to fluster her.

She studied him coolly. "Well, that's a story Francis didn't hear."

"Or didn't repeat."

"He only heard that there were two of them. Do you miss them?"

Spencer frowned. "Two of them?"

"Dancers, I think. They were at the same time, too—or so Francis heard. But do you *miss* them?"

She didn't even blush, though he realized

with mortification that *he* did, just as if he were guilty.

"Your bailiff repeated such a story?"

"No—his wife did. I think she was trying to convince me that I had made the right decision in not marrying you."

He could tell by her wrinkled nose that she wished she'd not said so much.

He stood up and stepped nearer, asking in a low voice, "Did you need convincing?"

"No," Roselyn quickly said, her back to him.

She wore her hair pulled tightly up beneath her cap, and he wondered what she would do if he started unpinning it, setting it free curl by curl to bury his face in it.

"Margaret *thought* I needed convincing," she continued. "I think the Heywoods told me stories of you out of some misguided sense of . . . consolation."

He wanted to run his tongue down her spine; he wanted to slide his arms around her and cup her breasts, and watch her face while he caressed her.

"Did it work?" He blew softly on her neck.

"Did what work?" she asked in a faltering voice.

"Were you comforted by the thought of me being so . . . scandalous?"

"I—I—"

He leaned forward and pressed his open

mouth just behind her ear. She gave a little gasp and a start, and when she would have ducked away, he slid his arm about her waist to hold her still. Her buttocks were pressed to his thighs, and he almost dipped to rub his erection between them.

They suddenly heard a voice from the courtyard. "Roselyn!" It was the girl, Charlotte.

For a shattering moment, Roselyn didn't know what to do—her body had betrayed her by almost melting against Spencer, and even now she wanted to drop her head back against his shoulder and kiss him.

He stumbled away from her and sat on the stool just as Charlotte entered. The girl looked stunned—and disappointed—at seeing him in Roselyn's bake house.

And Roselyn felt as guilty as if she'd let him bed her right there on the floor. What else could the girl think when she looked on his handsome face?

"Hello, Charlotte," she forced herself to say. "Was today the day we agreed on for a baking lesson?"

"Yes . . ." she began uncertainly. "But I don't wish to intrude."

"Intrude? Why saints above, no. I just have a terrible memory lately. You remember Mr. Sanderson? On my walk this morning we encountered one another again, and I offered him a meal."

Spencer nodded. "The cook in my barracks is normally a stable groom. Now I know exactly what the horses eat."

Roselyn was amazed—and troubled—by how easily he adapted to any situation. He looked utterly innocent and spoke in so charming a manner, that how could Charlotte *not* be fooled?

Yet still the girl only gave him a bewildered smile and turned to study Roselyn.

"Shall we get started?" Roselyn asked brightly.

Spencer soon made his excuses to the women and left them to their lesson. Wielding his cane with a little more confidence, he chose a direction he'd never gone before.

Clouds scudded across the sky, and though the day was considerably cooler, he still worked up a sweat. Soon he'd be ready to leave and face his fate in London.

A twinge of regret took him by surprise, but he ignored it, finding a path through fields of cut grain. Coming up over a slope, he saw a little stone chapel nestled between fields, and a small graveyard beside it.

A sense of fate called to him, and he drew

closer. He wandered the well-tended graveyard, not knowing until he found Philip
Grant's grave that he was looking for it.

He was stunned to see a second name on the
headstone.

Chapter 17

Spencer's uneasiness increased as he read the inscription on the headstone:

MARY GRANT
AGE 2 MONTHS

He awkwardly knelt down. Roselyn had lost both a husband *and* a child—why had she never told him?

With almost grim self-punishment, he thought back to his comments on her mourning clothes, as if she didn't have a right to mourn.

He had had little time to mourn his father before he left for Spain. To survive, he'd been forced to adopt another identity. He had put his family—even his father—away in his mind, as if they didn't exist.

He had left the comforting of his mother to Alex, and could only hope his brother had been up to the task.

But who had comforted Roselyn? Who had been with her when she'd held her dying child—or had she been alone?

As the sun disappeared behind a cloud, he leaned forward and touched the letters spelling the baby's name. There were dying flowers laid on the grave, as if Roselyn couldn't visit frequently. It had been a year now, and maybe the hurt wasn't as fresh—and he himself had kept her busy.

But how did a mother get over the death of a child?

At the nearby crackling of dried grass, Spencer whirled about on his knees to find a thin, older man staring down at him, wearing a large mustache on his lined face. Spencer was aghast that he'd allowed someone near without hearing him, and that he'd never thought to carry his knife for protection. Had Roselyn so befuddled his mind?

The man made no threatening moves, so Spencer took his time using his cane to stand.

"I am Francis Heywood," the man said gruffly, "the bailiff of Wakesfield Manor. You seem to be the soldier my daughter Charlotte met."

Before Spencer could speak, Heywood continued, "But I must say, I asked at the garrison about you, and there is no soldier with a broken leg." He looked pointedly at the splint on Spencer's right calf.

"Determined, aren't you?" Spencer said.

The bailiff shrugged. "It is my duty to protect those on the manor—especially the women. My daughter warned of a man bothering Roselyn Grant. Now who are you, and why do you keep wandering this estate?"

"I am Spencer Thornton." What was the point of keeping his identity secret from the Heywood family now, when even the Spanish knew where to find him?

Heywood's only visible reaction was a slight widening of his eyes. "How long have you been on Wight, my lord?"

"Over a fortnight."

"Why did you not come to Wakesfield Manor?"

"So you knew about the betrothal contract?" Spencer asked.

The older man nodded.

"Why didn't Roselyn know that this manor is now mine?"

"When she came here, her husband and child were dying. This was the only place she could go—how could I tell her that it was no longer in her family? Wight is so far from London, that I did not think you would visit often." He paused. "I assume she knows the truth now?"

"She doesn't believe me—she doesn't believe her father could do such a thing without telling her."

Heywood looked grim. "Lady Roselyn usually sees the good in people—and when she doesn't see it, she pretends it is there."

"Did she pretend with Philip Grant?" Spencer asked, surprised at how tense he felt.

"Why do you care, my lord?" Heywood studied him with an uncomfortable intensity. "I thought you did not desire marriage to Lady Roselyn."

"She made her own decision on our marriage. But what about Grant?" He pointed to the grass-covered grave between them.

"My lord, I still don't understand why you're here—"

"Let us make a bargain, you and I. I'll answer some of your questions if you'll answer some of mine."

"Some?" Heywood repeated, his mustache twitching with the beginnings of a smile.

"Let's not make promises we can't keep, Heywood."

After a slight hesitation, the bailiff said, "Very well, my lord. But perhaps you would like to sit."

Spencer limped away from the grave and sat down on a stone bench in the chapel's shade.

With knees creaking, Heywood sat beside him. "My lord, might I ask the first question?"

Spencer nodded.

"Where have you been staying? No one in the village has seen you."

Spencer knew a lie would be best, if only to protect Roselyn, but Heywood would never do anything to harm her. "I'm staying at Roselyn's cottage."

Heywood stiffened. "My sons never saw you."

"I assure you, I was in no condition to do harm to your Lady Roselyn. She tells me I almost died."

"A fortnight ago, the channel was filled with ships," Heywood said slowly.

"My ship went down during the battle, and I washed ashore. I was bleeding from a sword wound in my chest when Roselyn found me on the beach."

"How fortunate to come ashore near your own estate."

Spencer smiled. "Believe me, I knew where the battle was taking place, that I had somewhere to go."

"But you *didn't* come to the manor—you stayed with Lady Roselyn. Surely you must not look upon her in a kind light."

"When I finally discovered her identity, I was

less than gracious. I felt her caring for me was perhaps . . . an atonement for her sins." Spencer stretched out his leg, wondering what Heywood would think about *that* statement. "So tell me what happened with Roselyn's 'marriage.' "

"They are her secrets to tell, my lord."

"I don't ask you to reveal Rose's secrets, Heywood. Just tell me what you saw."

"Rose?" Heywood echoed softly.

"A slip of the tongue," Spencer said with a shrug, feeling as uncomfortable as if he'd revealed his own dark secrets.

"Lady Roselyn and Philip Grant were handfasted in London, where they lived for almost a year."

"Roselyn says he taught her the baker's trade."

"Yes. And she insists on using it here to support herself."

"And you buy her bread," Spencer said.

"The estate buys much of it, yes. After Roselyn gave birth to Mary the Black Death broke out in London, and she brought her husband and child here, the only place she could think of that was safe."

"But they died of it anyway."

"Yes," Heywood said, gazing out over the rolling fields with a sad, faraway look. "She wouldn't let us help her as her husband and babe lay dying."

"She didn't want you to sicken." Spencer's voice was low, as he thought of Roselyn all alone, surrounded by illness and death. No wonder she seemed almost too calm at times. How else could she live with what she'd seen and felt? "Why did she stay?"

"She insisted she couldn't return to her parents, and I knew there was nowhere safer for such an innocent girl. She wouldn't accept my hospitality in the manor, so I gave her a cottage. She insisted on paying rent."

"I'm not surprised."

They were both silent, listening to the rustle of the grasses and the squawking of birds.

"My lord," Heywood began hesitantly, "now that we know of your visit, perhaps you will stay at the manor."

"No."

Heywood rose swiftly to his feet. "Surely you know it is unseemly to remain with Lady Roselyn."

"Perhaps," Spencer conceded, looking up at the bailiff, "but if you tell no one I'm here, who will know?"

"But she is only a poor widow—"

"Who was to be my wife," Spencer interrupted, but without the anger he'd come to ex-

pect. "Let us say that she and I have our own
bargain."

"Do you plan to marry her?"

"No," he said flatly, and was surprised by a
flash of regret. "There are things I can't tell you,
ways she is in danger. But I won't be here much
longer." *Only five days.*

As Spencer rose and began to limp away, he
said over his shoulder, "Remember—tell no
one I am here."

"My family will have to know."

"You have my permission," he said, thinking
wryly of John Heywood. He turned around to
pin the bailiff with his gaze. "But no one else."

"As you wish, my lord."

Spencer found Roselyn kneeling in her
kitchen garden, the hot sun making waves of
heat rise from her black dress. In between
weeding, she wiped her face with her forearm.

He stepped into the courtyard, knowing she
heard him. She didn't bother to get up, so he sat
on the bench and watched her.

"Why didn't you tell me about your baby?"
he asked in a low voice.

He saw her shoulders stiffen, imagined the
pain she must be feeling.

And then he understood.

He saw her serenity for what it was—a mask
to disguise her feelings, to keep everything in-

side. When she stood up to face him, she was as dry-eyed and remote as he knew she'd be.

"Who told you?" she asked.

"I found the graveyard."

Roselyn remained calm, letting the spasm of old grief slumber again. She wiped her hands on a rag and finally looked up at Spencer.

So now he knew. Would he mock her child as he'd mocked her marriage, calling Mary a—

But she stopped the word from even forming in her mind, and knew suddenly that he would not hurt the memory of a child.

"So why didn't you tell me?" he asked again.

"It is not the first thing I share with strangers."

Was his smile sad? she wondered, and felt the prick of tears she despised shedding.

"I understand you better," he said softly.

"Oh, do you think so?" she asked with a touch of bitterness.

"I met your bailiff."

She stiffened. "You didn't tell him—"

"He knows who I am. Aren't you happy not to have to lie to him anymore?"

A rush of anger shot through her, and she stepped closer to look down on him. "Happy that he's now in danger?"

"Roselyn—"

"One Spaniard followed you—who knows if there could be another? Don't you think I lie awake enough nights imagining—" She broke off as her voice cracked. She had tried so hard to protect the Heywoods. "And now they know I've been lying to them. What must they think?"

"Come here."

His low, rumbling voice set off a jangle of nerves inside her. "No."

He caught her skirt with one hand and pulled her between his outstretched legs. When she would have fled, he forced her to sit down on his thigh. Roselyn perched there, feeling awkward and ridiculous—and blinking back frustrated tears.

"Heywood is very worried about you," he began.

She felt his arm settle around her waist, while his hand rested on her hip.

"And maybe he thinks I'm cruel for imposing on you. But I made it clear you had nursed me back to health, and it was only my stubbornness that was keeping me in this cottage."

"Is it?" she whispered, glancing at him. His face was much too close, his dark eyes too powerful. Why did he touch her with such familiarity, when she knew he was only going to leave?

Spencer's gaze dropped to her mouth, and she felt that answering warmth, the way her body lit like a new candle.

"What else did you and Francis discuss?" she asked breathlessly.

He no longer seemed to hear her. His lips were near hers, and his free hand touched her knee.

She bolted from his lap and ran.

Chapter 18

The next morning, Roselyn dressed and left the cottage as silently as she could, so as not to awaken Spencer.

As the sun rose, she gathered together the breads and cakes the Heywoods had ordered into two large baskets, and set off across the estate to the manor.

She'd spent much of the night wondering what Francis must be thinking of her. Was he disappointed—or angry? Now she would have to face him and his family, and her stomach churned with tension.

When she reached the doorway to the kitchens, she stopped cold, her head aching with worry and fear. Would they hate her now, think her a fallen woman to be living with a man?

She'd done nothing wrong except exchange a kiss.

But in her heart, she'd begun to long for more

than just a kiss from Spencer Thornton.

But such worrying was only delaying the inevitable. She opened up the door—

And found them all sitting at the table solemnly watching her.

Roselyn stood frozen in the doorway, feeling her face drain of color, until Margaret Heywood rose from the table with a warm smile.

Roselyn felt the sting of grateful tears as Margaret took the baskets from her arms and said, "Come, dear, sit with us and tell us everything."

Charlotte made room on her bench for Roselyn, giving her an encouraging smile. Roselyn could have hugged her. When she glanced at Francis, she saw that although he wore a serious expression, his eyes were kind.

Thomas scratched his head. "So what is the new owner like?"

"Thomas!" Francis said sharply, glancing at Roselyn.

She sighed and looked at her plate, which Margaret filled with porridge and bread.

"Lady Roselyn," Francis said in a solemn voice, "forgive me for not telling you the truth about Wakesfield's ownership. When you first arrived, your husband and child were ill and I just didn't feel—"

"Francis, no!" she interrupted, taking hold of his hand. Her last hope that Spencer's claim to the estate was a lie faded into ashes. "Do not apologize for trying to spare my feelings. I should apologize to you for the lies I've been forced to tell."

Margaret put an arm around her shoulder. "If you'd told us you'd found a sick man, we could have helped you, dear."

"I couldn't," she whispered, finally glancing at John to face the disappointment that saddened his eyes. "I didn't know who he was at first, and thought he might be a Spanish sailor. How could I put you in such danger?"

"There is more you're not telling us," Francis said.

She hesitated, then whispered, "Yes," begging him with her eyes to understand. "I promise you'll know everything the moment I can tell you."

"Is it about the war?"

She nodded.

"Then tell us what you can. I'd like to know how you found him, how you saved his life."

She recounted the events of the last fortnight hesitantly, thinking through what she could tell them and what had to be hidden. She painted a picture of two people trapped together by circumstance, distant and polite, with nothing in common and nothing to say to each other.

When she was done, the Heywood family maintained a sober silence as they all began to eat their now-cold food. Roselyn listened to the clink of glass goblets, the clatter of knives and spoons, the lack of conversation. Her own stomach was so twisted that even Margaret's cooking did not tempt her to eat.

John suddenly rose to his feet, as if he could no longer pretend to eat. "I suppose Thornton plans to court you again."

His bitter voice was as painful to her as a blow to the stomach.

"I do not know his plans," she said in a steady voice. At least *that* was true.

"Then how can we leave you alone with him?" he demanded, bracing his hands on the table and leaning toward her. "Is this just merely a cruel whim on his part, some kind of punishment—"

There was a knock on the door, and Francis motioned for silence as he went to open it.

Spencer stood in the doorway, leaning on his cane. Roselyn paled, which was infinitely better than blushing. What had he overheard?

"Good day, Lord Thornton," she said.

"Good day, Lady Roselyn."

For once, he kept that deep, unsettling voice under control. In fact, he sounded . . . amused.

Francis stepped aside. "Please come in, my lord. This is your home."

Roselyn saw Spencer glance at her, but she met his gaze calmly, once again the mistress of her emotions. Her entire world might be falling apart, but she was not going to show how much it devastated her.

"Lord Thornton," she began, coming to her feet. "Allow me to present the Heywood family." As she made the introductions, she knew with certainty that none would question Spencer's motives directly, for he was now their lord on whom their way of life depended.

Margaret pulled out the chair at the end of the table. "Come eat with us, my lord. Surely you have not yet broken your fast."

"Thank you," he said, settling slowly into the chair, his broken leg out to one side.

Roselyn found herself seated to his left, where she began to force porridge down her throat as if it were just another normal meal.

"Miss Charlotte," Spencer began.

Roselyn watched the girl's eyes widen as he put every bit of his bountiful charm into his dazzling smile.

"Yes, my lord?"

"Please forgive me for not properly introducing myself when we met a few days ago. My presence here has . . . complications."

"Of course, my lord. You do not need to explain yourself to me."

Around the table, an uncomfortable silence hovered as Margaret served Spencer, and they all resumed eating. Roselyn couldn't stop herself from glancing at John, who kept his gaze on his plate. She sensed not only anger in him, but an incredible disappointment. How must her actions look to him, the man who wanted to marry her?

John suddenly set his knife and spoon down, and she held her breath as he raised his gaze to Spencer.

Spencer seemed as if he'd been waiting for such a move. He watched John with interest, but not outright amusement, for which she was grateful.

"My lord," John said stiffly, "please allow me to prepare the master suite for you."

Roselyn knew she wasn't the only one holding her breath, as Spencer turned his narrowed gaze on her. She suddenly thought of how her cottage had been before he'd arrived—the endless silence. But wasn't that what had drawn her there, the need to live alone, to create a new life for herself?

She thought of hearing no one breathe in the night, of not having his gaze follow her, of no longer waiting for him to touch her.

What kind of fool was she becoming? He would be leaving soon, and she knew better than to trust someone like him. There was only John to depend on.

"Did your father not tell you I wish no one to know I'm here?" Spencer said. "If I take up residence in the manor, everyone will know."

"Then allow me to prepare one of the cottages—"

"John," Margaret said with a sharpness Roselyn was unaccustomed to hearing from her. "His Lordship is still injured and cannot be left alone. But thank you for your consideration."

Roselyn almost gaped at the woman—did Margaret support her staying alone with a man?

"I've never been to London," Thomas suddenly said. "Do tell us what it's like to live there, my lord."

Spencer looked about the table, at Roselyn's strained face, at Francis's discomfort, at John's bitterness. What a smart lad Thomas was. He regaled them with tales of living in London— leaving out the bawdier side of life and how he used to enjoy it.

When the women had finished clearing away the meal, Spencer found himself out of things to say. Francis stepped into the silence.

"My lord, would you like me to send word to your family of your safe arrival at Wakesfield?"

Spencer tensed; the last thing he needed was to worry that someone would come after his family for information about him. "No," he said sternly, meeting the old man's impassive gaze. "I've already explained that no one is to know I'm here. I promise you will receive a complete explanation when I can give it."

He glanced at Roselyn, hoping she thought he meant only an explanation about the two of them. She gazed at him steadily and he wanted to linger, to make his eyes tell her exactly what he thought when he looked at her.

But not in the midst of the Heywood family.

"My lord," Margaret said, "please forgive our departure, but 'tis the first market day in Shanklin since before the fleets sailed past. Charlotte and Lady Roselyn and I should be going."

"The merchants have brought new supplies from the mainland?" Roselyn asked, then smiled when the old woman nodded. "Let me fetch my baskets."

Spencer sat back in his chair and nodded to the men as they each took their leave to begin the day. The women draped kerchiefs around their shoulders and adjusted their caps.

"My lord," Roselyn said, and he knew those two words did not sit well on her tongue, "will you be able to return to the cottage by yourself?"

"It will do me good," he assured her, standing up.

She nodded and turned away, and he found himself watching her hips sway as she walked out the door.

When they were all gone, he limped through the many parlors and halls on the first floor of

Wakesfield Manor, not knowing what he was looking for. But it seemed . . . empty. Just like his home in London.

Though threatening clouds began to build up in the western sky, market day in Shanklin remained a festive affair. Wooden stalls were set up throughout the common, and many farmers had brought their families into the village for the day. The tavern was doing brisk business, and Roselyn received many new orders for her baked goods. She would be spending much time in her bake house.

Would Spencer follow her there again?

She wanted to groan at the ridiculous wanderings of her mind; he had made it quite clear that he was leaving soon. She had failed so far in learning whether he was a spy or not, and was left with only a ridiculous fascination for him.

Stranger still, was the fact that Margaret hadn't even mentioned Spencer.

When Charlotte wandered off to look at hair ribbons, Roselyn said, "Margaret, I'm not sure I understand your good humor. I would have thought you would be quite . . . disappointed in me."

Margaret slid her arm through Roselyn's and smiled. "My dear child, you saved a man's life. What is there not to be proud of?"

"But I've been *lying* to you."

"Did you feel you were doing the right thing?"

Roselyn opened her mouth, though for a moment nothing came out. "Well . . . yes."

"Then I will not judge you, my lady."

Roselyn lowered her voice. "Are you condoning my living in the same cottage with Lord Thornton?"

A tiny frown gathered the wrinkles on Margaret's forehead. "He is your betrothed, my dear, and I only want you to be happy."

Roselyn was almost incapable of speech, which was lucky, since Charlotte was walking towards them, her face beaming.

"Mother, did you ever see such lovely colors? Father said I could have two—"

A sudden scream rent the air, and a stab of terror lodged in Roselyn's chest. A young woman, a farmer's daughter whose name Roselyn had forgotten, was running toward the common from the beach, tears on her face.

"There's a dead man down on the rocks!" she cried, burying her face in her mother's shoulder.

There were shocked cries and frightened whispers. The men of the village headed down toward the beach, while the women stood clustered together, counting their family members, praying it was no one they knew.

Roselyn stood back, and resisted the urge to say another prayer—because she knew with grim certainty whose body had returned from the ocean.

Chapter 19

L ater in the afternoon, Roselyn returned to her cottage and found Spencer pacing the courtyard. She watched in silent surprise as he began resting a little weight on his broken leg.

"You could worsen your injury," she said.

He whirled around, and she was stunned to see a dagger in his hand.

"Don't surprise me like that," he said sternly.

She continued to stare at the weapon. "Where did you get that?"

"At the manor. When Francis came upon me at the chapel yesterday, I realized I was foolish to be so unprepared."

She sat down on the bench. "You might have even more cause to be wary. They found the Spaniard's body on the beach today."

"Did the villagers think he was from the battle?"

"Yes, but it aroused everyone's suspicions.

Apparently there are strangers on the island, asking questions."

Spencer stiffened. "About me?"

"Not that I know of. But you must understand that every visitor to Wight is a stranger, especially during these times of war. A man could have asked for simple lodging and been viewed suspiciously."

He shrugged and resumed his pacing, occasionally resting weight on his broken leg.

Now he was certain to leave soon, and nothing was resolved. He was not telling her all the truth, and for a moment she debated giving him the pouch anyway.

But what if that was all he was waiting for? Could she live with herself if something dreadful happened, if he was the traitor she suspected?

And that was the true dilemma of her situation: she couldn't trust him, yet she was drawn to him with a power she never would have imagined. Just watching him move made her feel pleasurably languid, made her body not her own anymore, but his.

What was she to do—just let him go?

But then she'd never know one way or another what he was, what he meant to her.

Meant to her? Even if he turned out to be the most patriotic of Englishmen, he was still dangerous. She needed to get back to her sedate life, to her solitary cottage, to her ordinary days.

Roselyn eyed him speculatively. "Why didn't you tell me you would be coming to Wakesfield this morning?"

He leaned against the low wall and the beginnings of a smile played about his lips.

"I didn't know myself until after you'd gone."

"You couldn't bear the thought of your own company?" she asked, trying for sarcasm, and realizing she sounded almost playful.

He looked away with too casual an air. "Something like that."

Something caught and held deep inside her, something more than the attraction she felt for him. He seemed almost . . . sad. Did he miss his family, his old way of life? Maybe he wasn't used to being alone—though surely he could have had female companionship whenever he wanted.

The thought of him with other women unsettled her. How foolish! Of course he would have other women, probably even a wife, once he broke their betrothal contract.

He turned his head and looked at her. She almost gasped at the intensity of his heavy-lidded, smoldering gaze, the black depths she couldn't begin to understand.

Almost without volition, Spencer found himself walking toward Roselyn. He waited for her to run from him, from what he represented, as she'd done so many times now. But she sat unnaturally still on the bench, only her head moving as she tilted back to keep their gazes locked.

Had he embarrassed her this morning? Was it because of her reputation, as she kept insisting, or something more?

He stopped before her, so close their knees brushed, and her skirts covered his boots. Her storm-cloud eyes glittered as she challenged him—or herself—by holding his gaze, while her chest rose and fell at a more and more rapid pace.

Not fear, no.

She *should* fear him—everything inside him demanded he put her on her back on the table, take her here in the sunshine, regardless of who would see.

Was it possession he wanted, or just proof that she lusted as much as he did?

And if she pulled away, it would tell him nothing about what she protected—her reputation or herself or even her family.

Ah, but he wanted to touch that creamy, freckled skin that he could still remember wet under the starlight.

As he stared down at her, Spencer heard

himself say, "Your carpenter wasn't pleased to see me."

"How would you feel if another man overheard you courting a woman?"

"Especially when he was overheard by the woman's betrothed." He regretted the words almost immediately.

She drew a deep breath and her eyes glittered, but he quickly covered her mouth with his fingers.

"I didn't mean to start another argument," he began. "I didn't want—"

But the soft, moist feel of Roselyn's mouth beneath his fingers stoked the blaze of the irrational desire he had for her. All his focus suddenly concentrated on keeping his hand from trembling; there was no will left to stop his fingers from wandering.

Bending low, he cupped her face with both hands, letting his thumbs follow the curve of her full lower lip. Her eyelashes fluttered and lowered, and her breath was almost a gasp now.

A sudden desperation welled up inside him. He thought of leaving her in four days, of going to London to face possible death. For the first time, he didn't feel in such a hurry. Was it solace and comfort he wanted, he who knew better than to expect that from any woman? He'd never *wanted* it from any woman—until now.

His thumbs traced her eyelids, then the light brows that arched across her forehead. The fragile line of her cheek aroused him, and suddenly he was dying to taste her there. He dropped to his knees, the pain from his healing leg just a vague call in the distance. Leaning against her tightly clasped knees, he held her face before him, then pressed his lips to her cheek.

Inhaling brought an exquisite, painful pleasure—she smelled like Roselyn, like baking bread and wildflowers and woman.

He leaned more against her legs, but still her knees did battle, though her hands remained clenched in her lap. Ah, how she struggled against herself. The familiar rush of excitement, of the forbidden, held him in its grip.

With his hands on her shoulders, he arched her back against the table, until her throat was bare to him. His lips nibbled wandering paths across her white skin; he licked at the little hollow where her pulse thrummed at the base of her throat.

Her black garments hid the rest of her from him, and he felt a primitive urge to rip them from her, claim her there.

Claim her? What claim could he have anymore, what promises could he offer? Besides money, what had he ever had to offer? *She* had realized that long ago.

Spencer straightened, placing his hands on the bench on either side of her with the greatest care, as if he didn't trust his fingers to stop caressing her.

Her thighs suddenly parted, and he found himself falling between her legs. Roselyn's face was a bare whisper away, and before he could register any shock, she kissed him.

There was an innocence to her kiss, but she was only tentative, not shy. She *wanted* to kiss him, and that knowledge sent his lust roaring to new heights.

Their open mouths clung together, their tongues searching and tasting, their bodies straining for even greater closeness.

He was mindless, drowning, lost, and he allowed his hands to find their way beneath her skirts, to skim up over her stockinged calves. He shuddered at the bare flesh behind her knees—then froze as he realized what he was doing.

Lifting his head, he looked down to see Roselyn's eyes closed, her head back, passion like a rose-colored flush across her skin.

All under the late afternoon sun, in view of anyone who might come by.

Her eyes opened, then blinked with a slow, languid awareness that made him think of awakening at dawn in her arms.

"What are we doing?" he whispered, while his fingers crept upward behind her thighs.

"I—I should go. I have so many orders from the tavern to bake."

She stumbled over her words, and he wanted to kiss them away. Instead he teased even higher, until he could feel the roundness of her backside against his fingertips.

She gave a little squirm and a gasp, and everything shuddered inside him, off-balance.

Still on his knees, he moved back, then pulled her knees shut. She stood so quickly that she almost knocked him over.

"I have work to do," she murmured, not looking at him.

Spencer watched her stride to the gate. More and more he realized she was not like other women. And there was the danger—to them both.

Roselyn did not return to the cottage until close to midnight. She released her breath as she saw that Spencer was asleep.

Her arms ached from kneading; her fingertips were sore from peeling fruit.

And her nerves were at a fevered pitch.

She had spent every moment waiting for him to come to her. Wild Roselyn, her old self, had taken possession, pushed away all her rational objections. She wanted to experience everything she never had with Philip.

But the new Roselyn she'd fashioned was so afraid—her voice was like that of a child wailing alone out on the open moor, growing ever softer, ever more plaintive.

When she awoke the next morning, Spencer was already gone. He was probably meeting with Francis, or going on one of his long walks.

But a deepening feeling of dread made her rush through her morning rituals.

It was all going to be over soon—she'd done what she could, short of confronting him or handing over the pouch to the authorities.

A restlessness gripped her that had nothing to do with his questionable loyalty—she was overcome with needs she hadn't imagined existed. This was a more powerful lure than anything that had drawn her to Philip.

But she had to attend to her business, or risk losing the tavern owner as a customer. She had baked far too many goods to be carried in baskets—she would need to borrow a workhorse and cart.

As Roselyn entered Wakesfield's main barn, she pulled a carrot from her pocket for Angel, but found the stall empty. Before she could even wonder who had taken the mare for a morning ride, Spencer rode into the barn on Angel.

She stood still, awed and impressed. He looked whole, well, a powerful man in his prime. She felt too warm and flustered as he grinned down at her.

"I saw you come in," he said, pulling Angel to a halt. He patted the mare's neck, but his gaze caught Roselyn's, then wandered leisurely down her body. "She's truly a beautiful animal. It was a lot easier to mount her today."

She wished she could take back the wild coloring sweeping her cheeks, but she didn't look away. "You're healing, so naturally you're stronger," she said, keeping her voice as normal as possible.

"Do you mind if I exercise her this morning?"

She shrugged, trying to ignore how her palms were sweating and her heart raced as if she'd just ridden the length of the island.

"Very well," he said. "I shall see you at dinner."

She stood watching him as he rode off, knowing he might as well be riding out of her life.

She was overwhelmed with a sudden regret—had she made a terrible mistake when she'd abandoned their wedding?

No, she had found the right life for her—the safe life. When Spencer was gone, everything would be normal again; she would know how every day would unfold, without this horrible, aching uncertainty.

But after she hitched a workhorse to a small two-wheeled cart and led it back toward her cottage, she couldn't help watching Spencer gallop across the horizon.

By the time Roselyn returned to Wakesfield in the early evening, the heat was oppressive, and dark clouds seemed to capture the air and hold it still. Her gown clung to her back as she walked along beside the horse, whose head drooped forlornly.

As they neared the barn, she heard the distant clash of metal on metal. She thought at first that the blacksmith might be working inside, but this was a lighter, deadlier sound.

She left the horse tethered outside, then went around to the rear door of the barn, which let her into the shadows behind the stalls.

Spencer was holding a sword on Thomas Heywood.

For a moment, Roselyn's dread became an all-encompassing pain that threatened to shatter her. By her foolish desire, had she brought danger to them all?

Spencer grinned. "Now, see how I'm holding this, Tom? Try my grip."

Her mouth dropped open, but when she noticed the sword in Thomas's hand, she felt like her bones had melted clear out of her. Spencer was *teaching* the young man.

She wanted to giggle in sheer, draining relief and collapse back into the straw. But that lasted only a moment—she found her eyes drawn to Spencer, and she realized with a start that he had altered his cane, nailing a piece of wood perpendicular to it, like the hilt of a sword. His right knee rested on the cross, holding him up and freeing his hands. As long as he didn't try to walk, he could balance and fight.

She stayed hidden within the empty stall, watching. Of course he would be good with a sword—he would naturally have had to defend himself after any number of his famous scandals.

But the patience he showed impressed her. He didn't belittle or scold the boy for his lack of knowledge, even though she knew that at Thomas's age, eighteen years, Spencer must have been far superior with the weapon.

Their voices became murmurs as she found herself studying his body, watching the way every muscle moved. She remembered his naked chest, gleaming during his bath. Cocooned in these new and heady sensations, she wasn't surprised when Spencer looked over Thomas's shoulder, right toward her hiding place.

She was trapped in his gaze, knew he could see her, but he merely smiled and continued teaching Thomas.

But his awareness of her was potent, power-ful, and when he complained of the heat and re-moved his shirt, she knew he did it just for her.

She could see the lines of his hipbones disap-pearing into his low-slung breeches. His skin glistened beneath the scattering of hair across his chest.

Roselyn knew with wicked certainty that if Thomas left, her wild self would emerge from long slumber, and she would draw Spencer into the shadows with her, and pull him down into the straw. She licked her dry lips and clenched her shaking hands, and wondered what he was thinking as he glanced at her again, his face intent—and not on sword fighting.

Chapter 20

❦

"Thomas!"

Spencer was so caught up in the heat of Roselyn's gaze that he was barely aware of Thomas, let alone who called the boy's name.

But he recognized John Heywood's voice immediately, although the anger in it was unfamiliar. John strode into the barn, staring at Spencer and his brother with an uneasiness he could barely conceal.

"He's teaching me to fight," Thomas said excitedly.

"That is kind of him," John said in a clipped, tight voice. "But right now, Father needs you out in the orchard."

Spencer watched Thomas leave, then turned to eye John. This hardly seemed like the same man who had courted Roselyn so gently—but that was when John thought he had no rival.

With a sudden stab of pain, Spencer realized

that he really *wasn't* John's rival, that Roselyn deserved so much more.

John folded his arms across his chest. "My brother doesn't need your help, Thornton. He's learned well enough here with us."

Spencer reached for his shirt and pulled it over his head. "Every man could use a more refined technique, Heywood. He saw me practicing and asked me to work with him."

"And why are you bothering to practice? You can't even stand unaided."

Spencer lowered his broken leg to the dirt floor, and leaned on his cane. "In case you have not noticed, there's a war going on. I need to be able to defend myself, especially like this."

He had meant no insult, but John took it as such, and drew himself up with anger. "Are you implying that I did not do my part against the Spanish?"

"No," Spencer said calmly, but clearly the young man felt some degree of guilt.

"I trained with the soldiers at the garrison, and I was ready to join them should we be invaded."

"Good of you."

John took a step forward. "Are you mocking me, my lord?"

Spencer rubbed his hand across his face—this wasn't going at all as he wanted. "I mean nothing of the kind. I'm glad you were here to protect Wakesfield—and Roselyn."

John eyed him warily. "I don't understand."

"She obviously needs protection. She can do wild, foolhardy things without thinking."

"Roselyn?" John said in bewilderment.

Spencer realized that John didn't really know her at all, because she had so thoroughly succeeded in changing herself into this perfect, proper widow.

"You don't think that running from our wedding was a bit impulsive?" Spencer asked dryly.

"I think it was intelligent."

Spencer gave him a grudging smile, wondering what Roselyn was thinking about all this. He knew she was still here.

"Perhaps. But it caused her much grief, as well. I would hate for her to put herself through something like that again."

"I won't allow that to happen," John said. "Unless you plan to interfere, my lord."

Spencer wanted to be sarcastic, but the words wouldn't come. He felt suddenly old and tired, and knew time was running out for him. "No, I won't interfere. She deserves to be happy."

But *hadn't* he been interfering these past weeks? His plan to arouse and then reject her seemed childish, the scheme of a man who thought only of himself. Now when he looked at Roselyn, he wanted comfort, solace, but he had no way to ask—and no right to.

When John bid him good-night and left the barn, Spencer barely heard him. He suddenly felt alone, dreading returning to London in three days. For a moment he thought of abandoning his plans, of escaping into the wilds of the Scottish highlands where no one would ever find him.

He heard a sob, and as he turned Roselyn darted past him, wiping tears from her face.

"Rose?" he called, his voice soft and urgent, but she ran out into the darkening night. He followed her as fast as he could, stumbling over rocks and into holes he could no longer see. He knew where she was going, the only place she had to call hers—the place he'd threatened to take from her, like a selfish monster.

Roselyn didn't know why she couldn't stop crying. As the heavy skies finally opened and rain came pouring down, it mingled with her tears. Still she ran, knowing that Spencer was leaving, that he wouldn't stand in the way of her marriage to John.

Wasn't that what she wanted? So why did her chest feel as if it were torn in two and she couldn't breathe?

She heard Spencer behind her, the rain muffling his voice. She reached the cottage and fumbled frantically with the latch, but before she could get the door open, he was near, calling her in a voice so tender it made her weep all over again.

She gave up trying to open the door and ran to the back of the cottage. Her solace, her courtyard garden, was sodden, still steaming from the day's heat, the graying dusk making everything look as bleak as her soul felt.

"Rose."

She whirled about, stumbling back against the stone wall, staring at Spencer. His hair was plastered to his head and brushed his shoulders in dripping strands. His wet shirt clung to him.

But it was his dark eyes that held her trapped. She couldn't—wouldn't run. There was a plaintive appeal in those eyes that she'd never seen before. It cut her deep to see him vulnerable, to see him needing—what?

"Go away!" she whispered raggedly.

"Why did you run?" He stepped toward her, his hand reaching for her.

"I don't know!" Her voice broke and she whirled away, covering her face with her hands.

And then he enveloped her from behind, his arms crossing to hold her tight, his chest pressed so closely to her back that she didn't know where she ended and he began.

He whispered, "Rose," against her ear, and

just the vibration of his voice deep in his chest
shot a sudden need through her.

With a cry, she tilted her head back, and then
his mouth was against her throat. The heavy
rain on her face was the final blow that un-
leashed the wildness she'd tried to deny in herself. She wanted this—needed this.

She arched back against him, desperate for
his heat and strength. His hands grasped her
waist, then slid slowly up over her ribs, pausing, hesitating, until she wanted to press her
breasts into his hands.

She held still with aching need as his palms
slid over her breasts and cupped her tight. Her
gasp was a demand that he continue, and he caressed up and over her breasts repeatedly, until
the sheer pleasure of it created a full ache between her thighs. Never had she felt this need
to be with a man, to take anything he could
give her, to give all she had of herself.

Then he found her nipples through the garments, and he plucked at them until they
pressed hard into his hands. It was as if he
played a lute, and each strum of his fingers
made her entire body vibrate. She could only
drop her head back on his shoulder with a
moan. His tongue licked along her ear and
cheek, then she turned her head to meet his
mouth with her own. They took sustenance
from each other, tongues meeting and straining

and stroking, and all the while his hands molded and shaped her breasts.

But it wasn't enough—she wanted to feel his wet skin, the heat and power of him. She pushed back against him, rubbing into him with her hips, and his ragged groan took her by surprise. She caught her breath when his hands dropped to her waist and pressed their hips together.

"Rose—" he said into her ear. His tongue followed.

"Don't speak! Just make me feel . . . Stop this need that I can't control."

He lifted his hands to her hair. She didn't understand at first, then she felt the plucking of the pins buried tightly in her hair, and she stilled. Each tug of his hands sent an answering quiver through her. When the heavy mass of her wet hair fell about her shoulders, she heard Spencer groan, felt him bury his face against it.

It made her knees weaken, and she sagged against him. "Spencer—"

From behind her, he whispered, "I want to see your skin bare and wet again."

"I—I don't understand—"

"That night when we kissed—I stood at the window and watched you bathe under the stars."

Roselyn imagined him watching her, and she felt a rush of desire so heady it made her dizzy.

The laces suddenly loosened at her neck, and her black gown gave way at her chest, which rose and fell rapidly.

"Before your bath, you removed your dress first, and I thought your smock seemed to glow as if you were a sea nymph sent to torture me."

"I torture you?" Her own voice was breathy, trembling.

"God, yes," he said, and with a tug her gown fell to her waist.

Her smock was so wet she could see her nipples through it. She felt Spencer lean over her shoulder, and his gaze took in her near-nakedness while he pressed soft kisses against her shoulder and neck.

The knowledge that her body could hold power over him overwhelmed yet strengthened her.

"Spencer—"

Her gown fell in a heap at her feet, leaving her clothed in only the soaking wet smock. The rain continued to fall around them, cooling the heat of the day, but inflaming the heat building inside her.

"Please," she moaned, "let me face you—"

"Not yet." His whisper trailed across her back as his hands skimmed down to her waist. The tugging began again, and she watched, holding her breath, as the smock moved down her shoulders, clung wetly to her breasts, then dropped into the grass.

Cool rain suddenly beat against her back as he stepped away.

"Face me now," he said, and though his voice was as harsh as a command, she knew he begged her.

And that was all it took. Roselyn turned to see his tense, passionate face, illuminated by the weak light spilling from her cottage window. His hot eyes seared her as they explored her body, lingering on her breasts. She clenched her hands against the rock wall, the only thing that held her up.

Spencer's gaze dropped lower, and she knew he gazed at where her thighs joined, the part of her that felt so hot and throbbing and needy. Never had she wanted this joining of a man's body to hers, craved it more than her own breath.

"Yes," he whispered. "This is what you looked like that night—all wet and glistening and too beautiful for poets to imagine."

Her throat tightened, tears stung her eyes—but it must be only the rain dripping down her face. She remained still as he limped toward her, tugging at the laces of his shirt.

"I have seen you wearing nothing," she whispered, as he pulled the shirt over his head and dropped it to the ground. "But it was not the same as this."

"This what?" His voice caught.

"This—this—this wonderful torment. What is wrong with me? Why do I feel so—so—"

"Achy?" he asked hoarsely.

Her mouth dropped open when his hands went to the fastenings of his breeches.

"Does everything inside you feel hot and heavy?" He slid the snug breeches over his hips and down his thighs. The splint fell away with his garments.

"Yes . . ." She watched with wide eyes as his erection spilled free and hung heavy before her.

He came closer, and her gaze rose to his face. She gave a little gasp as their lower bodies brushed, then pressed. Spencer slid his arm around her waist, holding her close.

Roselyn felt as if she were falling backward, and she clung to his shoulders.

He kissed her hair, her brow, her lips, arching her farther and farther over his arm. His lips taunted her throat, trailed across her wet skin, then closed over her nipple.

The world spun wildly as she cried out and clung to him. His hot mouth on her rain-cooled breast sent stabs of pleasure shooting throughout her body, until she was mindless and moaning beneath him. When she thought she could take no more without bursting into a thousand pieces, he moved to her other breast and started all over again.

The urge to rub herself against him, hip to hip, overpowered her. She had never felt such a sensation before, and was almost frightened of it. With a groan she pressed against him, his hard arousal nudging between her legs. She spread her thighs, guided by a primitive need she'd never experienced before.

He half groaned, half laughed against her breasts. "Not like this. I'll fall on top of you."

"I want you on top of me."

He lifted his head to stare into her eyes as his smile died. He turned her and she felt the world rush away as she fell back, caught in his hands, crushing daisies beneath her. Their scent wafted around them as he followed her down, pressing his body the length of hers.

With a moan she brought her knees up and settled him where she wanted him, hot between her thighs, rubbing against the womanly places that throbbed for him. She could have drowned in the dark seas of his eyes, so much did she yearn to be a part of him.

He brought his mouth down on hers, and as his tongue thrust into her mouth, so did he bury his shaft deep inside her.

She stiffened, waiting for the pain, yet knowing she would bear anything to be close to him—but there was no pain at all. Just a wonderful feeling of fullness, of completion.

Spencer felt her muscles tighten all around him, and knew a dawning dread. "Did I hurt you?" he rasped.

The relief was overwhelming when she shook her head. "It feels . . . perfect."

Perfect—that's what Roselyn was. He held himself painfully still inside her body, waiting for her to adjust as he looked on her flushed face, wet with the rain. He spread kisses across her face, her neck, then rounded his back so he could lave her breasts with his tongue.

He pulled out and thrust again deep inside her, wanting to touch all of her. He felt a need so deep for her that it frightened him, and his pace sped up until they rocked together in the darkness. She made panting, incoherent sounds against his chest and neck, and the first touch of her tongue sent him over the edge and into an abyss that had eluded him for so long. Though he tried to stop himself, his long celibacy worked against his control. With a groan, he shuddered and poured himself into her as her arms held him tight.

When at last he lifted himself up on his elbows, it was to find her staring at him a little wide-eyed.

"You didn't enjoy that," he said, kissing the tip of her nose.

"Oh yes, it was wonderful."

Roselyn, a widow, was yet an innocent to all she could feel. He knew more about what her body experienced than she did.

"No, you didn't enjoy that," he repeated, lifting up and then burying himself inside her again.

She gasped and wiggled.

He grinned. "But you soon will."

Chapter 21

Roselyn wanted to lie still, to enjoy the sensation of him deep inside her, the absence of pain. She wanted to shiver at the deliciousness of his lips just touching hers, the teasing, gentle way he smiled at her. This was how it should be between a man and woman—and she never wanted to go back to spending her nights alone.

This intimacy changed everything—surely he wouldn't leave her, surely he wouldn't mind that she'd withheld the pouch. He must have plausible answers for everything.

Spencer lifted himself off her body, and the shock of the cold rain on her heated flesh made her gasp. He pulled her to her feet, then suddenly lifted her up, his arms beneath her knees and back.

She flung her arms around his neck. "What are you doing? You can't carry me inside!"

"I most certainly—" He broke off, and she

giggled at the puzzled look on his face. He was standing on one leg, and he swayed precariously until he leaned back against the wall.

Roselyn clung to him tighter. "Don't drop me! Maybe I should carry you."

"We'd better do something, because this rock wall is biting into my ass."

She buried her face against his neck and laughed until her chest ached with the unfamiliarity of such abandon. He lowered her legs until just her toes touched the earth, and her body was pressed to the length of his. She could feel every inch of his skin, as hot as hers, rough with hair that teased her sensitive nipples.

She looked up into his shadowed face, her smile dying as he held her still with a gaze so hot she felt seared with passion.

"Our clothing—" she began.

"Leave it."

His husky voice sent a shiver across her skin, and they quickly walked toward the cottage. She barely felt the stones pricking her bare feet, or the watery puddles in the grass.

Inside the tiny cottage, there was only a glow from the embers of the dying fire. As Spencer knelt before the hearth to add wood, she ignored the doubts that tried to assail her. Wild Roselyn still held sway over her body, and she wanted to immerse herself in all the pleasure Spencer could teach her.

When the fire began to crackle with warmth, he turned to look up at her.

"Rose, you're cold," he whispered, leaning over his pallet for a blanket.

He pulled her down into his lap and wrapped her securely in the blanket and his arms. She rested her head against his chest and looked into the fire, trying to memorize everything about him and this evening.

She closed her eyes as he began to rub her back gently with the blanket, then squeezed the water from her heavy hair.

"I need to apologize," he whispered close to her ear. "I finished rather . . . abruptly out there in the courtyard."

"Abruptly?"

"I could have made things so much better for you."

"I don't see how," she said, tilting her head to look up at him.

To her surprise, Spencer's face looked red. "I haven't lost control like that since my youth."

"Lost control?"

He groaned and cupped her cheek. "How to explain such things to an innocent?"

"But I'm not—"

"In many ways you are. I rushed too fast, and didn't give you the same pleasure you gave to me. My only defense is that I have not been with a woman since last year—"

He broke off, and Roselyn saw the sudden shuttering of his face, as if he were a stranger again. The icy fingers of guilt and doubt crept closer.

"Last *year*?" she whispered, feeling herself stiffen. If the stories were true, he should have been in London with his many mistresses not six months ago.

"I meant to say last month," he said quickly, and his voice sounded forced.

But he hadn't meant that at all. *Last year*?

"I've just been so busy with the war and my estates. It befuddles the mind, you know."

He sounded so perfectly normal that it made her skin crawl.

"You've been too busy for your many mistresses?" she asked faintly, wishing she knew the truth from the lies. Her throat seemed too tight to swallow as she scrambled to her feet and wrapped the blanket tightly around her.

"This last month has been—"

She shot him a heated glance and he stopped talking.

Using the stones of the fireplace for leverage, Spencer got to his feet and stood there naked before her. She wished he'd cover himself, so she wouldn't have to see his magnificent body or remember how he'd made her feel special.

But she wasn't special—he treated her as he treated every other woman. He lied.

"I cannot discuss this now," she suddenly said, and to her horror, tears spilled from her eyes. She felt cold and wet and too devastated by what he'd made her feel out there in the rain.

"Rose—"

"No!" She didn't want to face the reality that she'd given her body to a man she couldn't trust. At least with Philip, she'd *thought* she could trust him. "We can talk in the morning. I'm tired."

She brushed past him and climbed into the loft. He said nothing to stop her, which only made her weep harder as she collapsed onto her pallet.

Stunned, Spencer stood before the fire and listened to Roselyn's sobs. After a year and a half of watching every word that left his mouth, he couldn't believe that an hour of intimacy with her had him making the most basic of mistakes.

He'd thought he could keep his secrets from harming her—but instead she'd been attacked by a Spaniard following him, and he himself had seduced her while withholding all the important truths.

He pulled on a dry pair of breeches, then sat before the fire, awash in guilt and despair. How could he have allowed himself to forget—even for these most incredible moments with Roselyn—that he was a hunted man?

Somehow they'd begun to care for each other, something he never could have predicted. And then he'd allowed lust to rule him, the biggest mistake of all. He'd given bedding her more thought than he had to the dead Spaniard washed ashore, or the rumors of strangers asking questions.

He had to leave her—*right now*—before she was ensnared any further in his deceptions. And how would she feel to see his head mounted on a pike? She'd think him worse than a seducer—a betrayer.

He allowed fragile hope to fill him: Rodney Shaw might not have left the armada alive. But such thoughts were foolish. Strangers were asking questions on the island, a Spaniard had been sent for him—and his own Spanish heritage practically ensured that no one would believe the truth without proof. And perhaps Shaw had already created his own proof.

He had to go back to London and finish what he'd begun, before anyone else was hurt.

For just one moment he considered telling Roselyn the truth, but he knew that would only be selfish. It was better for her to hate him for his sins than to agonize over his fate.

He silently dressed, trying not to feel the overwhelming ache in his chest, which was surely because of her tears. In an old trunk he found Philip's cloak, and after looking at the meager food stored in her cupboards, knew he could take nothing else from her. He would go to Francis Heywood for supplies and a horse.

For another hour Spencer waited, staring into the fire as if the flames could sear his guilt away. When he was certain Roselyn was asleep, he pulled the cloak about him and strode to the door.

He stopped with his hand on the latch, then grimly limped back to the ladder. Setting his cane aside, he pulled himself up a few rope steps, until he could see her tearstained face pillowed on her bare arm. He stared at her for a moment, feasting one last time on the sweet sight of her.

"Be safe," he whispered.

He descended the stairs, wrote her a note on a torn scrap of parchment, then left the cottage.

Roselyn awoke slowly, with dreams of Spencer's gentle hands caressing her clinging to her consciousness. She lay between the dream world and reality, puzzled by her reluctance to fully awaken—

And then she remembered. She had allowed him to make love to her—no, she'd begged him. She was repeating her worst mistakes all over again, with the impulsiveness she thought she'd put behind her.

And to make matters worse, she'd caught him in another lie. How could she have been so foolish?

She lay still, fighting tears, trying to find the courage to descend the ladder. What would she say to him? Could he think she would now willingly satisfy his needs whenever the urge overtook him?

And by the saints, how would she stop herself from doing just that? Even now the memories of his hands on her body were full of such exquisite pleasure that they made her shudder. He'd said there was even more—how could she resist that discovery?

But she would have to.

She lay still, biting her lip, dreading their first encounter—until she noticed the stillness that hovered in her cottage. Wouldn't he be up by now, practicing his walking, readying himself to leave—

A shock of pain made her stiffen. She told herself that he would be at the barn or at the manor, but even as she scrambled down the ladder wearing only a blanket, she knew what she would find.

There was a piece of parchment on the table that had not been there before. With shaking fingers, she lifted it.

I had to leave for London. Thank you for everything.

S

Roselyn slumped onto the bench as the parchment fluttered to the floor.

Thank you for everything?

She wanted to laugh, but she felt frozen, distant. She had given Spencer Thornton solace in every way she could—and then given the last precious thing she owned, her body.

He'd waited until he had that conquest before leaving—had it been his final revenge?

Her eyes were painfully dry, and her chest ached too much to sob.

Had he gotten everything from her that marriage would have given him, all so he could claim her an adulterer in the end?

She suddenly felt so cold. She hugged the blanket about her bare arms and realized with dawning horror that she could already be carrying his child.

In anguish, she dropped her head back and squeezed her eyes shut. If she was with child, what could she tell the Heywoods, especially John?

She tried to let the numbness take over, to soothe her wounded spirit and pride. But her hands shook as she poured hot water into a basin, and washed the smell of Spencer from her body. She scrubbed the stickiness between her thighs with particular virulence.

Then she dressed and walked outside, where the late summer sun shone as if belying the rainstorm that had swept her away the previous night. She picked up their wet garments and hung hers over the wall to dry—and hid his on a rack in the bake house.

Returning to the cottage, she told herself she had to eat to keep up her strength, but the stale bread and hard cheese made her nauseated.

A knock rattled her door, and Roselyn squashed the flare of hope that immediately flickered in her chest—Spencer was gone, and he wouldn't be coming back.

She opened the door to find Francis, his eyes grave. With a polite smile, she invited him inside.

"Would you care to share my meal, Francis?" she asked, sitting at the table.

"Lady Roselyn," he began in a hesitant voice.

She realized that he already knew Spencer was gone. But did he know everything? Did he know what kind of a woman she was, what she'd done—

"Lord Thornton came to me in the middle of the night," Francis continued.

She nodded slowly, not looking at him. "I discovered him gone when I awoke."

"Did he not even say good-bye?"

In too intimate a way. "Oh, his note was very polite. I have it here somewhere—ah, it fell on the floor." She picked it up and handed it to him.

Francis read it silently, then raised his eyes to her. "He said nothing more than this?"

She shook her head. "Are you certain you wouldn't like some bread? I baked it yesterday—"

"My lady," he interrupted, "I gave Lord Thornton supplies and a horse for the journey. He asked me to have you live at the manor for protection. Why would he say that?"

Roselyn shrugged, though even now she could remember the Spaniard's filthy hand covering her mouth. "Thornton is gone, and I can see that I was right not to marry him."

She couldn't bear the sympathy in the old man's eyes.

"My lady," he said softly, "will you tell me everything?"

She thought of the pouch that incriminated Spencer, of the dead body—of her own glad surrender.

"There's nothing to tell," she said, feeling only weariness as she tried to smile. Suddenly the thought of daily facing all the cottage's memories seemed too much for her.

"Very well, I'll come back with you to Wakesfield. I know you'll only worry if I don't."

Francis waited as she gathered a few belongings and then shut the door firmly behind her.

Later that afternoon, Roselyn worked alone in Wakesfield's kitchen, preparing mutton for dinner while Margaret and Charlotte worked in the garden. She kept her mind blank but for thoughts of the baking she had yet to do for her customers.

She heard the echo of a loud knock from the front hall, and wiped her hands on a towel as she moved through the dining chamber. When she opened the front door, she almost took a step back in surprise. A man stood there, dressed in a fashionable embroidered doublet, with padded trunk hose bulging at his hips. In one hand he held a riding whip, and nearby was a well-lathered horse, its head hanging.

She had never seen him before, and suddenly remembered the murmurs in the village about a stranger.

"Is your master at home?" he asked shortly.

She gave him a polite smile. "The viscount is not in residence, sir. Would you care to speak with his bailiff, Francis Heywood?"

He didn't return her smile as he brushed past her and stepped inside. "See to it."

She found Francis in his office, then bobbed a curtsy to the two men before leaving the front hall. But in the dining chamber, she put her back against the wall and remained to listen.

"How may I help you, my lord?" Francis asked.

"I understand a dead Spaniard was found in the village."

Roselyn winced and closed her eyes. The man didn't even introduce himself first, just got right to the point. Something was terribly wrong.

"Surely the soldiers at the garrison would be of better help to you than I, Sir . . ." Francis trailed off.

"I'm asking everyone, Heywood. How do you know the body was that of a Spaniard?"

"By the weave of his garments, my lord. He wore the clothing of a Spanish seamen. Other than that, there wasn't much left to identity."

"There was only one Spaniard?" The man's voice was impatient now.

"Only one body was found."

"That you know of."

His low voice made Roselyn shiver, and she held her breath.

"Is there something you wish to say, my lord?" Francis asked slowly.

"There have been reports that a Spaniard might have lived."

"Surely that would be difficult to hide."

"Perhaps. But a good spy could blend in."

She tilted her head back against the wall and squeezed her eyes closed. Could this be confirmation that Spencer was the traitor? Had he been in hiding because he knew they were after him?

She thought again of the Spaniard who had died before he could talk.

"I will continue the search," the stranger said. "What is the name of the next village to the south?"

"Bonchurch, my lord."

Something wasn't right, Roselyn argued to herself as Francis ushered the gentleman from the manor. Why send a nobleman after a spy?

Listening to Francis's footsteps disappear down the hall, she remained still, biting her lip, unsure of what to do.

If Spencer was a spy, he had already left to commit whatever treason he'd planned.

But if he was innocent, he was being followed by an enemy.

Sir Rodney Shaw mounted his horse and glanced once more at Wakesfield Manor, muttering a curse. What should he do now? Whatever trail there'd once been of Thornton was long gone.

At first he'd thought Thornton might have died after falling overboard, considering his injuries, so he'd ordered Rodriguez to swim to land and make sure he was dead.

Rodriguez was supposed to send word back through fishermen, but there'd been no reply. So when the Spanish fleet was scattered and fleeing up the French coast, Shaw had left the doomed expedition, found passage back across the channel, and come to Wight himself.

The incompetent Spanish would not be invading English soil, and Shaw had to make sure no one knew he'd been negotiating with both sides.

Had Rodriguez died that first night in the ocean? Then why had the body only been so recently found, considering the battle had been well over a fortnight ago? Had Thornton also made it to shore, then killed Rodriguez?

With another curse, Shaw kicked his horse into a gallop. He had to be certain of what had happened to Thornton. He would travel on to Bonchurch and ask his questions there.

Though he would prefer to kill Thornton himself, Shaw could only afford to wait so long. If it came down to a race to London, he wanted to be the first one there, to persuade the queen that Thornton had let his Spanish blood rule him—and that Thornton deserved to die a traitor's death.

Chapter 22

Roselyn felt Francis's scrutiny all through supper, and she wondered if he connected the stranger's warning about spies to Spencer. When she tried to retire early, he followed her to the staircase and drew her to a halt.

"Lady Roselyn, we should talk."

"Francis, could we do this in the morning?" She managed to sound as tired as she felt, and lifted her gaze to his with a silent plea. She couldn't explain without perpetuating her lies, and she didn't have the strength left for it.

Francis searched her face, then finally sighed. "Very well, my lady. After we break our fast, we will talk."

Roselyn leaned up and kissed his cheek, and suddenly she knew it would be the last for a long time. She ascended the stairs to her room, but she didn't turn the bed down, didn't remove her clothing. She only paced, her stomach tight with panic.

She had to find Spencer.

She would have to go out in the world, leave safety behind, take chances again. If he was guilty, she couldn't let the entire country pay for her foolishness in not turning him in.

And if he was innocent, he deserved to know that a man might be following him, thinking him a traitor. She owed him at least that.

It was time to confront him and learn the truth, though the thought of seeing him again after she'd surrendered her body made her ill.

She could no longer hide on her island and let the rest of the world's problems pass her by.

Long after midnight, when the house was silent, Roselyn crept down the staircase and left Wakesfield through the kitchen door. At her cottage she gathered supplies and the coins she'd saved, then looked down at the black gown she wore.

Slowly she unlaced it. The gown fell to her feet, and she folded it with infinite care, set it inside a chest, then picked up one of the plain brown garments she'd worn as a married woman.

Her hands suddenly started to shake, and she could barely slide it over her head. She was leaving behind everything she'd built of her new life. She might have nothing to come back to, for the Heywoods might never forgive her for leaving on so dangerous a journey without telling them.

Roselyn left the dark cottage behind, walking quickly, then soon running until she reached the graveyard. She collapsed on her knees before her baby's grave. She was so frightened—frightened of herself, frightened of taking another risk that might subject her to even more heartache.

With trembling fingers, she touched Mary's headstone and wondered forlornly if she was already with child. She began to cry with the pain of the life she'd chosen two years ago, the decisions she'd made.

What if she was making another poor choice—if running after Spencer only put her in even more danger? And if he turned on her . . .

The thought of beginning all over again, starting anew somewhere else alone, made the tears fall even faster down her cheeks.

But she alone had made the decisions that led to this crossroads in her life; she alone could make everything right again. There was no other choice.

She returned to the shed where she'd first hidden him and dug through the drying grass for the pouch. When she finally held it in her hands, she wondered whether it exonerated Spencer or incriminated him. She didn't know yet what she meant to do with it, but she couldn't leave it behind.

Soon she was astride Angel on the road to Cowes and the ferry that would take her to Southampton. It was the quickest way Spencer could have gone if he truly meant to travel to London.

And if he never arrived there?

Then she would know the rumors were true, and that he'd betrayed his country.

Spencer cursed his bad luck as he gulped another mouthful of ale. He could not start for London this night.

Yesterday he'd arrived in Cowes too late in the day to make the last ferry, and ended up wasting precious coin at an inn on the island.

Then he'd overslept out of exhaustion—he never would have guessed that putting in long hours on a horse could aggravate his leg so badly—and almost missed the first ferry across the Solents. It was a rough journey, and both he and his horse were wet and bruised by the time they made Southampton. He had no choice but to wait another day to give his horse time to recover. He spent the remainder of the afternoon watching drunk sailors chase less than virtuous women.

At least it kept his mind off Roselyn. Just thinking her name made him shudder with self-loathing. What was she doing now? What did she think of him? She must surely despise him for bedding and leaving her.

In such a morose mood, he had to force himself to stop drinking, lest tomorrow's trip be delayed while he recovered from a drunken stupor.

The waterfront inn left much to be desired, but the chamber he'd rented for the night seemed decent enough. He was about to head upstairs when the door opened and a small figure entered, well wrapped in a cloak.

It was hardly cool enough for such clothing, and out of boredom, he continued to watch from his bench in the corner. He could tell it was a woman by her walk and fragility, but he ignored the first warnings that rang in his head.

When she dropped her hood to speak with the owner, Spencer swiftly inhaled, then smothered a curse behind his tankard of ale.

Roselyn.

For just a moment a shot of pleasure moved through him, and he remembered her warm and naked in his arms, giggling against his chest like a woman who'd never known sorrow.

He shook his head to clear it. She could be nothing but a distraction to him now. He had tried to keep her safe, and she'd upset everything by following him. Surely she had brought along some of the Heywoods for protection.

But as she continued to talk with the innkeeper, no one else entered, and Spencer's anger simmered at an agitated pace.

She had followed him—alone? She was about to stay in this disreputable inn—alone? Didn't she realize what could happen to a woman on the road?

He took another swig of ale and glared at her from beneath lowered brows.

She carried only a small saddlebag with her, held against her side. The cloak dwarfed her, making her seem ridiculously small and fragile. She waited patiently at the bar, ignoring the boisterous men who called to her from various scattered tables in the tavern.

When the innkeeper returned Spencer couldn't hear what he said, but he saw Roselyn's shoulders slump momentarily before she straightened in obvious defiance. Perhaps there were no rooms to be had. What would she have done if he'd not been here? Slept out with her horse—or wandered the town alone looking for a place to stay? She deserved to see what a foolish mistake she'd made by following him.

So he remained quiet, keeping to the shadows. The innkeeper pointed to an empty table near the bar, and she primly seated herself, keeping her cloak about her like a shield between her and the men who leaned to get a better view of her.

She was the most obviously proper woman there, and stood out like the noblewoman she was, even in the plainest of garments. Her light brown hair was pulled tight beneath a plain white cap, but a few tendrils had fallen against her neck and one cheek, softening the severity she wore as protection. When the innkeeper wiped beer puddles from her table she gave him a grateful smile, and it was as if the room lit up with a hundred candles.

Spencer winced, because he was not the only one to notice. The remarks began soon enough.

"Come eat wit' me, miss. I be a lonely man."

"Surely ye need a chap to join ye."

"The seats all seem to be taken but at your table, miss."

Spencer sat up straighter, because the last voice sounded a bit too proper to be a Southampton sailor. The gentleman wore an expensive short cloak, and as he doffed his hat to Roselyn, his teeth gleamed in a knowing smile.

She didn't reciprocate. "I appreciate your offer, sir, but I prefer to eat alone."

There were hoots and jeers from the leering sailors, but what made Spencer tense was the fading smile on the gentleman's cold face.

Spencer slammed his tankard down on his table and got to his feet, with an appropriate sway for balance. "By the saints, woman," he roared, "ye didn't have to follow me!"

Roselyn's wide-eyed gaze fixed on him in shock as the tavern erupted with laughter. The gentleman remained at her side.

Spencer grabbed his cane and walked towards them. "I told ye I'd find a better place to stay than that roomin' house."

She inclined her head. "You were taking too long."

With a shrug, the gentleman turned toward the bar, and Spencer felt a bit of his tension ebb. Though he was pleasantly surprised at how well she'd taken up his story, it was still easy to give her a scowl.

"Well, I already got the room," he said. "Let's go."

"But I just ordered my meal—"

"The innkeeper will send it up." He took her elbow and practically pulled her out of the chair. He glanced at the innkeeper, who gave him a nod and eyed him with sympathy.

Spencer said nothing as he dragged her up to his garret room on the third floor, with the sloping roof on one side and a tiny fireplace on the other. He slammed the door, then turned Roselyn around and put her back against it.

She stared up at him, her eyes as gray as a cloudy day at sea. He knew he should yell at her, demand to know why she'd risked her life to follow him.

But instead he pressed her against the door and kissed her.

Chapter 23

Part of Roselyn melted inside at the delicious passion of Spencer's kiss, the weight of his body pressing her into the door. Another part of her wanted to bite his lip for his betrayal and for running away from her.

She pressed her hands against his chest to push him away, but it was like trying to move a wall. She was finally able to turn her head aside, and as she gasped for breath, she felt his lips nibbling on her ear.

"Spencer, stop this," she said with a stern voice, while visions of their joined naked bodies flashed through her mind.

"I'm trying, believe me," he murmured, his mouth on her throat.

"Not hard enough."

He gave a low chuckle. "But I'm already hard enough."

"Stop!" She ducked beneath his arm and whirled away to face him, her hands on her hips, fighting her own need to fling her arms around him. She had felt so alone all day—the only woman on the ferry, the only woman in the tavern—that just seeing him made her want to sink into him with relief. But she refused to give into such weakness.

Spencer picked up his cane and came toward her. She could see the dark clouds of anger rising in his black eyes.

"Roselyn, you should not have followed me," he said, wearing a thunderous frown.

"That kiss did not come from a man who wished I wasn't here."

He scowled. "What I wish I could have and what I deserve are two different things. Thank you for stopping me."

I didn't want to, a sly voice whispered inside her.

"You would have stopped yourself," she said. "After all, it was easy enough to take what you wanted from me and then leave without a word of explanation."

Spencer pierced her with his gaze. "I didn't mean it to be like that."

His low voice still sent shivers through her, and she had to fight the tears stinging her eyes. "Then how was I supposed to interpret it?"

He reached to cup her cheek. "I haven't stopped thinking about you since the moment I left your side."

"That comes from not having relations with a woman in at least a year."

Roselyn waited for him to deny it, but when she saw the pain in his eyes, she enveloped his hand with her own and held it tightly to her face. "Spencer, *tell me!*"

Across his face flashed more emotions than she'd ever seen from him. There was a war inside him, and she so wanted to be one of the victors. She held her breath, keeping his warm hand in hers, begging him with her silent gaze to finally tell her the truth.

"There is such danger to you," he whispered, drawing her up against him.

She looked up into his face, clasping his shoulders in her hands. "Please, tell me. I can't go on thinking what I'm thinking."

When he released her to pace away, she felt cold with fear. Did she really want to hear all of this? Could she even believe him after all his lies?

But he'd been worried about the danger to her . . .

He gave a tired sigh. " 'Tis a long story. Seat yourself and I'll try to explain."

There was only one stool, so he took that and she perched on the end of the bed.

"I'm not certain where to begin." He ran his hand down his bearded chin and closed his eyes.

Roselyn held her breath. Below her she could hear the boisterous noise of a party, while outside the open window came the clanging of bells from the docks. But when Spencer began to speak, all of that faded away beneath the images conjured by his words.

"This last year and a half, I've been a spy."

She closed her eyes and felt despair tighten her throat and sting her eyes.

"Before my father died, the queen approached him about sending one of his sons to Spain. Since I speak Spanish more fluently than Alex, he asked me to do the queen's bidding."

She opened her eyes, feeling hope flood through her. *The queen's bidding?*

"It gave me a reason to escape London; our botched wedding was proving too much to deal with."

When she tried to offer an apology, he raised a hand. "That's behind us now; let me finish. You have to understand what it felt like to be an asset because of my heritage, and not scorned. I thought maybe I could prove myself to everyone at court, to be of use for something besides a scandal."

"Oh, Spencer," she whispered. "I *do* understand what you mean."

"I sailed with Admiral Drake early last year, and while he raided the Spanish coast, I was left off near Cadiz. I spent the next year among the soldiers of the armada. They were a sad, desperate lot, with not enough food to eat or garments to wear. When we sailed up the English Channel, I had already planned to leave the ship near Wight, to bring my information to London. But on the journey, the other British spies began to turn up murdered."

Roselyn felt a lump of fear in her chest at the thought of what he must have gone through. But still, her doubts would not leave her.

"The murderer was Rodney Shaw, the last British spy but for me. On board ship, I discovered his plot to blame me for everything. He and his henchman beat me, but before they could kill me I threw myself overboard."

"And washed up on Wight," she murmured. His story fit perfectly—too perfectly? She didn't dare bring up the pouch. How could she hand it over if she wasn't certain of his loyalty—certain of him?

"Needless to say," he continued dryly. "You and I did not get along. At first I couldn't trust you with this—and then later I realized I couldn't put you in danger by telling you."

"But I was always suspicious," she said coolly. "When you were delirious, you spoke in Spanish."

"My mother is Spanish—why should this alarm you?"

"You wanted no one to know where you

were; you didn't even want me to send a message to your family."

"But—"

"And you wanted to remain with me, a woman you despised, in a humble cottage instead of at the grand manor you considered yours by betrothal contract."

"I never despised you," he said softly. "It just took me a while to get over my anger."

Spencer studied Roselyn's calm eyes by candlelight. She'd become a part of him, someone he would sense even in the dark, even when he was lost.

"You stayed in my cottage," she continued. "Why?"

"I couldn't risk being seen. The more people who knew where I was, the more danger I was in. And I must admit, I took some satisfaction in forcing my presence on you."

She arched one eyebrow. "And then the Spaniard came. Did you know him?" she asked softly.

Ah, she still had her doubts. But now that he was telling her everything, she *had* to believe him. She needed to understand the danger there could be for her in London; she needed to return to her island and let him finish the mission he'd begun.

"I knew who the Spaniard was. He was in the

employ of my enemy, Shaw. He was one of the men who held me while Shaw beat me."

She touched his arm, and he felt the shudder that moved through her. He put his hand on hers and she didn't pull away.

"Shaw sent the Spaniard to finish the task, but instead he hurt you," he said.

Though Spencer knew Roselyn didn't want his touch, he couldn't help sliding his arm around her waist, pulling her close. She didn't resist, nor did she relax against him.

He pressed his lips to her temple and closed his eyes, inhaling the smell of her, feeling the blood speed through his veins as he remembered her welcoming body beneath him in the garden. It had been so difficult to leave her, even though the danger to her frightened him.

He tilted her chin and loosened the clasp on her cloak. As it fell from her body, he noticed that her widow's weeds were gone.

He smoothed his hand up her waist, then gently cupped her breast. "You're wearing new garments."

He could feel her heart flutter near his fingers, felt the beat pick up and match pace with his own.

"These are for traveling," she countered, whispering.

Spencer watched her lick her dry lips; just the

sight of her pink tongue made him stir to life. His hand on her breast trembled, and he could no longer control the longing that swept through him. "You would have traveled more safely as a widow."

When she didn't answer, he tipped up her chin. Her wide eyes gazed at him, and her lips were parted with her rapid breathing.

"Are you finished with mourning, Rose?" he asked in a hoarse voice.

"No."

"Yes," he whispered, then leaned down to press his mouth to hers. Roselyn was trembling, ready to flee his embrace, or perhaps wanting to stay. It was as if he was being given one last chance to make amends the only way he knew how.

He gently parted her mouth with his tongue, willing her to receive him, to receive all of him. He stroked the roof of her mouth, her teeth, her tongue, each time probing deeper until her head was pressed to his shoulder, her body quivering in his arms. He slid his hands down her back and cupped her backside, pulling her hips hard against his.

He groaned, wanting to grind himself against her, to be a part of her, to surrender to these new feelings that swept through him.

Only Roselyn had ever made him feel like

this; only Roselyn could make everything else go away but the two of them.

With a little cry, she turned her head from his kiss and buried her face in his shirt.

"We must stop," she said haltingly.

He brought his hands back up to her breasts, caressing her through her clothing. "Rose—"

"But there is more you must know!" she cried, tipping her head back.

For just a moment he saw her hunger for the pleasure he could give. He let his thumbs rub her pointed nipples in little circles. "Tell me later," he whispered.

She broke away from him, bumping into the beams that supported the roof. "No, you must hear it all now. A man came looking for you yesterday."

Spencer felt as if he'd jumped headfirst into an icy pond as he stared at her flushed face. "Who was it? Did he ask for me by name? By God's precious soul, did he hurt you?"

"I am fine. He didn't give his name, and made me feel suspicious. After I brought Francis to him I hid nearby to listen. He never said your name outright, but he had heard about the dead Spaniard, and was looking for another Spanish spy. He left soon after."

Spencer sat down heavily on the stool and rubbed his hands down his face. Weariness crept over him, but he could not give in to weakness, not with Roselyn in harm's way. "You're certain he never said his name?"

"I'm certain. But he wore the clothing of a gentleman, not a soldier—which I found peculiar—and he had brown hair and an arrogant manner."

"It must be Shaw. Did he say where he was going next?"

"To ask questions in Bonchurch, farther south on the island."

"I was worried my broken leg would enable him to catch us, but there's still time—perhaps even a day or two," he said, swiftly coming to his feet. "I was going to send you back to Wight for your safety, but that would put you right into his path. We have to go—tonight."

Chapter 24

"Leave?" Roselyn protested. "But it's late! Surely dawn would be soon enough—"

"We can't risk it," he said, picking up her cloak and bundling it around her shoulders.

She felt like a little girl as he lifted her chin to attach the clasp.

"Here's your saddlebag," he said, handing the pack to her so quickly she almost dropped it. "I had not yet unpacked, so I'm ready."

She stared at the scabbard he strapped about his waist, the hilt gleaming dully in the candle-light.

"Spencer," she said, striving for a calm voice, "you need your rest. Surely your leg—"

"I've been resting since I arrived in Southampton this morn. I'll be fine, but will you?"

"You don't mind taking me with you?"

"I'll not send you back into the path of Shaw," he said grimly, grabbing her hand to

305

drag her while he limped down the stairs with his cane. "We need to put as much distance between us and him as possible. I only hope the horses are up to it."

As they reached the taproom, he slowed to a more moderate pace and motioned Roselyn before him.

"Just follow my lead," he whispered. As they entered the crowded room, he raised his voice. "But I tell ye, wife, 'tis a good chamber!"

She fixed a suitable frown on her face. "It's not large enough."

"But they don't 'ave more," he said, looking at the innkeeper, "do ye, sir?"

The man with the large apron over his belly shook his head. "That's the last."

"Well, it won't do," she said firmly. "Give the man the key. And I'll not be needing supper, either."

Grumbling, Spencer did as she asked.

Outside, his good-natured frown vanished, and he walked as fast as he could to the stables. Only when their horses were saddled and they were on the road did he seem to relax.

The night was dark and overcast with the threat of rain in the air, which made Roselyn sigh in resignation. The horses picked their way through the narrow, garbage-strewn streets of Southampton, and the occasional late night reveler stumbled out of their way.

Finally the road widened, and the trees encroached to the edges, and they left behind the comforting lights. Spencer slowed his horse until she caught up and rode beside him.

She sighed again. "I don't understand why we could not at least sleep for a few hours."

"If we'd stayed at the inn, I would not have given you the opportunity to sleep," he said in a low voice.

Even in the darkness, she felt smoldered by his glance, and a warm blush stole across her cheeks. She should be angry that he thought he could so easily seduce her again; instead she imagined that dark garret room beneath the eaves, a narrow bed, and the two of them entwined on it.

"But Rose, we also don't know how long Shaw kept looking for me on the island," he continued in a more sober voice. "If he reaches London first and tells the court his lies, how will they know whom to believe? 'Tis my word against his—and what if he's somehow concocted convincing proof?

"The sooner we get to London, the sooner I can have you safe in my home. My brother will take care of you while I see the queen."

"We'll need sleep at *some* point," she said with exasperation.

"Yes, and now Shaw can't be certain which road we'll take. I promise we'll make an early stop in the evening."

"You mean *tomorrow* evening?"

"Yes. But don't worry—if you fall asleep, I'll make sure you stay in the saddle."

Fine comfort that was, she thought irritably. They plodded along for several minutes, and Roselyn stole glances at him. She couldn't stop thinking about what he'd told her, wondering how she could know the truth.

"Spencer?"

"Hmm?"

"What was it like to spy against Spain?"

In the moonlight she saw the grim set of his mouth.

"Lonely."

She would have thought "dangerous" to be the first word he'd use.

"I had to pretend I was one of them," he said. "Sometimes I . . . lost myself, what it felt like to be Spencer Thornton. I had to become Miguel de Velasco, to think—even dream—in Spanish, for fear of making a mistake that could get me killed."

"It sounds terrible," she whispered, wishing she could lean across and hold his hand.

"The worst part was being able to trust no one. My assignment included very little contact with other British agents. My sole duty was to get myself aboard whatever fleet sailed for England, and to report on their ability to invade us."

"So you had no one to talk to for well over a year?"

Spencer looked down at where he gripped the reins. "My duty *was* to talk to people, to find out things. Along the way there were soldiers I worked beside, men who had no say in what their government did, who only wanted to survive."

"But no women," she said softly.

"No women." He gave her a bitter smile. "It would have been too dangerous—what if I somehow compromised my identity?"

He seemed so sad that Roselyn felt the need to lighten his mood. "So you gave up all your mistresses."

She thought his smile softened. "Yes, it was a hardship. I thought of them constantly, of course."

"Of course." She wished she could wholeheartedly believe his words. She wanted to comfort him, to take him into her arms and hold him through the dark night.

"You must know about loneliness," he said in a hesitant voice. "Since Grant and your baby died, you've deliberately kept yourself alone. Why?"

The old pain had mellowed, and she smiled wistfully. "You already understand the answer. 'Tis easier, isn't it? When you don't care about much, you have nothing much to lose."

"You cared about Philip Grant."

He didn't even ask it as a question.

"At the beginning, certainly, but not after that."

"But I thought he was what you wanted?"

"So did I. But it was all a ruse to obtain my dowry. After my parents disowned me, he became very bitter."

Spencer's stillness was loud. "Did he hurt you?"

"No, not how you think. But the absolute withdrawal of his affection hurt me worse than a blow. It had been what I cherished about him. I continued to work hard at his side to at least win his respect."

"Did you?"

She shook her head and gave a sad smile. "No. And when Mary was born, we were *both* a burden to him."

She felt strangely relieved to be saying the words.

"Tell me about her," he whispered.

She glanced at him. "I don't understand."

"I know she was young, but I would like to hear about Mary."

She stirred in the saddle, feeling confused, sad—but grateful. The Heywoods never mentioned her name, as a way to protect Roselyn, of course. Yet she had felt as if she was supposed to pretend Mary had never been born.

"She was a good baby," she began, and before she knew it, she was telling Spencer Thornton about Mary's smile.

By the time the sun dawned, Roselyn's backside ached with every movement of the horse. It had been two years since she'd regularly ridden, and she was paying for it now.

Yet she said nothing to Spencer, who with each mile grew more and more somber. He often looked over his shoulder and would give her a bracing smile when she caught him at it. He pushed their pace as hard as he dared, resting only when he felt the horses needed to.

She knew that it was worry for her rather than himself that drove him. It warmed her, yet made her feel terribly confused. He never complained that she was slowing him down, or that he was sorry she'd followed him. Although he was the one using a cane, he helped her from Angel's back whenever they rested, made sure she was comfortable before seeing to himself.

No one except for the Heywoods had ever treated her with such consideration, and it made her feel adrift in feelings she was afraid to explore.

By nightfall, even those thoughts were driven aside by bone-deep weariness. She would do anything to get off Angel, and when Spencer called a halt at a small inn in Guildford, she gladly tumbled into his arms and let him steady her.

With wobbly legs, she followed him to the stables, but he insisted on seeing to the horses himself while she watched. Again, he implied to the innkeeper that they were husband and wife, and she accepted it without even a twinge of guilt, her hand resting in his bent elbow as if it belonged there.

They would be in London on the morrow, and she could tell by Spencer's shadowed eyes that he dreaded it as much as he welcomed it.

They ate dinner quietly in their room, which had a tiny table before the hearth. But he ate little, and soon began to pace from the door to the window, as if he expected an attack at any moment.

There were enemies behind Spencer, and enemies before him, and Roselyn knew he would find no peace this night, or probably rest, either.

She suddenly knew what she would do, without a conscious decision.

She set the wooden tray of supper dishes outside their door, and locked it. Then she slowly began to unbutton her bodice. He did not notice what she was doing, and she felt nervous about his reaction as she shrugged the gown off her shoulders and let it fall, revealing the linen smock that hung to her knees.

Yet she also felt heady with the knowledge of what she meant to do, the chances she was ready to take. By following Spencer she'd once again become wild Roselyn, and she couldn't—wouldn't—stop now.

Chapter 25

Spencer must have sensed something, because he slowly turned and looked at her, his gaze heating as it moved down her body. Neither of them breathed.

With trembling fingers Roselyn loosened the laces of her smock, then let it slide down to the floor. He inhaled a breath that widened and lifted his chest, and the sweet softening of his gaze made her feel all strange and wobbly inside.

"Rose," he breathed, lifting a hand toward her.

She walked forward and placed her hand in his. They stood still, just a single candle flickering at the bedside table, their hands joined the way she so desperately wanted their bodies joined.

Spencer pulled her against him, and she gasped at the rough feel of his garments against her bare flesh. He caught her face between his hands and leaned down to kiss her, so softly, so gently, that she sighed her pleasure.

"Rose, are you sure?" he whispered against her lips.

In answer she spread the laces of his shirt and pressed her mouth against his chest. With a groan, he held her tight to him, and shuddered in her arms as she licked his nipples. How she savored the knowledge that she could affect him, how much pleasure she took in touching him!

Roselyn removed his garments one by one, then stepped again into his embrace, moaning at the heat of his skin down the length of her body. She looped her arms around his neck and stretched on tiptoes to kiss him. As his tongue joined hers, she felt a growing ache inside herself, a restlessness for more. She wanted to be one with his body, to feel a part of him.

Spencer gently pushed her backward onto the bed, holding her so she didn't fall. She held out her arms to him, but instead of lowering his weight onto her, he stretched out at her side.

She gave a little moan of disappointment and turned toward him, but he pressed her back onto the bed.

"We're here for the night," he murmured, leaning down to kiss between her breasts. "I promise not to rush this time."

She hadn't felt he'd rushed the first time he'd made love to her, but her protests died when

he closed his mouth over her nipple and suck-
led her.

A fierce burst of pleasure spread out through
her, and she stiffened beneath him. Over and
over he licked and kissed her, until her body
moved restlessly, no longer obeying her. He
turned to her other breast, and with a moan,
she ran her fingers through his soft hair and
held him to her.

His free hand caressed her hips, her thighs.
When he parted her knees, she thought he
would rise above her, but instead his fingers
teased the sensitive skin of her inner thighs,
moving nearer, nearer to the center of her, until
her body quivered with excitement and longing and uncertainty.

Suddenly his fingers slid into the curls between her thighs, and she stiffened at the wave
of passion that shimmered through her body.

"Easy," he murmured against her breast.
"You'll enjoy this."

Their gazes met, and his was filled with the
knowledge of what he could make her feel, if
only she'd let him. She relaxed, and was rewarded with the most exquisite feelings of
pleasure as he began to stroke her, his fingers
sinking inside her, then moving out again to
circle and tease and press.

Roselyn felt the buildup of such a mindless,

driving urgency that she was drowning in it, overwhelmed. Every caress of his tongue against her nipples, every probe of his fingers between her thighs, made her feel ever more desperate, ever more tense, until suddenly everything she was seemed to come apart in the most wonderful sensation of all. Only afterward, when she was trembling and sated, did she open her eyes.

Spencer's forearm rested against her chest, and his chin rested on that. His smile held warmth and humor and something else, something so soft and genuine she was afraid to think about it.

She blushed. "That was . . . that was . . ."

"Your first *real* experience with lovemaking," he said softly, giving her a crooked grin.

"I hadn't thought so, but . . . I guess you're right. I didn't know I could . . . feel that way."

"Might *I* feel that way now?" he asked, his voice growing husky.

She smiled and put her arms around him. "Oh yes, please."

But instead of rising above her, he rolled onto his back. "Come here."

"I don't understand," she whispered as her gaze strayed down his candlelit body.

"Come up on your knees and straddle me," he said.

Roselyn felt awkward and silly, but she did as he asked, then caught her breath as she settled against his erection. His soft groan affected her as much as if he'd caressed her. Then he did, reaching up to cup and play with her breasts. Between her legs, he throbbed and seemed to grow even larger, and she again felt the shudder of rising desire.

"Guide me inside you," Spencer said, his voice strained.

When she lifted her hips up and touched him, she didn't know what she'd expected. He was certainly hard, but the skin itself was soft and hot. For a moment, she let herself explore down his shaft.

"This is lovely," he said tightly, "but if I'm not inside you soon I shall explode, and that is not nearly as much fun."

Smothering her laughter, she did her best to guide him between her legs. She wasn't sure if she was in the right position until he grabbed her hips and pulled down, sheathing himself inside her.

With a gasp, she fell forward and rested her hands on his shoulders.

"Are you all right?" he whispered.

Roselyn looked down into his eyes, narrowed and dark with passion, and felt raw power held quiescent beneath her, at her mercy.

She lifted her hips and sank back down. His eyes closed and he shuddered.

"Did I hurt you?"

"God, no," he said hoarsely. "Please, please continue."

She smiled with pleasure and satisfaction, and he gave her a wary look.

"Be gentle with your servant, my lady."

She leaned down until their lips almost brushed. Up close, she watched his face again as she lifted and lowered her hips. He arched beneath her, and she felt him so deeply inside her that aching wonder shook her.

"Spencer," she whispered, then pressed gentle kisses to the corner of his lips, to his cheek, even to his eyelid. He was so precious to her that tears stung her eyes at the beauty of her blossoming feelings for him.

For a moment dark thoughts intruded, as she wondered how long it could last, but she pushed them aside and took control of their lovemaking, riding him until he cried out her name and shuddered beneath her. Roselyn fell down into his embrace and rested atop him, feeling him beneath her, inside her.

Finally she slid off him and lay at his side. He turned in her embrace, pillowing his head against her shoulder as she slid her arms about him. She brushed his hair back from his face.

His eyes were closed, his long, dark lashes resting on his cheeks.

She wanted to question him about their journey, about their relationship, but before she could work up the courage he gave a soft snore. She smiled, feeling warm and peaceful and strangely grateful, as she continued to stroke his hair.

"You were the first man to kiss me," she whispered.

He didn't react to her words except to snuggle his head against her and pull her more tightly to him. His face seemed open and vulnerable in sleep.

She felt braver now. "You were the first man to care for me." Then softer: "My betrothed."

She pulled the blankets up over them both and fell quickly to sleep.

Before dawn, Spencer awoke as if swimming up from deep water. At a level just below true consciousness, he remembered the words Roselyn had whispered as he'd fallen asleep.

She'd never been kissed.

What kind of monster had that stable groom been? When she had lost everything in her gamble for happiness, had he only punished her?

Spencer opened his eyes and looked down at where she cuddled at his side. He'd already known she'd never experienced pleasure in her husband's bed. As he imagined how unpleasant sex must have been for her, he felt a strange ache in his chest. He wished he could have kept the pain from her, that he could remove all those ugly memories.

He smoothed her hair back from her cheek, and just the sight of her sweet face made his heart come to pieces in worry for her. Had he brought her deeper into danger?

He realized then that he loved her.

The thought made him all the more terrified for her safety. Aye, he loved Roselyn, loved her bravery in choosing her own life and living with her decisions, no matter the outcome.

He cursed himself for not even bothering to get to know his betrothed, to see how they might have made the best of their parents' command. He had not thought a woman could love him, and was still uncertain if Roselyn did.

He slid his hand down her warm stomach. He ached for her that she'd been a mother so briefly. Even now she could be carrying *his* child.

What if they executed him for treason? Roselyn and their child would be banished, outcast, and it would all be his fault.

How could he tell her he loved her, when he might be dead soon? Better she hate him and think he used her, than to know he'd gone to his execution loving her.

But he was still a weak, selfish man, and he woke her as he wanted to wake her, caressing her body to welcoming life, then forgetting his sorrows briefly in the shelter between her thighs.

Afterward, Spencer washed quickly in the cold basin. It was difficult to keep his mind on the day when Roselyn lay warm and dreamy on the pillow they'd shared.

She laughed softly. "Your body tells me you're not ready to leave my bed."

"This freezing water will soon change that." He limped to his saddlebag and changed into fresh garments. "I'll bring you food, my lady. Be up and about when I return."

"Stop calling me that," she murmured.

He could see the blush that flowed from her face down her neck. "How far does this lovely rose color go?" he asked, peeking beneath the blankets, then planting a kiss between her breasts as she laughed. "Right to there, I'll wager. Any lower?"

"Spencer!"

"Ah, I guess this is not the time for exploring. And you *are* a lady," he added soberly. He wanted to say "my lady," but knew it might hurt her in the end.

After they'd broken their fast, he handed her a dagger and scissors he'd borrowed from Francis.

"What are these for?" Roselyn asked warily.

"I need you to cut my hair and beard."

"But why?"

Her frightened eyes made him ache to reassure her, and he smiled to hide the knot of grief gripping his chest. "I need to enter London as myself, to prove that I have nothing to hide."

She trimmed his hair and beard, and he took a sharp knife to the whiskers left on his face. He'd been wearing that beard for well over a year. As he looked into the cloudy hand mirror, he could see that his skin was paler where the beard had been.

He suddenly felt more like himself, more confident that he could convince the queen and her government that he had only done their bidding.

He definitely enjoyed Roselyn's startled look as she studied his face, and the blush that she tried to hide.

As the sun set and the sky reddened across long fingers of clouds, Roselyn rode beside Spencer into the narrow streets of Southwark on the southern bank of the Thames, where she and Philip had lived. Returning reminded her how much she hated London, from the traitors' heads mounted in warning on London Bridge, to the rats and refuse overflowing the trenches in the center of every street.

In London itself she had always ridden by carriage, but as a resident of Southwark she had walked everywhere. Now, mounted on a horse, she felt the overhanging floors of the houses pressing in on her. She'd forgotten the smells of a crowded town, forgotten the constant noise of vendors calling, "Hot apples," or "Fresh herrings," and the never-ending sound of hammer on metal.

Everywhere people pressed in on her, startling Angel. Roselyn wanted to crawl into Spencer's lap and let him hold her, but that would be cowardly. So instead she concentrated on him, on the stunning face revealed under his beard. His handsomeness awed her.

He ducked beneath a tavern sign, then rode down a narrow alley. She tapped Angel's flanks to catch up with him. A courtyard and garden opened up behind the tavern, with a crowded stable for guests' horses.

"This is it," Spencer said, dismounting, then limping over to help her to the ground. "I know the owner well. We'll leave the horses here and continue across the Thames by wherry."

"Why by boat?"

He put his arms around her and nuzzled her ear. "Because my home is best approached that way."

"Of course," she breathed, suddenly excited

and nervous to see his home. Surely if he were guilty, he would have fled London, not shown his clean-shaven face and taken her proudly to his family.

She knew then that she trusted him, that he was telling her the truth. Wouldn't a man being chased by his enemy run the other way, instead of facing his accuser? She would give Spencer the pouch, in hopes that it would help him make everything right, and then they would have plenty of time to discuss their life together.

After he had made arrangements to temporarily stable their horses, they moved off through Southwark, picking their way through the garbage on the streets.

"Where are we going?" Roselyn asked as she clutched his hand and balanced her saddlebag with the other.

"To the river. I think the best place to hire a wherry is down this street."

"No, this way," she said, veering opposite the way he meant to go. "I lived near here."

She saw his face pale, then he put his arm around her and gave her a fierce hug.

"You're a brave woman," he said hoarsely, "but I still say this is the street."

She tugged on his hand. "But I'm certain—"

Her voice faded away as three dangerous-looking ruffians emerged from the shadows of an alley behind Spencer. Spencer's own face was wiped of all emotion just as a man's hand gripped her elbow and yanked her back against him. Her nose felt assaulted by the smell.

"Gentlemen," Spencer said smoothly, wearing an amused expression. "I suggest you let the lady go and be on your way."

The hand gripping her elbow only tightened, and a rumbling voice said, "We'll be takin' yer purse, man. The odds be four to one, eh?"

Spencer swiftly brought his cane up hard, cracking it against the temple of one of the brigands, who promptly collapsed into a sewage-filled trench.

"Three to one," Spencer said.

Chapter 26

Two of the brigands grabbed Spencer, and Roselyn screamed as the third covered her mouth. She tasted dirt and beer and something so vile she wanted to gag.

Though she fought, the man dragged her down a dark alley. The last she saw of Spencer, he had pulled the sword from its scabbard, and was threatening one man while trying to dislodge the other who had an arm wrapped around his neck.

Though tears of despair fell from her eyes, she forced herself to remember the pattern of the muddy streets, growing narrower and darker the farther from the riverbank they went.

She had the saddlebag with her, and began to fear that the letter Spencer so desperately needed might be taken from her. Was he even alive to care? She couldn't give up hope yet.

The thief's hold had weakened slightly, as if

he believed her powerless. She desperately lifted her foot and kicked backward. She missed his groin, and hung off balance by one arm until he whirled her around toward him. He was laughing as she met his gaze, and she lifted her free hand and raked her nails down his face.

With a hoarse scream, he let her go and covered his eyes. She ran, clutching the saddlebag to her chest, darting down twisting, narrow streets and dodging people until her lungs burned.

Only when she believed she'd lost him did she slow down. If she returned immediately to Spencer, the two remaining thieves could still overpower them both.

But if she had help . . .

It took her a while to regain her bearings, but soon she was trudging through familiar streets. She knocked on the door of her friend's home, a woman who'd sold fresh fish from a cart near Philip's bakery. If only the family hadn't moved.

The door was opened by a shabbily dressed man.

"George?" she whispered, then looked beyond him to see his brother Walter and George's wife. "Ann?"

By the light of one guttering candle, she saw

four tiny children watching her from behind the woman's brown skirts.

George gave her a gap-toothed grin. "Be that you, Roselyn?"

She nodded happily, and he gave her a hug that lifted her from her feet. When he let her go, Ann turned her around and wrapped warm arms about her.

"Roselyn, when did ye return to London? Why did ye not tell us ye was comin'? And where is Philip and sweet Mary? Surely the babe must be—"

Something in her face must have made Ann stop.

"Ann," she said gently, "Philip and Mary died of the Black Death soon after we left London."

Ann's eyes widened and filled with tears as she took Roselyn's hands. "Oh, my dear," she began.

" 'Tis all right. I've been living on the Isle of Wight, earning my living by baking. But I just returned to London today with—"

By the saints, Spencer could be unconscious—or worse—right now!

She whirled around to face the brothers. "I need your help. My companion and I were attacked on the street, and I don't know how he fares. We must find him!"

"But Roselyn—" Ann said.

Roselyn gave her a quick hug. "I promise I'll return and tell you everything on another day, but I must go to Spencer. He could be badly wounded."

The return journey was undertaken with the creeping approach of darkness, guided by the occasional guttering lantern hung outside a shop door.

Spencer was not where she'd left him—and a fresh patch of blood stained the ground.

Roselyn resisted the urge to imagine the worst. Where could he have gone? If the brigands had killed him, surely he'd still be lying in the street—

An icy calmness doused her mounting terror as she turned to George. "If the watch had taken him, where would he be?"

"One of the prisons be not far away," he said slowly. "We'll take ye back to Ann first, and then do yer lookin' for ye."

"We must check the tavern where we stabled our horses. He could be there."

By midnight, Roselyn realized that Spencer had completely disappeared from Southwark. She tried to convince the men that he had gone home, but George refused to hire a wherry at this time of night, insisting that his brother Walter would row her across in the morning. Besides, he said, London at night was no place to

be, what with the Spanish out there somewhere, waiting to attack. She just shook her
head and closed her eyes.

She sat beside the small hearth, trying to pay
attention to Ann's reassuring words, while desperately wishing that morning would come.

When Rodney Shaw arrived in London close
to midnight, the third horse he'd used in the
last two days almost collapsed beneath him.
But what was another horse, compared to ar-
riving in time for Lord Forman's party? Every
noble family would be represented—perhaps
even the queen, the old bitch, would deign to
come.

Shaw himself would be seen by all those who
mattered. Although only the government knew
of his mission to spy on Spain's armada, he
would make certain he hinted in a few noble-
men's ears where he'd been this last year.

Nothing would stop him from convincing
the government that Thornton was the traitor-
ous spy.

And when the queen bestowed her favor and
a prestigious title on him, even Shaw's mother
would be invited to the ceremony, which
would please her endlessly.

His mother had done her duty to further
both of their ambitions. She'd sent missives to
inns and taverns along the coast, telling him the

exact day and time of Forman's ball, so that wherever he landed on English soil he'd be prepared.

When Shaw arrived at Forman's estate on the Thames in Westminster he had no formal invitation, but the gardens near the river overlooked tall, wide doors he could easily slip through. The great hall sweltered with heat and too much perfume, while the expensive garments worn by both men and women glittered in the candlelight.

He knew his clothing was stained from travel, and caught the disapproving eye of many guests, but on the morrow all would know he was a hero. No one would dare look askance on him again—they would pay him the deference he deserved.

But for now, he contented himself by wandering the great hall and the surrounding parlors. He came to a halt on the edge of the dance floor, stunned to see Spencer Thornton partnering a woman in the dance. Thornton had been too injured to have reached London before him! Had he already spoken to the queen? Was Shaw even now about to be arrested?

As Shaw stood there, feeling the first clawing of terror, the dance brought Thornton close to him. Their eyes met and Shaw stiffened, his mind racing for the words he'd use to throw

Thornton's inevitable accusations back in his face.

But Thornton merely looked down at the stunning woman in his arms and whispered something in her ear. She giggled and patted his chest as if chastising him. Then they were gone, swallowed in a sea of dancers.

Shaw was engulfed with uneasy bewilderment. Could Thornton have a plan that even now he was setting in motion?

Shaw had survived too much to give up so easily, had risked his life to become indispensable to two countries. He had only one country left, and he would not abandon the dreams he and his mother shared. He would see her in the finest silk as she deserved, the mother of a true nobleman.

He left the party as quickly as he could, determined to go to Sir Francis Walsingham, the state secretary who'd recruited him and Thornton to spy on Spain.

And he wouldn't wait until morning.

As dawn lightened the sky, Roselyn sat in a damp boat on a wooden seat facing Walter, who rowed upstream through the foggy mist. Holding her saddlebag in her lap, she concentrated on remembering which home was Spencer's.

She had seen it only once, when her family's barge had sailed past, and her mother had pointed it out with greedy pride. She could only pray Spencer had arrived there safely.

They glided past the tall, crowded buildings on the northern bank, dodging other boats and barges carrying passengers from farther upstream, hearing the occasional watermen's cry of "Eastward ho!" or "Westward ho!" Soon the riverbanks became open stretches of well-groomed land, with archways standing sentinel before elaborate gardens. Many wealthy homes had steps rather than docks leading to the Thames.

Walter was almost certain he knew where the Thornton estate was, and he guided the wherry up against the steps. Through the arched gate, she could see a two-story manor in the distance, white stone with darker edging.

She looked at Walter uncertainly as he took off his cap and rubbed the top of his balding head.

"I be waitin' a bit for ye, mistress. You come back if it be the wrong house."

When she tried to pay him for his service, he refused, and she gave him a grateful smile.

Roselyn stepped out of the wherry, straightened her shoulders, and started up the steps. The stone walkway leading up to the house was deserted, and she began to feel uneasy. The gardens looked slightly unkempt, drooping in the early morning mist. The walk seemed to take forever, as the manor loomed larger and larger. When she knocked on the front door, the echo sounded cavernous—as if through an abandoned house. She waited a long time before a maidservant finally opened the door.

The girl yawned and leaned against the door frame. "A bit early, ain't it, luv?"

Roselyn blinked in surprise and tried to reserve her judgment. Spencer had told her that his brother was taking care of everything for him, but much about this estate was amiss.

"Forgive me for intruding," she began, "but is your master in attendance?"

The girl smirked. " 'Course he is, but surely ye don't expect him to be up and about at this hour."

Roselyn's relief almost staggered her, and she braced her hand on the door. Spencer was home and well, not lying injured in some hovel in Southwark—or worse. "I need to see him. It is extremely urgent."

The maidservant rolled her eyes. "I bet it is, luv. Wait here and I'll see what I can do."

Before Roselyn could react, the girl shut the door in her face. She fumed for endless moments until she finally realized that she'd been abandoned.

Holding her breath, she lifted the latch and

pushed the door inward. No sound greeted her, not the murmur of servants' voices nor the clinking of pots somewhere distant in the kitchens. It was as silent and empty as any monument to wealth.

She hurried up the broad stone staircase to the second floor, then stared in dismay at the long line of closed doors. When she found an imposing set of double doors, she slowly swung one open and peered in. The draperies were closed, letting in only murky light. An enormous four-poster bed occupied the far wall, with bed curtains tied back to the posts and a mound of rumpled sheets and blankets and satin coverlet in the center.

Roselyn closed the door behind her and tiptoed toward the bed, where a man's head was buried beneath pillows.

"Spencer?" she whispered, then hesitantly lifted a pillow.

She could see black hair draped across a slumbering face whose contours she'd memorized by sight and touch.

Relief made her tremble as tears filled her eyes.

"Spencer," she whispered, reaching down to shake his naked shoulder.

He gave a little groan and turned away from her.

She frowned, wondering how he could sleep

so deeply. Wasn't he just as frantic about her disappearance as she'd been about his?

She shook him harder. His eyelids fluttered, then he rolled onto his back and shaded his eyes as if bright light had suddenly pierced the gloom.

Roselyn just smiled at him, and he slowly smiled back.

"Good morning," he said softly.

"Spencer, I was so worried," she began, kneeling on the edge of the bed. She reached out and brushed the hair from his face, then allowed her fingers to stroke his cheek. "When I couldn't find you, I—" She pressed her lips together and struggled not to cry.

"Shh," he whispered, drawing her down to lie against his side. " 'Twill all be fine now that you're here."

Safe in his arms, sheltered in his big bed, she allowed herself to relax. He grinned and came up on his elbow, then leaned over to gently kiss her lips. With a sigh, she slid her hands up into his hair and held him to her, slanting her open mouth across his, suddenly hungry for the taste of him. Though they had been separated for only one day, it seemed a lifetime.

But . . . something was wrong. Spencer's kiss was different—even his weight pressing her into the bed was wrong.

She twisted her head aside, and he trailed

kisses down her cheek. "Spencer," she said sternly, "look at me."

"Oh, I've looked, believe me," he murmured against her ear.

She pushed at his shoulders until he propped himself on his elbows above her, grinning down in a carefree manner that made her fears grow.

"Something is wrong," she said slowly.

As her gaze wandered down his chest, she gave a sudden gasp and put her hands where a scar should be—but wasn't.

Before her shocked mind could comprehend, the door opened, and a worried voice said, "Roselyn?"

The voice was Spencer's—and he still wore Philip's old garments and a bemused expression.

Roselyn gaped at the identical face grinning down at her in the bed.

Chapter 27

The man who looked like Spencer—but wasn't—tugged her closer. She gave him a quick elbow to the stomach, and as he collapsed with a groan, she rolled out of bed and onto the floor.

Spencer was immediately there to pick her up and draw her into his arms, and while she clung to him, she stared at the other man, now lounging back against the pillows and watching her beneath half-lowered lids.

"Spencer, you said you had a brother," she finally said, "but you never said he was your twin."

Spencer squeezed her tighter. "It never came up. This is Alex—who'd better keep his hands to himself from now on. Roselyn, I've been so worried! Where have you been? How did you escape?"

She still frowned at his brother. "But I called you Spencer, and you didn't correct me!"

"*I've* been Spencer more often during the last two years than he has, apparently. It didn't even occur to me to correct a beautiful woman for such a simple mistake, not when you were so . . . concerned for me. I just wanted a little brotherly kiss."

At his wicked grin, she felt a blush of mortification suffuse her cheeks. She leaned back in Spencer's embrace and looked up at him. "I thought he was you—"

Spencer sighed and framed her face with his hands. "Do not apologize. Alex has always enjoyed pretending to be other than he is."

"And you have not?" Alex scoffed. "We were both always so good at pretending—'tis what landed us so secret a mission."

"Us?" Spencer echoed.

Alex spread his arms wide. "But it was so treacherous and difficult to pretend to be you—especially after that scandal of your interrupted wedding."

Roselyn stiffened and Spencer shot his brother a frown.

Alex's eyebrows rose. "Ah, so you are *that* Roselyn."

"And there have been so very many Roselyns?" she teased Spencer.

"Of course not," he said gruffly.

Alex smiled. "Maybe not for you then, but now . . ."

Roselyn could not keep her gaze from straying to Spencer's brother. Though their faces were identical, Alex wore his hair shorter, swept back off his face to reveal a pearl earbob dangling from one ear.

"So you were the 'Spencer' behind every scandal that reached my ears," she said slowly.

"Only the recent ones," Alex answered with a grin. "Before that, Spence managed all his own scandalizing."

"Roselyn," Spencer murmured against her hair, "I'm sorry I did not warn you about my brother. But tell me now how you escaped? I searched for you for hours, thinking—God, I cannot bear to repeat what I was thinking."

He shuddered against her and she held him tighter.

"I came here to recruit men and organize a wider search," he continued. "Then I began to hear that someone had been searching for me, and I left messages for you—" He glared at his brother. "And *you* were off at another party, and were no help to me at all!"

Alex straightened. "And how was I to know you'd returned?"

"Spencer," Roselyn interrupted, "I was lucky enough to escape the thief and find friends in Southwark."

He heaved a sigh and held her even more tightly. "I'm so glad you're well," he whispered, and the hoarseness of his voice made a sweet ache tug on her heart.

"By the time we returned for you, you were gone." She closed her eyes and let the feelings she'd denied flood her mind.

She loved Spencer.

There could be no other reason for this trust she now placed in him without proof, no other reason that she'd felt like giving up if she lost him. He'd had the courage to answer his country's call, even when he'd been hurting. He had kept his humor and charm, even when he thought he might die.

Roselyn was back at the beginning, giving her heart to a man and hoping he could be trusted. But Spencer was not Philip Grant, and she was no longer the immature girl who reacted angrily when she didn't get her way. Spencer was now a part of her, body and soul. She loved him.

"We're both fine now," he said softly, and she clung to him with gratitude to God for keeping him safe.

Alex pointedly cleared his throat. "My turn for answers. So you're alive, Spence. I was beginning to wonder."

As Spencer faced his brother, Roselyn stayed beneath his arm, at his side. She realized that this was the first time the brothers had seen each other in well over a year. But there were no hugs, no warm greetings. She sensed a wariness between them.

Spencer briefly told his brother everything that had happened to him as a British agent, as well as Roselyn's encounter with Rodney Shaw.

Alex's frown deepened and he rested his head back against the pillow. "So this Shaw is going to claim that you murdered all those British spies, and you're going to claim that he did it."

" 'Tis not a claim," Spencer said tightly. "I saw it—and he tried to do the same to me."

"But if you can't prove it, you'll lose your head at Tower Hill."

"How kind of you to remind me."

Alex swung his legs over the bed and stood up, wrapping the sheet about him with such obvious practice that Roselyn didn't even have time to be embarrassed.

"And because I aided you in this deception," Alex continued coldly, "This could very well be a twin execution."

Leaning on his cane, Spencer stepped in front of Alex. "Do not worry yourself, brother. The queen knows how small your part in this has been. If anyone loses his head, it will be me."

"Gentlemen," Roselyn quickly said, stepping between them, "we have a problem to solve, and I think I know just how to do it."

But before she could procure the Spanish letter, they heard a sudden pounding, then the splintering of wood. The brothers looked briefly at each other, before Alex dropped his sheet and reached for his clothes.

With a gasp, Roselyn covered her eyes.

"Sorry, but I'm not going to meet our guests quite so exposed," Alex said.

In the distance, they heard a maidservant's cry, then the pounding of booted feet on the stairs. Spencer suddenly grabbed her arms and held her still.

"Do not say a word to them," he said urgently.

"But who is it?"

"Probably soldiers. You are not a part of this and I will not have you endangered."

"But Spencer, I have something to tell you!"

Before any more words could leave her mouth, the door was thrown open and the room was suddenly full of soldiers wearing plated brigantine and waving muskets and pikes. Spencer shoved her behind him, and she wanted to scream when he was pulled from her and forced to his knees while they bound him from behind.

"On whose authority do you imprison me?" Spencer demanded.

"By Her Majesty's authority, my lord," said one of the soldiers. "You're to be held for questioning."

Alex, wearing only a shirt and wide, loose breeches over his hose, was similarly restrained. "Let me at least put on my boots," he said with a growl.

"*I* am Spencer Thornton," Spencer said. "You want me, not my brother."

Although Alex shot Spencer a speculative look, the captain merely said, "We cannot tell the difference between you. Better that we make a small mistake than a large one."

Roselyn stood beside the bed, clutching one of the tall posts, wondering if the queen had turned against Spencer. She felt useless, able only to cower like a weak woman while the brothers were led toward the door.

"Where are you taking them?" she demanded.

She immediately regretted her bravery when more than one soldier turned her way. Spencer looked over his shoulder, giving her a narrow-eyed warning.

"Lord Thornton has a broken leg!" she said. "Please, at least take his cane."

To her utter surprise, the soldier holding Spencer motioned to another, who picked up the cane from the floor.

They pulled him toward the hall, but came up short as a small woman blocked their way. She was dressed in a fine black gown, and her gray hair was neat beneath a smart black cap and veil. Though Roselyn couldn't see Spencer's face, his entire body became rigid.

"*Madre*," he said simply, with a short nod of his head.

This formidable woman had obviously faced too much in her years in England to be cowed by mere soldiers. In a lightly accented voice, she said, "You heard the young lady. Where are you taking my sons?"

As the company of soldiers moved past her, escorting Spencer and Alex from the room, their leader said, "They go to the Tower, my lady, where we take all traitors."

The fear that spread through Roselyn was like a slow death in icy water, but she had sworn to herself that no longer would she hide away from the real world. She would take chances, brave danger—anything to free Spencer.

She lifted up her skirts and began to run, catching up with the company of soldiers as they reached the door leading to the gardens. She clutched the door frame and called, "Spencer!"

He looked over his shoulder, as the soldiers pulled him toward the river.

"I can help you!" she cried. "Trust me!"

"No!" He turned toward her, but was dragged backward. "This is my battle and I will win it. Go back to Wight—go back to John. Stay safe!"

She stood in the doorway long after the soldiers had loaded Spencer and his brother onto a barge. Though she knew he was only trying to protect her, his words still angered her, as if after all the intimacies they'd shared, she would abandon him.

With a sigh, she finally closed the door, then turned and found the hall scattered with servants watching her with expressions ranging from disgust to interest to amusement.

She lifted her chin, hoping they'd disperse without her insisting on it. But they continued to stare until an older gentleman smartly attired in blue and gold livery stepped forward.

"I think it is time you left, mistress," he said calmly.

"Left?" she repeated, using the haughtiest tone learned from her mother. "I have business here."

"I am quite certain the master no longer needs your particular business."

He thought she was a harlot! Before she could defend herself, a woman's voice called, "Hold!"

Spencer's mother stood at the top of the stairs, as regal and unsmiling as the queen. Roselyn felt a tremor of worry, imagining how

she would explain her actions to the viscountess.

"Young lady," Lady Thornton said, "I believe we have met before, but your name
eludes me."

Roselyn walked forward and stopped at the
foot of the stairs. "I am Roselyn Harrington
Grant, my lady."

There was a moment of tense silence, and she
was certain that Lady Thornton must be feeling
nothing but hatred for her.

Lady Thornton glanced at the man who'd
asked Roselyn to leave. "Allbright, please have
the servants return to their work. See to it that
within two days this house is as I last saw it."

There was a sudden flurry of movement, and
the hall was soon deserted but for Roselyn and
Lady Thornton. Roselyn remained still, waiting
for anger and condemnation as Spencer's
mother descended the stairs, but the older
woman only said, "Please walk with me, Lady
Roselyn."

With Roselyn silent at her side, the viscountess toured the hall as if she'd never seen it before. It was difficult for Roselyn to hold her
peace when she wanted to blurt out the danger
Spencer was in and beg for Her Ladyship's
help.

Lady Thornton came to a halt before a recessed shelf set in the wall, lit with candles. Proudly on display was the statue of her naked son—with wings.

Lady Thornton shook her head. "*Madre de Dios*, but he makes it like the shrine of a saint, does he not?"

Roselyn couldn't help the smile that tugged at her lips. "I think it was done in pride and jest, my lady. I understand that Alex presented it to Queen Elizabeth, though it seems the queen did not wish it displayed long."

She was beginning to realize who was the truly scandalous twin.

"You seem to know much about my sons, for someone who wanted no part of this family."

"I have only met Alex today, my lady, but I have spent much time with Spencer this last month."

"I did not know he had returned from Europe," Lady Thornton said, eyeing Roselyn with narrowed dark eyes. "Perhaps you would care to tell me what led to this . . . injustice."

Roselyn told Lady Thornton about Spencer's mission, and how he had recovered from his injuries on the Isle of Wight. She left out the details of their new relationship.

Lady Thornton had brought her into a drawing room during the explanation, and both now sat upon cushioned chairs. "I knew some of what Spencer was involved in, because I insisted Alexander reveal it."

Roselyn smiled.

"For one day only, Alexander pretended to be his brother in front of me. As if I would not know the difference between my own sons," Lady Thornton sniffed. "Alexander told me that Spencer was performing a secret duty for the queen, but spared me the true extent of the danger. I preferred to continue my mourning in Cumberland, but weeks ago Alexander sent for me to keep me 'safe,' or so he claimed, should England be invaded. But I believe he felt guilty, because Spencer made him promise to visit me often, and it usually . . . slipped his mind."

She wore a faint, amused smile, and Roselyn saw the love she bore her sons.

"Lady Thornton, if you have no more questions for me, I must journey to the Tower. I might have evidence to convince the queen that Spencer is innocent."

"Of course he's innocent," Lady Thornton said, waving a hand dismissively. "But first I must know why you followed him to London."

"But I already told you about Rodney Shaw. He could be in town already. I must—"

"No, there is another reason."

Again Roselyn felt the power of penetrating black eyes, so like Spencer's, and she shifted uncomfortably.

"Two years ago you broke the betrothal contract rather than marry my son."

Roselyn stiffened. "Yes, my lady."

"Why do you help him now?"

"We both had done things we regretted then. I knew Spencer didn't love me, and his treatment of me . . ." She trailed off, hesitating to offend his mother.

"Was abominable," Lady Thornton finished with conviction. "And I could not understand why. His father and I raised him to respect women, and his reluctance to marry made no sense to us."

"I think I finally understand it," Roselyn said. "He never thought he could have the kind of marriage you and his father had. He implied to me that his heritage often left him feeling that no woman would want him. He had no way to tell you this without hurting you, so he . . ."

"He hurt you instead," Lady Thornton whispered.

Roselyn saw the sheen of tears in those proud eyes.

"But you have forgiven him?" Lady Thornton asked.

"Yes."

"Do you love him?"

"Yes," Roselyn said without hesitation.

The older woman relaxed her shoulders the slightest bit. "Does my son love you?"

"He has not spoken the words, my lady, so I cannot say for certain. He is too conscious of the danger to you and Alex, and to me."

"Very well. We will worry about this matter at another time," Lady Thornton said in a firm voice.

Roselyn thought she might be hiding a smile, and felt herself warm to this woman who loved her husband and sons so much she braved the enmity of a foreign land.

"Now we must set these mistakes to right," Lady Thornton continued. "I will ask for an audience with the queen."

"No, my lady, you must let me do this. And please don't think it is because the war is with your people."

Lady Thornton stood up, her back straight with pride. "I am an Englishwoman now, Lady Roselyn. Why would I think such a thing? But how can you help my sons?"

"Because I might have the proof that will convince the queen of Shaw's guilt. And I could use your help."

Soon the two women were back in the master suite, their heads bent over the letter written in Spanish. Lady Thornton frowned as she read.

"What does it say?" Roselyn asked anxiously.

"These are orders to kill a Mr. Smythe, a British agent who was discovered. It is signed by Señor de Alcega. Do you know this name?"

"No," she said, refusing to acknowledge the panic that made her fingers tremble upon the letter. She pointed to the top of the parchment. "Is this not a name?"

"No, formal greetings only," the Lady Thornton said, shaking her head. "Bah, murderers who politely greet one another."

"Then there is no proof." Roselyn felt as bereft and cold as if Spencer were already dead.

"What did you say the name of the traitor is?"

"Rodney Shaw," she whispered, then half-heartedly looked at where Lady Thornton pointed.

Though the curling handwriting made it hard to see, at the end of a sentence was the word "Shaw," as if the writer had addressed his cohort by name.

"That's it!" she breathed, grinning at the viscountess. She gave the older woman a hug, then blushed as she quickly pulled back. "Forgive my impertinence, my lady."

"It is not impertinent when you are trying to help my son," Lady Thornton said with a smile.

"But what if we're too late? What if—"

"The queen will want to deal with Spencer herself—he was a great favorite of hers. But she will most likely let him languish and contemplate his sins for a while."

"Then I will send her a missive asking for an audience, to show her the proof of Spencer's innocence."

"You can try, *querida*—but she might make you wait as well."

Chapter 28

When Spencer was shown to his quarters in the Beauchamp Tower within the Tower of London garrison, he could not believe such a spacious, well-windowed room was a prison. But when he looked out of the windows to the east he could see the White Tower, where they could rack him in their search for answers; to the northwest he could see Tower Hill, where they could remove his head if they weren't satisfied with his replies.

And he could still see the Thames, where the barge had carried him beneath Traitor's Gate, which had dropped down behind him with a finality that would ruin many a night's sleep.

But for two days no one came to question him. He was provided with ample food and a feather mattress and blankets for his bed; he could even talk to Alex through a loose floorboard—when Alex would speak to him. Such lax treatment of a prisoner made no sense.

355

And gave him too much time to dwell on Roselyn.

He imagined her riding Angel, bound for the island, safe at last from the dangerous politics he had swirled about her.

But part of Spencer worried that she wouldn't flee, that she'd think she could help. In the past few short weeks, she'd become a woman who took foolish risks just for him— and he didn't know what to make of it. It contradicted everything he ever believed a woman could mean to him.

So he continued to pace, pondering Rose and his love for her and the impossibility of it all, until Alex pounded on the floor beneath him to make him stop.

After sending a missive to Queen Elizabeth asking for an audience, Roselyn waited two days for a reply. Each hour of each day made her more and more certain that Spencer was being tortured for information, that the soldiers were looking for any excuse to have him killed and the problem of his treason finished.

She couldn't sleep; she could barely eat—and then only when Lady Thornton personally watched each mouthful that passed her lips.

"If only I could see him," Roselyn said yearningly as she broke her fast on the third day of Spencer's imprisonment.

"You know I cannot allow that," Lady Thornton said.

"But with the proper bribe, I know the guards will allow me to see Spencer. I have heard of such things."

"Perhaps, but my son would not wish you to place yourself in danger. You must trust Her Majesty in this matter."

"Trust?" she said, coming to her feet. "How can I trust—"

There was a discreet knock on the door, and Lady Thornton called for the visitor to enter. The steward, Allbright, opened the door and bowed.

"My lady, there is a message from Whitehall. Her Majesty intends to formally accuse Lord Thornton of treason this afternoon." He paused for only a moment. "I have ordered your barge prepared."

Lady Thornton and Roselyn almost collided in their haste to leave the dining parlor.

"Change your gown, Roselyn," Lady Thornton said breathlessly as they ascended the stairs to the second floor. "We must look our best for the queen."

"I'm retrieving my cloak only, my lady," she said, glancing down at the dark green woolen gown she wore. "I will not pretend that I have returned to my old life; the queen will know that as a falsehood."

"But her respect—"

"I will earn her respect again," Roselyn said firmly as she disappeared into her own chamber.

But when she tried to work the clasp on her cloak, she found that her hands were shaking uncontrollably. This would be her only chance to save Spencer. What she did this afternoon could result in his death—or a life with him.

But not until Roselyn stood in the arched doorway to the queen's privy chamber did she realize just what she had to face.

Two years before, she had made herself an outcast to these people who now turned to look at her with contempt. Every courtier and nobleman was dressed in bejeweled satins and silks, puffed and painted.

Her parents, the Earl and Countess of Cambridge, stood near the queen as if they'd been invited to watch Roselyn's final defeat. Though she thought her father might feel sympathy, he wouldn't dare to show it beneath the cold, watchful eyes of his wife.

To face it all again hurt more than she could have imagined. It was as if beneath these condemning eyes, she relived every mistake she'd made and was judged anew for them.

But for Spencer she would bear it all; for Spencer she would make public every misery

with which she'd been punished for her recklessness: poverty, neglect, even the death of her
child. She could only apologize for her past
mistakes, and pray that the queen would listen
to her.

Roselyn lifted her chin and walked slowly
down the path opening between the courtiers,
with Spencer's mother at her side. Soon she
could see the raised dais where Queen Elizabeth sat on her golden throne beneath a canopy
of estate. She wore elegant black and white
satin, encrusted in garnet and rubies that glittered when she moved, along with the jewels
that decorated her ears and throat and fingers.
Beneath her red wig, the queen's whitened face
wore a stern frown.

To the queen's right, Spencer and Alex stood
unbound near a phalanx of guards. The brothers still wore the same rumpled garments, but
looked unharmed. Roselyn's relief nearly
brought her to tears, and she shook off Lady
Thornton's restraining hand to run to Spencer.

When he did not acknowledge her she
searched his beloved face, but he looked over
her head. The agony of his rejection made her
feel light-headed with bewilderment. She saw
Rodney Shaw's smug face at the front of the
crowd, surrounded by the smirking expressions worn by all the courtiers.

Once again she'd embarrassed herself before them all.

Roselyn straightened her spine, gathered her courage, and turned back to face Spencer. She refused to believe that every bit of gentleness and consideration he'd shown her had been false.

While the crowd tittered, she gazed into the eyes that had so often concealed things from her, and saw desperation. She knew suddenly that he was trying to protect her from association with him, that he would deny himself her comfort and help if those things meant dragging her down with him.

And she loved him so for the attempt.

With the return of her courage rushing upon her like wind filling out a ship's sails, she walked to the queen's dais and swept into a deep curtsy.

Spencer knew that everyone in the privy chamber could see the tension in him, and sweat trickled down his temples. He didn't care if it made him look guilty; it was all for brave Roselyn, who presented herself as a target in a futile effort to protect him.

He knew every courtier here—had wooed the women, teased the dowagers, fell into his cups with every young rakehell. But only Roselyn dared to stand by him—Roselyn, who had more cause than anyone to despise him. Before the entire court he had rejected her, yet still she would not leave. She was ready to destroy herself to save him, and he was humbled by her bravery.

He would do anything to protect her from scorn—and he would give anything to be with her always, to prove that he was worthy of her.

Queen Elizabeth's expression did not change as Roselyn straightened from her curtsy. "Lady Roselyn, what have you brought us?" she demanded.

Spencer watched as his mother came forward and stopped Roselyn's hand before it could enter the pouch at her waist. She put a small box in Roselyn's hands and pushed her forward.

One of the ladies of the privy chamber brought the gift to the throne. While Queen Elizabeth admired the rope of pearls and diamonds, Spencer could only stare at his mother, who stood at Roselyn's side like a guardian in black. He finally understood that it was easy for her to accept the scorn of others, as long as she could be with his father. He was ashamed of himself for worrying about her heritage, when he should have been ashamed of his own behavior.

"Lady Roselyn," the queen said, "why did you interrupt the business of our government?"

"Your Majesty," she answered in a clear voice,

"I have evidence that will help you clear Lord Thornton and his brother of these false charges of treason."

"It is impertinent of you to suggest that we need your help," the queen said haughtily.

But her gaze slid to Spencer, and though he kept his face impassive, he could not help wondering what Roselyn was talking about, and worrying that she would make herself a formidable royal enemy should her "evidence" be contrived.

Queen Elizabeth glanced back at Roselyn. "Nevertheless, we shall view this evidence you have brought us."

Roselyn reached into the pouch at her waist and withdrew a folded piece of paper. Again one of the queen's ladies brought it to Her Majesty.

"What is this?" the queen demanded.

"The letter is from Rodney Shaw's superiors in the Spanish army, ordering him to kill a British spy."

Spencer's mouth dropped open only a fraction before he remembered to shut it. Roselyn had had the pouch all along! But he could hardly be angry with her, or blame her for not trusting him. For the first time in weeks, he allowed hope to blossom in his heart.

Rodney Shaw stood frozen before all the

court, his pale face suddenly dotted with perspiration.

"Your Majesty, 'tis a forgery!" Shaw cried,
looking about him for support. "Would I have
come straight to Sir Walsingham if I were a traitor? I tell you, I found Thornton standing over
the corpse of the last British agent!"

The only people paying him any attention
were the courtiers, who now began to back
away from him.

Roselyn stepped closer to the queen. "The
letter is in Spanish, Your Majesty. Lady Thornton would be happy to translate it for you."

Queen Elizabeth eyed her over the letter.
"Think you that we are untutored, Lady Roselyn? We read many languages."

Roselyn bowed her head and curtsied again.
"Please forgive me, Your Majesty."

Spencer saw a snarl cross Shaw's face, and
he wished desperately that Rose were not so
near him.

Then Shaw drew his sword.

Chapter 29

The privy chamber rang with shrill screams as the courtiers stumbled back from Shaw's wildly waving sword. Before the soldiers could even react, Alex grabbed one of their swords and tossed it to Spencer, who rushed to put himself between Roselyn and Shaw.

Queen Elizabeth rose to her feet. "By Christ's wounds—"

But Spencer heard nothing else as his sword crossed with Shaw's and he felt the consuming power of redemption and victory so near at hand.

"Give it up, Shaw," he ground out as they circled each other. "No one can save you."

"A nasty limp you have there, Thornton. Let me put you out of your misery."

In a flurry, Shaw launched wild blows that Spencer desperately parried. More than once, he barely missed being skewered before he finally cut Shaw's sword arm. When Shaw tried to turn and run men blocked his escape, and he was forced to face Spencer, who held his sword at the ready.

In a low voice, Spencer said, "No longer are there men to hold me in place. That was the only way you could defeat me."

With a cry of rage, Shaw brought his sword down toward Spencer's head. Their blades met and slid together and they glared at each other across them.

"You gambled with your loyalty and lost," Spencer said. "Give up."

"I'd rather you kill me!"

"Coward." He knocked the sword from Shaw's hand, and stepped back as the soldiers surrounded the traitor.

Spencer turned slowly around to see the proud smile on his mother's face, and the tears on Roselyn's. He wanted to pull her into his arms, to tell her of his love and beg her to allow him to remain at her side forever.

But there was still the queen to deal with, and granting permission to marry was something she insisted on. And he still had so many questions.

"Your Majesty," Spencer said, "if you needed to see proof of my loyalty, why was no effort made to question me these past days? I lived practically in comfort."

The queen regally seated herself. "Lord Thornton, we were merely keeping you safe."

"Safe?"

"Sir Rodney had been under suspicion because of the behavior of his mother, who had recently begun to live well beyond her family's means—and made sure all knew it."

Shaw gaped up at the queen. "But . . . Mother insisted . . . she made me . . . she wanted . . ."

"In the end, it was your choice, Sir Rodney," the queen said coldly. "We were forced to protect Lord Thornton from your desperate acts, and Lady Thornton obliged us by guarding Lady Roselyn well. The final proof was that letter. Well done, Lady Roselyn."

The soldiers led Shaw from the chamber.

Spencer looked at his mother, who remained near Roselyn. "*Madre*, you knew everything?"

"No, my son, but one does not disobey an order from Her Majesty."

Queen Elizabeth smiled. "Lord Thornton, you have performed admirably in our service, and the crown thanks you. Do you have information for us?"

"Yes, Your Majesty. The Spanish will not be invading."

The court was suddenly silent, as if the security of the country rested on him.

"They could not join forces with Parma's

army in the Netherlands," he continued, "and by the time I left the ship, they were already running out of food and powder."

The queen raised her chin. "It is as we suspected. British power rules in the end."

Queen Elizabeth rose from her chair and stepped down to the floor, her vivid gown glistening under the candlelight. "Lord Thornton, did our royal mission finally lift you out of your sulk?"

He stared at her. "Your Majesty?"

"We thought what better way to distract you from romantic woes than to give you noble purpose—and to make a man out of your brother by giving him the responsibility of a title to protect."

She walked toward Alex, whose face had flushed in obvious anger.

"The ladies of the court did not recognize Sir Alexander's masquerade. Your faces resemble one another, but the difference between you is obvious when one looks in the right place."

She suddenly grabbed Alex's backside, and he jumped away from her, breathing heavily and glaring at the laughing courtiers.

"A man's body in dance always gives him away," the queen continued smoothly, moving back to sit upon her throne.

Spencer stared helplessly at his brother, who

had been the viscount for a year and a half. Alex would now go back to being the second son, although Spencer's claim as heir was only by minutes.

He saw at once how difficult such an adjustment would be—and the queen's humiliation only made matters worse. "Alex," he said, "how can I ever thank you for your help?"

Alex only nodded and stalked away without the queen's permission, and Spencer realized with regret that their relationship had been damaged further.

When the queen turned her formidable gaze upon Roselyn, she knew that her time of reckoning was at hand.

"Lady Roselyn," she said in a voice sure to carry throughout the privy chamber. "We understand that you fled from the marriage we had sanctioned, and pledged yourself to a less worthy man without our permission."

Roselyn moistened her suddenly dry lips, but before she could speak, Spencer did.

"Your Majesty, Roselyn was but a young girl who followed her heart when my own behavior proved so abhorrent. The fault is mine, not hers."

"Spencer, no," Roselyn quickly said. "Your Majesty, I have indeed paid dearly for my mistakes, but I pray you will say that I have redeemed myself in your eyes by my actions here today."

"You wish much of us," the queen said in a cool voice.

Spencer slid his hand into Roselyn's, and she gripped it tightly.

"Your Majesty," he said, "I come to you freely and beg for this woman as my wife. She means more to me than life itself, and if you do not give your permission—"

"Lord Thornton, do you threaten us?" the queen demanded. "Surely you do not dare to marry without our permission?"

"Your Majesty already granted it to us, two years ago. Will you not, in reward for my service, grant it again?"

Roselyn was aghast that Spencer would demand such a thing from the queen, all for her. Did he feel he owed her a debt, or could he actually be in love with her?

But the queen was frowning down at her. "Lady Roselyn, this man you pledged yourself to without our permission—he is dead?"

"Yes, Your Majesty."

"Then since you did not carry out our wishes two years ago, we will see it done now. Let us retire to our chapel and conduct this wedding." She rose to her feet and swept from the dais.

Roselyn stared in stunned dismay. This was happening so fast! She needed to be certain marriage was truly what Spencer wanted.

Spencer slid his arms about her, and she resisted the urge to surrender to the comfort of his embrace.

"You do not need to marry me," she whispered. "I lied to you about the letter, when you would have been grateful for the peace of mind it could give you."

He caressed her cheek. "You merely protected yourself and our country. I thought of nothing but marrying you every moment I was in the Tower, Roselyn. God—and the queen— has granted me a second chance to make you my wife, and I will let nothing stop me."

She slid her hands up his chest and cupped his face. "Tell me why, Spencer, after all we've done to one another, you still wish to marry me."

He kissed each of her hands. "Such an easy task you ask of me, my heart. It is because of love that I would wed you, the love that even now makes everything worth the price. Can you love a man who betrayed you in more ways than one?"

"Oh, Spencer," she whispered, standing on tiptoes to kiss him. "How I love you." She kissed each of his cheeks, then brought up his hands to kiss as well. "We were both young and foolish, too blind to see what we could have. I only thank God that we saw the truth. Now I can finally be a part of your wonderful family."

A darkness seemed to pass over his face. "Rose, I don't know how I can ever ask my mother's forgiveness."

"I think you misunderstand yourself," she said, brushing his hair tenderly from his eyes. "You were afraid that we'd never be as blessed with love as they were. By being scandalous, you ensured that no one would want to marry you. You warned every woman away—including me—before any could be hurt."

"Rose." His aching whisper touched her.

"On Wight, after we made love, you left without a word to *make* me hate you. But . . . something has changed. You're no longer afraid to love, to trust."

"Only because you made me see that life without you was meaningless. When I put you in danger, when you could have died—"

"Shh," she whispered, leaning up to stop his words with her mouth.

He murmured, "I love you" against her lips, and they clung together, body to body, soul to soul, joined in their hearts.

"Lord Thornton!" Queen Elizabeth called from the ornate doorway where she stood tapping her foot. "This wedding is only part of the business the court must conduct this day. Bring your betrothed to us! There will be time for kisses later."

Laughing, Roselyn let Spencer take her arm and lead her through the privy chamber.

He leaned down to press his mouth to her ear. "We shall be married, my heart, but I must request that before you ravish me this evening, you allow me a bath."

She chuckled and leaned her head against his shoulder.

With a rakish grin, Spencer said, "I'm quite certain I have a tub that we'll *both* fit in."

Epilogue

April 1589

Roselyn stood on the cliffs near Shanklin, looking down on the storm-swept beach where she'd first found Spencer. She hugged her cloak about her against the wind and turned when she heard her name called.

Spencer strode toward her, and even after so many months, just the sight of him made her eyes sting with tears of gratitude and love.

She turned back toward the channel and quickly dabbed at her eyes.

"Rose, 'tis too cold out here," he said against her hair, putting his arms around her from behind.

"Winter has been too long, and I missed my walks. I still can't believe that soon my brother and sister will be visiting us."

"The *least* your parents could do was give permission for the rest of your family to see you," he said gruffly. "You have heard not a word of explanation from them since they pretended such a gracious reunion at our wedding."

She stood silent in his embrace for a pensive moment. "Have you heard from Alex?" she asked even as she thought of John Heywood, who'd wished her well when he'd left to explore the world beyond England.

"No, but Alex will come around. He'll find someone to love"—he slid his hands over her round stomach, holding their baby—"and he shall know peace," he finished in a whisper. "I love you, Rose."

With a smile, she leaned against him and stared out over the water that had brought them together again, making them whole.

Avon Romances—
the best in exceptional authors and unforgettable novels!

Coming Soon from
HarperTorch

CIRCLE OF THREE

By the *New York Times* bestselling author of
THE SAVING GRACES

Patricia Gaffney

Through the interconnected lives of three generations of
women in a small town in rural Virginia, this poignant,
memorable novel reveals the layers of tradition and responsibility, commitment and passion, these women share. Wise,
moving, and heartbreakingly real, *Circle of Three* offers
women of all ages a deeper understanding of one another, of
themselves and of the perplexing and invigorating magic
that is life itself.

"Filled with insight and humor and heart,
Circle of Three reminds us what it's like
to be a woman."
Nora Roberts

"Powerful . . . Family drama that is impossible
to put down until the final page is read."
Midwest Book Review

"Through the eyes of these strong, complex women
come three uniquely insightful, emotional perspectives."
New York Daily News

0-06-109836-1/$7.50 US/$9.99 Can

COT 0401